After the Blue, Blue Rain

Comfort & Company, Volume 1

A.D. Price

Published by Glore House Books, 2022.

This book is a work of fiction. All of the characters, organizations and events in this novel are either products of the author's imagination or used fictitiously.

Cover design by Amy Dunkleberger

https://adpricebooks.com

Library of Congress Cataloging-in-Publication Data is available upon request.

ISBN: 979-8-986-8930-8-2

For my family

Blue rain, falling down on my window pane
But when you return there'll be a rainbow
After the blue, blue rain
And there's a blue star
Looking down asking where you are
But when you return there'll be a sunbeam
Hiding the blue, blue star
Skies will be much brighter than they were before
When you and love come strolling through the door
Then there'll be no more blue rain
Just the sound of my heart's refrain
Singing like a million little blue birds
After the blue, blue rain
Written by Johnny Mercer and Jimmy Van Heusen

PROLOGUE

Excerpt from "My Escape: A Confession" (submitted to O.P.M.G., February 1946)

Dear Reader: The following is an account of my last days in America. I have tried to be as honest and forthcoming with the specifics as possible. Engineers aren't known for their writing talents, however, so if I stray off-topic, neglect details or indulge in non-essential observations, I hope you will not judge my story-telling too harshly.

On the day I made my escape, the snow had turned to slush. I had been assigned to road duty a mile from the camp, supervising other prisoners in construction and ditch digging. For that I earned 80 cents an hour.

Based on the schematic I had been provided, I had mentally sketched out my plan some weeks before. I knew that at certain points the road we were building cut across a gas pipeline. Great care had to be taken to avoid striking the line, as it would explode if ruptured, and for weeks I had guided my team with cautious precision. On that day, however, I gave them orders for a perfectly timed miscalculation.

Under the fading winter sun, I lay out markers directing the bulldozer to dig across an area where only I knew the pipeline ran. It would be the last section dug before quitting time. The men were tired—I could tell by the lazy way their shovels hit the half-frozen earth—and in their fatigue they had lost focus. That was good.

Discreetly I tried to listen for sounds of the impact, of the bulldozer's blade hitting the gas line, but little could be heard above the screeching and rumbling of the engine and roller. After a few seconds, though, I noticed bubbles popping up in the ground behind where the bulldozer had just been. It was a sure sign of escaping gas, but I waited several seconds before yelling, "Gas! Run!"

My warning came a moment before the explosion. A fireball shot up where the volatile bubbles had been, enveloping the abandoned bulldozer. The prisoners and the guard on duty scattered in a panic, and taking advantage of the commotion, I took off, running away from the site.

I kept running as the wail of a fire truck siren filled the cold dusk air. I ran across snow-dusted fallow fields and through a patch of woods. I ran until darkness had fallen and an abandoned barn was in sight. Exhausted I stumbled toward it. The ground was hard and rough with weeds and wild grass, and I lost my balance when my toe struck the edge of a brick that had been obscured by a patch of snow. I flew forward, my chest and right arm striking more loose bricks as I landed face-first on the ground. After a stunned moment, I willed myself to my feet and limped the rest of the way to the old barn.

Once safely inside, I collapsed against the wall and let the pain from the fall wash over me. I had no means to deal with my injuries and little time for rest. As soon as I was able, I began to explore my surroundings. Whatever equipment the building might have once housed was long gone, save for a beat-up toolbox I discovered in a corner. Tucked inside was a rusty switchblade, which I used to cut the camp ribbon off my work coat. The coat had served me well, but the canvas only kept out so much of the cold and would stand out among civilians. I knew I would have to acquire something warmer.

I waited for the warning whistle to sound before boarding the last car of the idling train. Coatless, hatless and bagless, I didn't want to draw attention to myself, even in the dead of night. I tucked the discarded newspaper I had been hiding behind under my arm and slid into an empty seat in the corner. As I had hoped, everyone around me was either sleeping or reading and barely took notice of my entrance.

I had a few hours before sunrise to secure the necessary items. A little money (I had spent most of what I had saved on the ticket), a coat and, if I was lucky, a hat. Careful planning had gotten me this far, but quick thinking and luck would have to see me through the rest. I rested my head against the freezing window and, overcome with exhaustion, fell quickly asleep.

Excerpt from the Journal of Pfc. Stanley Comfort (Birmingham General Hospital, Van Nuys, California, January 2, 1946)

From the porch I watch the men pacing and shuffling about the front lawn, orderlies and nurses by their sides, herding them away from one another. Every day at seven and three, weather permitting, the psychiatric patients of Birmingham General are escorted outdoors for "recreation hour." The ones who can't or won't walk remain on the porch and watch the ones who can and do. Usually I walk, but this afternoon, I stay and make the most of my precious Chesterfield.

Doc gave me this journal and asked me to write down my thoughts and impressions. Pretend you're writing a story, he said, *your* story. It's true every soldier here has his own story, but in the end, all of them are the same. Some of us stutter, some shake, some cry. Some are in wheelchairs, some in braces. Some just look at you with dead eyes and a deader heart. But, just like me, they have all gone down the rabbit hole. Wacky, nuts, bonkers.

The first few weeks of my mental rehabilitation concentrated on the basics—the who, what, where and when of life, my life. You see, I have no memory of recent events, but I still understand how the world works. I know what a hospital is, what doctors do, what the beds and bathrooms are for. I know about families and "loved ones." I know my "loved ones." I know you're supposed to wear clothes but never frowns.

I know certain facts about myself—biographical details, as Doc likes to call them. I know my name is Stanley Franklin Comfort, Private Stanley Comfort. I know I enlisted and was shipped to the Pacific in December 1944, and my last battle was Okinawa. I know this because various doctors, nurses and aides have told me. I remember them repeating my name over and over, and me laughing. Your name is Private Stanley Comfort, Pfc. Stanley Comfort,

Comfort, Comfort. How could I forget a guy named Private Stanley Comfort?

But I have. Completely obliterated that Pfc. guy from my noggin. "We need to reintroduce yourself to yourself," Doc had said when we first met in his office back in November. "Everything's in there, it just needs to be found and coaxed from its hiding place." Doc then read out loud from my military file. "Date of birth, September 19, 1925. Place of birth, Los Angeles, California. Mother, Dorothy Schmidt Comfort, Father, Franklin Herbert Comfort, deceased."

I know I'd startled at the word "deceased." My mom had told me about the heart attack that had killed my dad—her ex-husband—on the day I was transferred to the Van Nuys hospital. She also told me about her new husband and her new house in Dayton. And how she wanted to spend more time with me and help me recover, but the new husband needed her in Dayton, so . . .

Doc had interrupted my thoughts. "And you have an older sister of course. Katherine. Kit."

Yes, I had seen Kit with my mother. "She's a private detective," I said, with a note of pride. "Comfort and Company, Private Investigators. She gave me one of her cards."

"Excellent. I hope to meet her soon."

"She likes to buy hats," I had declared out of nowhere.

Doc responded with a strained smile and a change of topic. "When you feel ready, you can re-read the letters you received while you were deployed. I think they could be very helpful."

"Letters?"

"Letters from your family. You saved them all and the Army sent them back with your other things when you left Hawaii. You can start with your mother's."

I take a last deep drag on my cigarette as images of my mother hugging me goodbye (at a train station?) flood my brain. But I have no words to describe the sensation of remembering, if in fact that's what I'm doing.

I'll read my mother's letters, written and mailed separately from my father's, and maybe tomorrow, I'll take a walk.

P.S. to myself: Be sure to ask Doc about the article below!

(Taped to the opposing page is the first paragraph of an article torn from the *Los Angeles Times, November 11, 1945)*

War Veterans Seeking Motherly Type Girls

Motherly girls—not the more glamorous selfish type—are being sought as wives by returned servicemen who are trying, unconsciously, to cure themselves of emotional upsets caused by war experiences. And this is a fact which all husband-hunters must reckon with because: Thirty percent, or some 3,000,000 of the discharged men will be suffering from mild or acute war neurosis. Marriage with the "right sort of wife" was the only specific cure for battle nerves advanced at Cedars Lebanon Hospital last week in a symposium on the state of mind of World War II veterans.

IT'S BEEN A LONG, LONG TIME

Monday, February 4, 1946

ONE

KIT

The downtown office of the Yellow Pages was so small Kit had to wonder if it had begun life as a closet or, more fittingly, a telephone booth. Its stale air, a mélange of competing scents, overpowered her like a wool blanket in July, and as the door closed behind her, she felt the perspiration gathering around her collar. To meet the ad book's noon deadline, she had dashed over from Comfort and Company with her copy, and the hustle had left her sweating. Almost a year into her ownership, Comfort and Company was still struggling, and since detective agencies rarely grew on word of mouth, a bigger, better Yellow Pages ad seemed her best—perhaps only—hope.

Undaunted by his cramped quarters, the ad salesman, Diego, read her dashed-off copy with the flair of a radio pitchman. He wore a dark brown double-breasted suit, and his tie was from the Salvador Dali collection, a striking orange and black affair featuring a swan against what looked like a castle and an upside-down mountain. Kit had a hard time looking away from it.

"'When you need the comfort of the truth, delivered with discretion,'" Diego paused, "'call Comfort and Company, Private Investigators, Trinity 6-5525. Missing persons our specialty. Walk-ins welcome.' Then the address, 333 South Spring Street, Los Angeles. Is that everything?"

"That should do it," Kit said.

"Any other text you want to add? Or photos? We could shrink the print a little, put a picture of you here, in the corner," he said, pointing to the upper right side of the layout.

"No, not me." she said firmly. As much as she hated to admit it, she knew that a picture of a woman detective would not bring in clients, or not the right sort of clients anyway.

"How about your partner?"

She frowned. "He'd never agree to it." Once a local celebrity, her partner, Henry, now craved anonymity. Kit was the Comfort in Comfort and Company, and Henry, the Company.

"How about a dog? Nothing says comfort and security like a dog."

"A dog? We don't have a dog."

"So? Who's going to know? Everyone loves Rin Tin Tin, don't they?" And to underscore his point, he extracted a glossy headshot of a handsome German shepherd from under his blotter.

"Is that Rin Tin Tin?"

"No, it's my dog. Valentino."

"He's an actor?"

"We're working on it," he said, a bit defensive. Then returning to the ad, he said, "We can put a bubble over the dog's head. You know, like in the funny pages. He could be saying something like, 'Missing someone? We're here to help' or 'You can put your trust in us.'"

"And what happens when a client comes in expecting to see a dog?"

Diego made a "pfft" sound. "Just say he's busy on another case. Or he's getting his nails trimmed." His grin was infectious. "Look, the dog's just to get their attention. They won't remember the thirty other detective ads they just looked at, but they'll remember the one with the talking dog. Take my word for it."

Kit couldn't disagree with that logic and took her business checkbook from her handbag. "Fine. Add Valentino. How much?"

As Kit turned onto Broadway from 8th Street, she was met by a sudden swirl of cool air whipping down the tall buildings. Although the gust almost claimed her favorite pillbox, slapped on while dashing out the office door, its sunshine-infused freshness was a welcome relief. The usual mid-day crowd, a mix of lunching workers, fashion shoppers and matinee goers, filled the street, and Kit soaked up their casual energy as she headed east toward 3rd. Despite years here, the umph of downtown had never gotten old for her.

Apparently not content with one impulsive purchase, Kit came to a halt when she reached the Broadway entrance of her favorite department store. Bullocks had a way of calling her when she was at her least solvent, and its elegant pull was particularly fierce that day. She had already picked out a navy gabardine suit and a matching pin-less turban, but her true desire was the fine straw hat that had caught her eye in the window.

She made her way to the millinery department and asked to try on the masterpiece. She almost gasped with delight when she saw her reflection in the counter mirror. The hat was edged with ruffled horsehair, and its delicate brim flowed out unapologetically, adding a hint of mystery to her angular face.

"That hat would look lovely with the Valentine print," the saleswoman gushed from behind. "The one with the big bow."

"It sure would," Kit admitted. The red Valentine cocktail dress, featured coyly in the store's Valentine's Day holiday display, had also caught her eye. Too bad the hat cost forty and the dress, sixty-five. "But I'm going to stick with the gabardine today," she said with a barely suppressed sigh. Gabardine. Better for blending in, she told herself, and wasn't blending in her primary mission these days?

"You can't go wrong with gabardine," the sales woman assured Kit as she handed over her purchase. "It's very versatile."

"I hear it's the number one fabric of corpses," Kit said without thinking.

The saleswoman blinked with startled disbelief and whispered, "Excuse me?"

"Sorry," Kit muttered. "I've no idea where that thought came from." She gave the clerk a quick smile and turned to leave. Truth was, she did know where the odd statistic came from, and right now, he was probably wondering why she wasn't in the office.

To Kit's surprise, Henry had already come and gone by the time she made it back to work with her Bullocks bag. Immediately she raised the blinds to let in as much afternoon light as the heat-less office could absorb. The snappy winter air, made chillier by that perpetual breeze of downtown, was sneaking in through a window with a broken latch, sending shivers through her lean body. She and Henry shared the tiny space, and when he was there by himself, he kept the blinds lowered and fully shut, no matter the season. As she had discovered at Empire Insurance, where she had typed reports for him before his short-lived retirement, Henry didn't approve of sunshine and thought Los Angeles had way too much of it. But on a brisk day like today, Kit couldn't get enough of it.

By unspoken agreement, Kit was the company's missing person specialist, and Henry, the adultery and fraud. Out of economic necessity, however, their efforts, and schedules, sometimes overlapped. As owner, she handled the invoices, rental agreements and what passed for advertising. If a case called for special photography, she was there. Henry "sleuthed," as he put it, and only "sleuthed." Of course, he also taught and guided her, but he would never take credit for being her "old wise guy."

As the Yellow Pages trip had reminded her, it had been only a year and change since she had taken on her first solo case. Back then, the agency was called—ironically as it turned out—Dependable Detective Agency and was owned by her former boss, Terrence Hennessey.

In his own mysterious way, Henry had warned her about getting mixed up with Terrence. Henry had no history with Terrence, but the world of private investigators was a small one, and he'd heard things. A single young woman working for an unattached man was always a loaded proposition, and Henry feared for her happiness. "He might not always be reliable," is how Henry put it in a master stroke of understatement. He made no mention of demons and illicit habits. That world had been unknown to Kit, and she never imagined her introduction to it would come via her boss. He had hidden it too well, she had thought after receiving word of his death. Now, though, she could see that all the indicators were hiding in plain sight.

Terrence might have been handsome at one time, she had concluded after meeting him. His graying slicked-back hair was thinning and his teeth showed signs of neglect, but under his black eyebrows, his wide-set eyes still glimmered a cold cobalt blue. His eyes were the only thing people really noticed about him, and at times they seemed to be living a separate life from the rest of his being. While his reedy frame sported the perpetual slump of the troubled, his eyes never stopped probing and assessing. No doubt they were responsible for his success as an investigator, because despite everything else about him, he remained an accomplished detective.

For her job interview, he had invited her to lunch at Cole's, explaining that he liked to double up on tasks. Terrence, she would learn later, regarded eating as an obligation, and he never passed up an opportunity to do two jobs at once. "I'm a natural-born one-man operation," he said over a plain turkey sandwich, "but even I can't be in two places at once. That's where you would come in."

He went on to describe the job in broad strokes, emphasizing that "evening and weekend hours" might be required. Kit assured him that she had experience working unconventional hours, but didn't confess to doing so for free. Before their complimentary pie slices had arrived (he ate so many meals there and was such a generous tipper the waitresses liked to give him free desserts), he offered her the position.

Also on the Hennessey payroll was a photographer named Bobby. His prior experience consisted of shooting group photos for his Simi Valley high school yearbook. What he lacked in expertise and worldliness he made up for in energy, which was fine with Terrence. "As long as the client can tell who's in the picture and what they're up to, that's all that matters," Terrence explained. "I'm not looking for Robert Capa here."

She learned later that the secretary Kit had replaced was just out of business school when she had started at the agency. As Bobby explained it, she quit after things didn't work out with Terrence and married someone else. "If I were you," Bobby said, "I'd steer clear of personal entanglements with Mr. Hennessey. He's a great investigator, but a lousy boyfriend."

Bobby had been with Terrence for a year before his draft number came up, and after he shipped off to the Pacific, Kit casually brought up her photography training. Terrence merely grunted and sent her off to get snaps of a target's clandestine entrances and exits. Without further discussion, he then made her his "on-call photographer, for the foreseeable future." The foreseeable future turned out to be eternal, as poor Bobby's ship was destroyed off the Japanese coast, two weeks before Hiroshima.

Though Terrence was beyond draft age, the pull of the war had weighed heavy on him. He had been an enlistee in the First War, and all talk of battles and combat made him go oddly quiet. When she mentioned that her brother had enlisted and was off to boot camp, Terrence shook his head, then sighed with resignation. A moment later, he got up from his desk and walked out of the office. She didn't see him again for two days, and he offered no explanations for his departure.

Several more absences followed, each one a bit longer than the previous. She covered for him as best as she could. Always when he returned he seemed diminished, but she couldn't put her finger on how. The clients remained happy with his efforts. When she mentioned the disappearances to Henry, he muttered something about benders and advised her not to poke about.

Then one Friday, Terrence left for the weekend and was still gone by the following Friday. Henry dutifully went in search of him, but came up empty. Weeks later, she got word that he had been found dead at the Ambassador Hotel, a few blocks from the office. Unknown to her, Terrence had a previous drug arrest, so when he turned up cold on a bed in one of the city's more notorious dives, the police didn't hesitate to rule his death a misadventure.

She had become the agency's sole investigator by default, an opportunity she both relished and feared. Her first client was a distraught young war bride named Sophie whose sailor husband had walked out the door one morning and never returned. They had married a week after they had met, and he had shipped out a week after that. Ten months later, he was injured at sea and granted an honorable discharge. Now Sophie was imagining that all sorts of mishaps and dangers had befallen her husband, never once suspecting that he had willfully deserted her. Her anguish was deep.

The police had made a half-hearted attempt at locating him, but since there was no evidence of foul play, they couldn't justify expending too many tax dollars on the matter. So, using her contacts at the Veterans Center, Kit tracked the wayward groom to a San Pedro flophouse. He was remorseful but unwilling to return home. The war still had him in its grip, he admitted at last. He had nearly died in a submarine accident after a fellow sailor had set off a depth charge too soon, causing an explosion and trapping him in the engine room. Any kind of loud noise caused him to replay the terrifying moments over and over in his head. He couldn't explain what was going on in his mind to his wife, who barely knew him in any form. "I've been missing since I got home," he said, "I just made it real finally, for Sophie's sake."

Kit had talked him into returning home and explaining himself to Sophie—inserting herself in a way her mentors had always warned against. The reunion was brief, and she found out later that the couple filed for divorce not long after. Despite the unhappy ending, Sophie had thanked Kit. "It's better to know than be a prisoner of your imagination," she said. For her part, Kit had completed her assignment and gotten paid. The money wasn't enough to make the office rent, but it was tangible proof she could do the job.

Now, as she glanced at the street below, Kit tried not to think about the hat she had just said goodbye to or the overpriced Yellow Pages ad she had just agreed to and instead focus on her unwritten, perpetual to-do list. And what was it she needed to do? Oh yes, find clients, preferably paying ones.

Some agencies operated "by appointment only," but Comfort and Company couldn't afford to be that picky. Walk-ins were indeed welcomed, as the new ad announced. Unfortunately, the office was tucked above a watch shop in the Holly Hotel, a location so discreet as to be invisible. The watch shop's owner had allowed her, for a fee, to place a business sign in his front window, but passersby weren't inclined to notice it and wander in spontaneously.

So, when Kit spied a petite, trim brunette in a gray gabardine suit and Stetson hat stop suddenly in front of the watch shop, her eye drawn to the square of cardboard tucked in the corner of the display window, she held her breath. The woman stared at the sign for several seconds and glanced up to the second floor. Then she zoomed off, quickly walking out of sight.

Deflated, Kit sighed and returned to her desk. Fifteen minutes later, however, the brunette was back, this time knocking on her door, and just like that, Kit had her first client of the week.

Dina Harris, who, Kit guessed, was in her mid-twenties, was round-faced with a slight overbite and overworked eyebrows, cherubic in that way that many men found attractive. Like a brunette Shirley Temple all grown up, she thought. Her black suede pumps with the gray bow, which Kit had noticed almost immediately, added an unexpected flourish to the simple gray of her suit. A pair of gloves was tucked under the handle of her matching purse, which sat squarely on her narrow lap. Kit had to admire her style—she made affordable look chic.

When Kit had greeted her at the office door, Dina had looked confused, and Kit pretended not to notice her reluctant handshake and quizzical smile. Even with ongoing wartime shortages, clients still expected, and preferred, to have a beefy male in the Philip Marlowe mold handling their investigations. Even Henry, who was long past his physical prime, would have gotten a more enthusiastic hello than she had.

While telling Kit about a man named Peter Novak and the train he apparently hadn't disembarked from, Dina squeezed her purse absent-mindedly. Kit made note of her manicured, ring-less fingers. So far Dina's story—that her wartime lover had stood her up at the downtown rail station—had a sadly familiar Sophie ring.

"And you're positive he got on the train in Chicago?" Kit said, settling in her own chair behind the office's one desk, and taking up her notebook and pen. Something about polished Dina Harris made her suddenly conscious of the clutter before her. Along with everything else, Kit shared the desk with Henry, who thought nothing of leaving his favorite darts, shot glass, and lucky hula dancer on the blotter.

"He sent me a telegram from Kansas City, saying he'd be arriving at Union Station at nine on Saturday." She glanced down at her purse. "I have it here, if you want to see it."

"Please."

Dina removed the telegram from her bag and handed it to Kit, who confirmed the delivery date as Friday and the place as Kansas City. The message: "On my way. Arriving Union Station 9 am Saturday."

"No one at the station had heard of any problems with the run that day," Dina said. "I asked. No accidents or detours. I phoned the Super Chief headquarters when I got home, but they couldn't tell me anything."

"What about family?"

"He has a sister and mother in Chicago. I phoned, but they hadn't heard from him either."

"Did you go to the police?"

"First thing this morning. They just laughed at me. Said it was too soon to worry."

Kit had no problem imagining that. Vets came from all over, lured by fragrant citrus and the gleaming factories that had sprung up during the war. Tens of thousands ended up homeless, and an unknown number had gone missing. Despite its good intentions, the police's new Missing Persons Division couldn't begin to handle the deluge. "I'm sorry to hear that. But are you sure you want to pursue this privately?"

"I'm a transcriptionist for a neurologist a couple of blocks away. I pass by here every day, but I never noticed your sign before. Today, when I passed, it caught my eye. I thought, how strange I should see it today, so close to work. So I went back to my desk and got this."

Dina then slid a folded newspaper to Kit's side of the desk. Kit glanced at the header, a July 1945 edition of the *Stars and Stripes*. It had been folded to highlight a photograph. In it, Kit recognized Dina, dressed in a WAC uniform, saluting the picture taker with a sly grin. Next to Dina was a dark-haired man with regular features, a wide, welcoming smile and a captain's insignia. The caption identified the duo merely as "medical officers enjoying a rare break on a Saturday night."

"That was taken at the officers' club the last night we were together in France," Dina said.

"He's a doctor?"

"Radiologist. I was his transcriptionist. We were both attached to the 27th Evacuation Hospital. I was discharged six weeks ago. He left a month later."

"Is this the only photo you have of him?"

"Unfortunately. We didn't have much time for picture taking. I'm sure his mother could send more."

Kit refrained from stating the obvious, that what Dina thought she and Peter had together was likely the romantic equivalent of a mirage. That her lover had panicked somewhere between Kansas and California and had no desire to resurrect their wartime fling. As Sophie and others had taught her, passion was just another casualty of war, coming and going. "Does he have friends here?"

"We have a couple of mutual acquaintance here. People we trained with. But no one close, that I'm aware of."

"Do you know if he has any friends or associates in Kansas City, or anywhere between here and there? Someone he may have stopped to see?"

"No one he mentioned," said Dina.

"Any tattoos, birthmarks, scars? War injuries? Any outstanding traits we could use to confirm his identity?"

Dina shook her head. "Sorry."

"Any prior marriages? Serious girlfriends?"

"No. I mean, I don't think so. Look. I know what you're thinking. But he's not like that. If he had changed his mind about us, he would have told me before he left Chicago. Something happened. I know it. Something went wrong."

Kit could have assured her that as long there was money for her services, she was above presumptions and judgments. "All right. We'll give this a try. I'll start today with my contact at the Veterans Center, in case he found his way there, and I'll have another go at the train station." She picked up the *Stars and Stripes.* "I'll need to keep this, so I can show his picture around."

Dina nodded. "So you think you might find him? The sign says you specialize in missing persons."

"We'll do our best. You do understand, though, that even if we find him, we can't just hand him over to you. It will still be up to him whether to see you."

"Yes, I understand. I just want to know what happened."

Dina paid the retainer—Henry insisted on getting one—and gave Kit her office number. As she was leaving, Kit couldn't help herself and said, "What lovely shoes. May I ask where you got them?"

"Thank you. Wetherby's. I bought them for the office Christmas party, 1943. Haven't had much chance to wear them since."

"No, of course not." She offered Dina a wan smile. "I'll call you if anything shakes out."

Kit sat down at her desk and opened her notebook to her fresh "Harris Case" entry. Unlike Kit, Henry wasn't a big note-taker—"it's all under the dome" he would say, his finger pointing to his pate. And to Kit's irritation, he never forgot a detail and could write (or two-finger type) accurate reports as easily as a shopping list. He claimed to have acquired this skill after years of attentive observation, but Kit suspected he was just a natural memorizer. He was also fond of mnemonic devices, giving witnesses and places alliterative nicknames like San Fran Sam and Alibi Al.

When he did engage in note taking, it was to distract or throw off a particularly stubborn interviewee. The notes would be cast off as soon as the interview was over. In his opinion anything that required the investigator to take his eyes off his subject, even for a second, was counter-productive.

Kit had acquired her dedication to note taking from their mutual former boss, Irwin, the head of investigations at Empire Insurance. She had been his secretary and Henry his senior investigator. A lifelong bachelor, Irwin treated Kit, fresh from business school and eager to please, like the son he never had, mainly because none of the young men in his orbit had the patience to listen to him.

Irwin would say, "When the customer"—it was always "the customer"—"sees you taking notes, he becomes more conscientious and careful with details. But you don't want to focus on the details per se."

"You don't?" Kit said.

"Don't focus on the details of what they tell you," Irwin would say. "Use the details to illuminate what they don't tell you."

"You mean read between the lines?"

"Not exactly. Say for instance the customer tells you he got home from work at seven and went to bed at eleven, waking up sometime after midnight when he smelled smoke. He's not necessarily lying, he's just not telling you what he did between seven and eleven, which might be significant."

"Or," he would say, miming turning a page in his notebook, "maybe the customer's wife neglects to tell you that the customer always comes home at six, not seven. She might not think his lateness on the night of the fire is significant, or she might be deliberately leaving that detail out. When you look back on your notes, those missing pieces will become more obvious."

Were there omitted details in Dina's answers? She had seemed straightforward enough. Kit's deception meter hadn't gone off as it often did with new clients, especially clients searching for disappearing loved ones.

No, there was nothing, and she had a feeling that was not a good sign. With a determined grunt, she slipped the notebook into her camera bag and headed back into the sunshine.

TWO
HENRY

Henry had hoped to see Bells of St. Mary's that afternoon, but his quarry had picked The Dolly Sisters instead. He liked Betty Grable as much as the next man, but she hardly compared in beauty and talent to Ingrid Bergman. As far as Henry was concerned, no one topped Bergman, not even Jean Harlow at her most sultry.

While Henry didn't approve of his mark's taste in movies, he had come to the conclusion that the man was innocent as far as the investigation was concerned. As he had done the four previous days, the mark—Emerick Johnson—had retreated to the public library after the show. Henry felt confident in reporting to Mrs. Johnson that, contrary to her suspicions, Mr. Johnson was not carrying on with his secretary or any other women. No, in fact, Mr. Johnson's recent odd comings and goings were the result of being jobless, a development Henry had just confirmed.

Like so many others, Emerick was a veteran who hadn't quite left the war behind, and the world he had returned to was too busy to make allowances for profane outbursts and unexplained absences on the job. Henry had witnessed similar reactions after the Great War, and it depressed him to see history repeating itself. Emerick had shone as a soldier, earning two Bronze Stars, but none of that mattered in post-war Los Angeles, where you couldn't throw a cat without hitting a damaged war hero.

He found Emerick in the periodical room, seated at one of the big desks, newspapers spread out in front of him. As Henry removed his hat and sat down across from him, he saw that Movie Mook, as he had dubbed him, was studying help wanted ads. He was what Kit would call "nice looking," attractive without being sexy, masculine without a trace of menace.

"So, what did you think of the movie?" Henry said in a theatrical whisper.

Emerick looked up, startled. "Excuse me?"

"Sorry. I noticed you at the show earlier. What did you think?"

"The movie? All right, I suppose. I wasn't paying that much attention."

"I found it amusing, but Grable can't sing to save her life."

"Huh?"

"Job hunting?" Henry said, picking up the sports section of the *Herald* from Emerick's pile. He flipped to the racing page to check that day's Santa Anita Handicap: At 5-2, Grandmere topped the three-year-olds, but Determinado was a determined 7-2.

Emerick gave Henry a cautious look before answering. "Yeah, but not here." He pointed down at the open "Help Wanted" page. "This is the Sacramento paper.

"The *Bee*?"

"That's right. They've got papers from all over here." He nodded in the direction of the corner reference area. "How about you? Retired?"

Henry accepted that his balding head, sagging, scarred cheeks and thick wire-frame glasses made him look a bit older than his actual years, but he had never been mistaken for elderly before. "No, I work odd hours."

"Oh, doing what? If you don't mind me asking."

"I'm a private investigator," Henry said, lifting his eyes to meet Emerick's. "I'm working a case as we speak."

"In the library?"

"I've ended up in stranger places."

"I bet." Emerick smiled vaguely and peered at Henry. "You look familiar."

"Maybe because you've seen me every day for the last week."

"I have?"

"Some days you come here; Mondays and Wednesdays you're at the Veterans Center; some days you buy a bottomless cup of coffee at Calson's. You always take in a matinee. You prefer comedies to dramas and Jujubes to Jujyfruits. You take bathroom breaks after the short." He paused for dramatic effect. "One place you don't go to anymore is Regal Insurance. Your wife thinks you have a mistress, and in my experience, your wife would usually be right."

"Huh? Maggie hired you to spy on me?" he said, more statement than question. "Where did she get the money to do that?"

"I didn't ask. Are you going to tell her what you've been up to?"

"Why? Isn't that your job?" Emerick's voice tightened and rose slightly, reassuring Henry there was still life underneath the wiry waves of blonde hair.

"The only thing she's paying me to find out is whether you're breaking your marriage vow. I can now honestly report that you're not. Imagine her relief." Henry refolded the sports section and slid it back to Emerick. "Don't you think it would be better if you told her, before she asks?"

"I was hoping I wouldn't have to. I thought I'd have another job by now, but my fucking boss is blackballing me all over town. Says I'm a hothead. Now I'm just hoping to find anything that will pay the mortgage."

Henry saw that flash of the anger that apparently had gotten the vet into trouble in the first place. "Regardless, your wife deserves to know. That's what they're there for," Henry said with easy conviction. "You're not fooling her."

"Obviously."

Henry scribbled a name on the back of a Comfort and Company calling card and shoved it across the table.

"What's this?" asked Emerick.

"You said anything."

"Thompson's Automatic Car Wash?"

"Grand opening next week. Brand new system. Conveyor belts, blowers. I know the owner. He's handy with machines but terrible with money. Tell him I sent you."

Emerick flipped the card. "Henry Richman?" For the first time, Emerick pinned his gaze firmly on Henry. "Why is that name familiar?"

Henry shrugged and stood up to leave. "Thompson's. Go there. You never know what the day might hold."

"Thanks, I guess. And Grable still has great legs. Who cares about her voice?"

Henry smirked. Perhaps he had underestimated Movie Mook after all.

On Main Street, blocks from Emerick and the downtown library, Henry walked up to his car to begin his bomb check. It was a ritual he had initiated following his near death in a car explosion years before. Anytime he left the Studebaker someplace public, he would give it a thorough inspection, checking any spot where a fatal tampering might occur.

The car's starter always came first. He lifted the hood, then bent his knees to get the part at eye level. Finding nothing amiss, he closed the hood and squatted to inspect the car's undercarriage. Again, nothing. Finally, he opened the driver's door and leaned in to give the steering column and dashboard a close examination.

He had purchased the sky-blue Commander a few years back, attracted to its pickup and compactness. Less space to stick a bomb in, he had thought as the car salesman prattled on about the Studebaker's comfort and elegance. Intellectually he knew it unlikely that the police—or anyone else—would go after him again, eight years later after the failed attack. Psychically, however, he needed the bomb-check because every time he approached the coupe, the seconds before the explosion would replay in his head like a demented newsreel.

The details of the memory never changed. Each time he would see himself opening the door, plopping behind the wheel, adjusting the mirror, reaching for the starter button. He would press the button while simultaneously leaning over to pop out the passenger side window. Then came the sudden heat of the blast and the noises, the most terrifying of which were Bea's screams. She had been about to drive to the market when Henry, worried she would wind up late for a visit from the plumber, had offered to run the errand for her. She had one foot back inside the house when the bomb went off.

From car to hospital, Henry never lost consciousness, but his post-explosion recollection was fuzzy at best. He recalled Bea's tear-streaked face, contorted by both relief and grief, staring down at him through the glassy remains of the windshield. The neighbors had come running out, some still in their bathrobes and slippers, and one had the wits to call for an ambulance. For weeks, the splintered ruins of his garage attracted a stream of curious locals, and the reporters who staked out their block took no pity on the already tender Bea.

His wounds were numerous (imbedded with 150 pieces of shrapnel, according to his surgeon who claimed to have counted them all) and life-threatening. No doubt about it, the bomb was built to kill. As the doctor later explained, his positioning on the seat had saved him. Had he been upright behind the wheel, his head and chest would have borne the brunt of the exploding fragments. Tipped over, his vital organs had been spared.

After his first surgery, Bea had refused to leave his side and kept a forceful vigil at the hospital. Not even the revolver that Henry kept tucked beneath his hospital sheets reassured her. "They'll just wait till you're asleep," she said. "They're police, who would stop them?"

They both knew that the bomb had been the work of the LAPD's hit squad, acting on behalf of Chief Davis, who was well aware that Henry and his reformer partner Calvin were closing in on their corrupt operations. Bribery, extortion, frame-ups—the LAPD under Davis had done them all, and bombing had been their preferred scare tactic. Before Henry, they had even set off a bomb in Calvin's house. No one had been hurt then, but the warning had been clearly delivered, if not heeded.

At his attacker's much-publicized trial, Henry had recovered enough from the explosion to make a dramatic appearance. Testifying from a wheelchair, Henry detailed his investigation of the mayor and police chief. At first, Henry's answers were terse and businesslike, as would be expected from an old cop and hired hand.

When the prosecutor got to the bombing itself, however, Henry had broken down on the stand thinking about Bea. The bombers had assumed Henry would be the one behind the wheel, but only a last-minute change of plans had kept his wife from being the victim. This twist of fate, the randomness of it, had proved a gut-punch to Henry's consciousness. After a few uncomfortable moments of courtroom silence, he pressed on with his testimony, but the truth, his truth, their truth, had been revealed. "Nothing will ever be the same," Bea had said later. "We survived, but our lives will never be the same."

On Main Street, Henry turned the ignition key in the Commander, his inspection complete, the prescience of Bea's words struck him hard once more. He released his held breath and pulled into traffic.

THREE

KIT

The Veterans Center on 3rd and Broadway tried hard to be welcoming in that efficient way the military was famous for. Kit headed down a wide hallway, passing rooms sporting floral couches and wing back chairs, arranged around cozy matching rugs, radios softly broadcasting Arthur Godfrey's morning show, until she found the staff lounge.

Seated at a table, a bowl of bean soup in front of him, Manny Salcido shot up as though at attention and greeted her with an unapologetic grin. "Hey, it's L.A.'s cutest private dick," he said, leaning in for a hug.

Kit obliged, welcoming the warmth of the stout man's embrace. "Gee, Manny, you sure know how to make a dick feel special." They had dated briefly in high school, back when she was innocent and he was muscular, and she knew he still pined for her, a fact she acknowledged but tried never to abuse. He was sweet and a fast talker. A bad back—the result of a car crash—had kept him behind a desk during the war, both in Europe and Los Angeles. If missing out on bombing Hitler bothered him, he never let on.

"Anytime. Have a seat," Manny said, nodding toward a folding metal chair on the other side of the table.

With as much grace as she could muster, Kit sat in the uninviting chair. "Early dinner or late lunch?" she said, nodding her chin at the bowl.

"Neither actually. I'd invite you to join me," he said, "but I had to steal this from the cafeteria. If I don't eat when I can get a chance, I don't eat."

"They're still running you ragged, eh?"

"Some days it takes everything I got just to keep it together."

"Sorry to hear that."

He waved his free hand dismissively. "What's on your menu today?"

"Just wondering if you'd seen this fellow recently." Kit handed him a copy of the *Stars and Stripes* photo. 'He's gone missing."

Manny concentrated on the photo but nothing registered in his eyes. He shrugged. "Don't think so, but like I said, a ton of guys have come through here the last few weeks. I mean hundreds. It's fucking depressing. Pardon my French. What's his name?"

"Peter Novak. He's a doctor."

"Doesn't ring a bell, sorry."

If Manny had seen the name, he likely would have recalled it, she thought. His memory could rival Henry's, almost. "But you'd have a record, if he had requested any services here under that name, right?"

"We would."

She tilted her head back and coaxed him with a half-smile.

He grinned back. "I guess I can sneak a look at the register before I leave this evening."

"Thanks. It's a long shot, but you know me . . ."

"Cross those t's and dot those i's."

She hesitated a beat before asking, "And while you're at it, could you check for the woman in the photo? Lieutenant Dina Harris? D-i-n-a."

"Sure. She's cute. Like Shirley Temple. Is she missing too?"

"No, she's a witness," Kit said as she retrieved the photo.

"How soon do you need the information?"

"Tonight?"

Manny shot her a look of playful reproach. "Only if you let me buy you a drink."

She laughed. "Deal. The usual spot?"

"I'll be there."

She rose and gathered her bags. "Hate to not eat and run, but I've got another appointment."

"Where you off to now?"

"I have a date with a shrink."

"From soup to nuts, eh?"

In the waning afternoon light, Birmingham General appeared flatter and less welcoming than it had the first time she visited. The military had taken it over and, as it was wont to do, turned the quaint Van Nuys hospital into a sprawl of barrack-like buildings. A thick bank of sooty clouds had settled over the complex, enveloping everything, including her mood, like a dirty shroud. Her brother's doctor, Luca Moreno, had suggested they chat outdoors before her visit with Stanley, and Kit had brought along her camera, hoping the sky and the facility's grounds would inspire her.

The doctor was waiting for her on the wraparound porch of the psychiatric unit, which was located in the older section of the hospital next to the steepled chapel. He was sporting a dark suit, and she almost passed him by, momentarily forgetting he was a civilian, hired by the Army on an emergency basis.

He waved her over with a polite smile, and as she got closer, she saw the suit was a pinstripe, neat but a little outdated. As her mother would say, he had a nice head of hair—dark, little waves slicked back—a cleft chin, slightly aquiline nose that looked like it had been broken at least once, and hazel eyes that could only be described as "bedroom." If it weren't for his mouth—broad with thin lips covering slightly crooked teeth—he would have been matinee idol handsome.

"Miss Comfort?" He offered his hand, which like his mouth was expansive and smooth. "Thank you for taking the time to speak with me. I suspect you're busy," he said, nodding at Kit's camera.

"I'm off the clock at the moment," she said with a breeziness she wasn't quite feeling.

"Good. Shall we . . .?" He gestured to a gravel path leading away from the entrance, and they stepped off the porch and headed there. "I imagine you see a lot in your business."

"Let's just say, I won't be joining the Optimist Club any time soon."

He gave a short, warm laugh and Kit relaxed. "I hope it's not too discouraging," he said.

"You want to believe the best of people, but then they go and act like . . . people. But sometimes they surprise you, and I guess that's what keeps me going—the surprises." She paused as they oriented themselves on the path that wound around the various units. "So you said on the phone you needed some information?"

The doctor nodded. "We don't normally involve family members in therapy, but given the particulars of Stanley's case, I thought it might be useful to talk to you. Stanley agreed."

"What are the particulars of his case? In your view?"

"As you've seen, Stanley's memory stops around the time he enlisted. We know approximately when he developed amnesia. We know when he suffered the blast concussion, but we still don't know why he's blanked out his entire military service."

"I take it that's unusual?" Kit asked.

"Usually with concussive amnesia the patient only forgets the period just before the event, not a year or more."

"And not remembering is a problem?" The question had been on her mind ever since Stanley had returned home. While the rest of the world was trying to forget and move on from the war, her brother was being compelled to remember and relive it.

"I would say it's *the* problem," the doctor said. "Or rather it's how the problem is manifesting itself. Some psychological damage is causing him to forget, and as long as the damage is controlling his memory, he can't function normally."

Kit didn't fully understand the doctor's explanation, but accepted it in good faith. She had witnessed Stanley's stupor after all, the mind that went in and out like a bad electrical connection. "What do you want to know?"

"I'm trying to get some insights into his pre-Army days, his relationships. His family life, any romances."

"I'm afraid I won't be much help with the latter. But go ahead."

After a pause, Dr. Moreno said, "Was Stanley close to your parents? Did they have a good relationship?"

"Define good."

"Healthy. Mutually respectful."

"Dad was hard on him, but fair," Kit said as they neared a small building with a ramp snaking from it.

"Demanding?"

"Sure. But he was that way with everyone, not just Stanley."

"Did he withhold affection?"

"I'm not sure he had any to withhold. That wasn't his way."

A man in a wheelchair passed them on the path, breathing hard with the effort. Dr. Moreno nodded a greeting, then said, "Would you say Stanley emulated your father?

"Not consciously."

"What about your mother?"

"Mom doted a bit. As much as Dad would let her. He is the baby after all."

"What about you? How would you describe your relationship with him?"

Kit chuckled. "My annoying little brother? I adore him." Her grin fell, replaced by a sudden gasp of grief. She stopped, overwhelmed. Moreno was silent as she gathered herself. "Is he making any progress, in your opinion?"

"I'm not going to lie. He hasn't responded as well as we had hoped. But there's another technique I've been trying with him—hypnosis."

"Hypnosis? That sounds very . . . Harry Houdini."

"If only it were as simple as a parlor trick." He smiled, and finally she could detect some kindness in his expression. They had come full circle on the path and were approaching Stanley's building from the back. "Clinical hypnosis is a bit more complicated. We've had some success using it for combat stress. But it works best when the clinician has some baseline information about the patient's mental history." He paused. "Which is why I hope we can have more chats like this."

"In my line, that's called gathering more evidence," she said. Then without thinking, she added, "But I'd like that."

Her answer drew a smile. "He'll be coming out in a second, the doctor said, nodding at the porch. "It was a pleasure meeting you, Miss Comfort."

"Likewise, but please call me Kit."

"Kit, of course," he said softly. "I'm Luca."

She half-blushed. "Thank you, Luca, for not giving up."

FOUR
STANLEY

As a familiar silence fell between them, Stanley led Kit out of the sun, toward a string of eucalyptus that ringed the old half of the hospital. Even by Los Angeles standards, it was warm for February. The winter had been brutally dry, with little rainfall to quench hillsides recently scarred by wildfires. While some complained about the arid air, Stanley felt strangely buoyed by it, as though figurative clouds were being lifted along with literal ones. When he had first mentioned this feeling to Doc, he had said in an apparent non sequitur, "Well, Okinawa's very humid."

Okinawa. Doc was always bringing up Okinawa, that place where he had apparently gotten lost, for real and in his head. The Army doctor back in Japan had given him sodium pentothal in the hope he'd be purged of enough demons to serve out his tour, the psychiatric equivalent of patch 'em up and send 'em back. It hadn't work.

Now here he was, back home in the loony bin, still fucked up, still groping for a toehold on his life. Although he remembered as much as the next guy about his so-called youth, the memories seemed to exist on an island far out to sea. He could make out the shape from the shore, but had no way to reach it.

They stopped under a canopy of eucalyptus branches and sat down on a carpet of slender fallen leaves. With his Zippo, Stanley lit a cigarette, and Kit studied him quietly as he took his first drag. He wanted to tell her about the feeling of familiarity that sometimes overwhelmed him, but as usual, his words failed him. So he moved on with the script.

"Did I have a girlfriend when I shipped out?" Stanley stammered, while Kit dug out a small camera from her shoulder bag.

"You were dating. I don't know that you were serious about anyone."

He watched as she released the camera lens. "What are you doing with that?" he said, slowly exhaling a cloud of smoke.

Kit fiddled with the camera's shutter. "I thought I'd take some pictures,"

"Of me?"

"Of you. This place. I like to have pictures of locations. For my work. Do you mind?"

Stanley shrugged. "Do you have old photos of me?"

"Tons. I'll bring them by next time. Maybe they'll trigger something."

Would they? He took a drag on his cigarette, then changed the subject. "Doc told me about Dad when I was in the hospital."

Kit nodded. "Heart attack. He'd been having chest pain, on and off, for some time, according to his doctor. But he never told any of us about it."

"What else about Dad?"

"What else?" Kit raised the camera to her eyes, its lens pointed over his right shoulder, and depressed the shutter.

"Were you sad when he died?"

"Very much so," she said with a catch in her voice.

"Should I be sad?"

The question seemed to confuse or perturb her in some way. "Should you? I suppose so," she said, positioning herself on his other side.

Kit moved with the same confidence as Doc, he thought. Maybe that was normal for normal people. "I mean, were we getting along?"

She drew the camera up to her face, obscuring her eyes. "You and Dad? Sure. Most of the time."

"But not all the time?" he said. The camera clicked.

"You were still a teenager. And his son."

"So he liked you better?"

Kit paused in mid-shot to consider the question. "No. He liked me . . . differently."

"Differently?"

"It's easier for fathers and daughters. No competition."

Abruptly he realized he'd been neglecting his cigarette. He flicked off the long ash. "He didn't mind you being a detective?"

"He might have minded me staying a detective, but during the war, he was too busy worrying about you and the plant to care about what I was doing."

"What about Mom? Did she approve?"

"No, but I wasn't expecting her to." Kit turned to look behind her, squinted with concentration, then snapped a picture of something that had caught her eye. "Has she called you?"

"She talked to Doc," he said flatly. "Doc's obsessed with mothers." Kit laughed. It was her first unguarded moment of the conversation, and Stanley felt a jolt of awareness. "He gave me all the letters you all wrote while I was away. I've only read Mom's and Dad's so far."

"How was it, reading them?" She sounded genuinely curious.

Again, he shrugged. "Kinda like reading a book, and you were all characters in the story." In the distance, he spotted a nurse walking briskly towards them. "Better put that away," he said, indicating Kit's camera with his chin. "Photography is strictly prohibited in this joint."

Kit smirked and slipped the Kodak into her bag just as the nurse reached them. "Your session starts in five minutes, Stanley," she said, all smiles and professional warmth. "Dr. Moreno's waiting in his office."

"I was just leaving," Kit said to the nurse, then to Stanley, she half-whispered, "See you soon, with the evidence."

“Looking forward to it.” Ignoring the nurse, he watched his sister retreat. “I think,” he mumbled before dropping the cigarette butt on the path and crushing it with his toe.

FIVE
LUCA

In the quiet of his office, Luca adjusted the playback speed on his reel-to-reel, eager to refresh his memory of Stanley Comfort's first recorded hypnosis session. Since they were creating a narrative together, with one session building on another, Luca knew that maintaining continuity was key. Along with refreshing his own memory, he needed to confirm that the information just shared by Kit, the sister, lined up with what his patient had already revealed about himself.

In the oddball world of military psychiatry, Luca was himself an oddball. For one thing, he was a civilian, recruited by the Army to help with the incoming tide of damaged psyches. At the start of the war, he had tried to enlist as a medical student but received a 4-F rating from the Selective Service System. In addition to his flat feet, a disqualifying trait inherited from the Moreno side of his family, Luca was a polio survivor.

He had contracted the disease when he was ten and living in an Italian tenement in Brooklyn. Unlike best friend Mateo, who ended up in a wheelchair, Luca suffered only a mild infection and was back on his feet after a few weeks. Polio could reappear in the body years later, however, so despite his recovery, the Selective Service had deemed him ineligible.

Luca had mixed feelings about his rejection. His parents' countrymen, after all, were fighting on the other side, and Luca's studies had led him to view war as its own disease. Early on, his pacifist tendencies did battle with his belief in justice and liberty, concepts drilled into him as the son of immigrants. If humans' capacity for violence served any positive purpose, wouldn't it be to defeat the vicious oppression of fascism? By the time he had finished at Yale, he understood that the Axis must be stopped, and all internal debate ended. He pledged his services to the Army.

But from his first day at Birmingham, Luca had generated suspicion among the military doctors. Their mission was to "fix" the fallen troops as quickly as possible. Their analytical techniques relied heavily on drugs and focused on what was wrong with the man, not what was wrong with war. Not all veterans succumbed to combat fatigue, but in Luca's experience, all veterans bore mental battle scars. Like polio, he thought, combat fatigue was an infection, not of the body but of the soul. And like polio, it could lurk inside men for eternity. In his estimation, what these veterans needed were tools, psychological tools like hypnosis, to launch counterattacks against invasion.

Luca's rejection of lobotomies and injections had raised eyebrows among his Birmingham colleagues, but so far, they hadn't tried to interfere with his treatment regimens. When he volunteered to take over Stanley's case, the unit's conservative director, in fact, had seemed cautiously relieved.

From Army records, Luca had learned that Stanley had been listed MIA a few days after the capture of Okinawa's Cactus Ridge. Weeks later, at the big battle's end, he was discovered miles away, having taken up with another squad. He was disoriented and speechless. According to the medic, he had suffered a head injury and most likely had been unconscious for some time. They ordered him to the field hospital for further evaluation. Then they dropped the Bomb.

From the start, he had told Stanley that to find himself, he must return to Okinawa, metaphorically speaking.

"The path to Okinawa, however, requires a starting point," he had explained to Stanley during their first session, "and since your memory stops when your military service began, the starting point isn't currently on the map. So to speak."

Initial assessments of Stanley's mental condition had been dire. One of Luca's colleagues had speculated that for his psychosis to be so acute, Stanley's ego sensitivity must be immense and therefore a lobotomy might be the only cure.

"But the patient isn't aggressive or even agitated, the usual prerequisites for a leucotomy," Luca had argued. "In my view, lobotomizing an amnesiac would be like curing blindness by turning off the lights. He won't know what he doesn't know."

Hypnosis, he had insisted to the hospital director, was the best therapeutic option for Pfc. Comfort. The director had been skeptical, but signed off on the plan once Luca reminded him that hypnosis was cheaper than surgery.

Luca's plan was to go heavy with Stanley's appointments that week—daily hypnosis sessions of about an hour, augmented by talk therapy. He wanted them intense enough to build momentum and keep Stanley moving forward in his recovery. Intense enough to construct the contours of his memory map. They would fill in the details at a more gradual pace later. That is, if all went according to Hoyle.

For their first session, Luca had wanted only to establish the margins of the lost memories, to construct a frame or foundation, as it were, for discovery. "It will be like watching a movie you can walk out of at any time," he had assured Stanley. "No harm will come to you. You'll only remember what I tell you to remember." Without hesitation, Stanley gave his consent.

Luca checked his watch—fifteen minutes before Stanley's appointment—and flipped the play lever on the tape machine. He heard himself explaining the induction process, instructing Stanley to close his eyes and focus on his breathing. His voice was calm and relaxing, his pitch and cadence like aural mirrors to his words.

"Slowly breathing, in and out, in and out. Easy, even, relaxed. Your muscles are relaxing. One by one, you're letting go. First your face, then your neck and your shoulders. Going down your arms to your

fingers. Now your hips, your thighs, knees, all relaxed. And finally your feet and toes.

Now I want you to imagine you're walking down a set of stairs. Slowly going down, step by step. Breathing with each step. With each step, you're drifting down, deeper and deeper. And as you drift down, you will feel more and more relaxed. You will feel warm. And safe. Warm and safe. How do you feel?"

"Warm and safe."

"Good. Now I want you to imagine you're standing in front of a set of doors. There's a sign on the door that says 'library.' Can you see it?"

Stanley spoke slowly, his voice expressionless.

"Yes, I can see it."

"I want you to open the doors and enter the library."

Silence filled the tape. Stanley was following Luca's instructions, lifting his right arm a few inches, then dropping it.

"Good. You're inside the library. All around you see shelves with books on them. On the right side of the room are books about your childhood, your parents, your sister, your school.

Your life before the war. You can't see what's written on the pages yet, but it's all there. Can you see the books?"

"Yes."

"I want you to go to these shelves and look for a book titled Family. When you find it, raise your right arm."

More silence followed as Stanley raised his right arm.

"Good. Now take the book off the shelf and open it to any page." [Brief pause] What do you see?"

"Saturn."

"The planet?"

"Yes. It's a gas giant, hydrogen and helium. That's what Dad says."

Stanley's voice became childlike, not so much higher pitched as unguarded.

"You're looking up at the stars?"

"Just Saturn. Through the telescope. At the observatory."

"Griffith Observatory? You're there with your father?"

"With Dad, Mom and Kit. We got here early so we could be first in line. Even Mom wants to see Saturn."

"How old are you?"

[Pause] "Ten."

"It's a family outing?"

"Dad really wants to see it. He's been reading newspaper stories about the construction and wants to see it in the flesh."

"And you?"

"Sure. I like that you're looking at the past. That's what Dad says. When you look through the telescope, you're looking at the past in the present."

"What does your mom think?"

"She likes it."

"Excellent. Now I want you to close the book and return it to the shelf. [Silence] You are now going to select another book from the right side of the stacks, but this one will be from when you were in high school. A senior in high school."

Luca stopped the tape and made note of the running time. At this point in the session, he recalled, he had checked Stanley's breathing and looked for signs of distress, before guiding him to his next memory:

"What do you see?"

"Dirt. Grass."

"Where are you?"

"Baseball mound. At San Diego. SC championship."

"You're pitching?"

"Yes."

"You're a senior?"

"Yes. It's my last game."

"Who else is there?"

"Kit."

Luca scribbles the name on his notepad and circles it. "Anyone else?"

"Dad. Dad's there."

"So, you're on the mound. What's happening?"

"Last out. It's tied. I'm up in the count, 1 and 2, but there's a guy on second. Luis is giving me signs to throw a curve. I'm thinking, no, fastball. I shake him off. He flashes the curve sign again. I shake him off. He tries a change-up. I shake him off. He finally flashes fastball. I nod. Then I throw the ball as hard as I can." [Silence]

"Stanley?"

"Hard single up the first base side. The runner's so fast. He's halfway home before Jack can get the ball out of his glove. The throw's not even close."

"Your team lost?"

"That's it. Game over."

The soundtrack filled with muffled noises. Luca recalled Stanley bolting from the couch, his face contorted with anguish, turning to stare at his office door.

"Stanley, what are you looking at?"

"Dad's gone."

"Gone?"

"I see him leaving the stands. He's just walking away. I should have thrown the curve. Why didn't I listen to Luis and throw the curve? He knew, he knew this guy was good at the fastball, but I didn't listen."

"All right Stanley, you can close the book now and return it to the shelf."

Luca shut off the recording and stared at his notes. He had intended the high school memories to be baselines only, bland and comforting. But clearly Stanley had a fearful fury running through his subconscious, an anxiety that predated his combat stress.

As Luca had instructed, when woken from his trance, Stanley had no memory of the details of his library trip, but the agitation produced by the baseball memory lingered in him. What had Kit said about the father? He was demanding. Hard but fair.

Luca rose and took in the scene outside his office window. The lawn was now empty and still, and in the fragile silence, he let his thoughts turn to his encounter with Kit. Not so much her words as her gestures, her walk, her face.

SIX

KIT

Literally at the end of the line—the trolley line—Cole's boasted cheap cocktails, patient bartenders and French dip. Weary workers descended for a quick drink before heading home, but the place emptied out around seven.

Manny, carrying a tray with a martini and a French dip, joined her in a back booth, where she was guarding a Tom Collins. "Where's your martini?"

"Tonight, my heart belongs to Tom," she said before taking a healthy sip of her drink. Unlike most men, who had "their drink," her taste in cocktails was eclectic and mood-driven.

Manny dipped one end of his sandwich in the beefy drippings and took a joyful bite. "Me, I'm in love with jus."

Kit groaned in mock disgust, and in response, Manny brandished the skewered olive from his drink and said, "Go on, take 'olive' me."

She giggled softly. Manny's relentless corny humor had always been his most appealing trait, she thought, even in high school. "Glad to see you haven't lost your touch."

'You inspire me, Kit. With everyone else . . . I'm a regular King Kong." He pounded on his chest in imitation.

"Please."

"Yep. I terrify the gals in the typing pool." "I find that hard to believe."

"You can see them tense up whenever I stick my head through the door."

"Well, you do have a big head."

"And a big bark, and an even bigger bite. They want nothing to do with me."

"You could try being nicer."

Manny scowled. "Too late for that. I don't suffer fools gladly anymore. I'm a rampaging jerk."

"They're lucky to have you over there." Uneasy at Manny's dark turn, Kit changed topics. "You got something for me?" She pointed to a folded sheet of lined paper acting as a coaster for the martini.

"No luck with Peter Novak. I checked our records and called around to some other centers. If he reported in, it wasn't in this county."

"It was a long shot."

"Shirley Temple, however, I did find." He raised the martini to his lips with one hand and tapped the slightly damp paper with the other. "Discharged a month ago at Fort Dix, by reason of Section III AR 615-361. She didn't have enough points for a standard discharge. She'd still be in Europe otherwise."

"615-361? And that would be . . .?"

"Inadaptability. Which in her case, given that she served for almost two years and rose to the rank of lieutenant, would most likely mean pregnancy."

"Pregnancy? Crap."

"I'm assuming the missing fellow is the father?"

"That would be my assumption. And it would explain why she didn't want to wait for the police."

Manny pointed to her empty glass. "Another TC? My treat."

"No, thanks. I should get going. Got an early morning."

Manny shook his head in mock scolding. "You know what they say about all work and no play."

"I know, but I'd rather be boring than bust." Kit started to slide from the booth, then stopped and gave Manny's hand a squeeze. "Thanks, Manny, as always."

Manny grabbed her arm. "Do you really have to go?"

Kit stared at Manny's hand and jerked her arm away. The harshness of the gesture surprised even her.

"Like I said," Manny mumbled, "King Kong. Sorry."

Kit nodded. "Night, Manny. Stay out of trouble."

Kit's house was one of the older structures on the tree-lined central Hollywood street. The modest Spanish stucco had been her childhood home, abandoned after high school for a downtown bedsit, then reclaimed after the sudden death of her father and the even more sudden remarriage of her mother. It sat in the middle of the block, between a sturdy Craftsman bungalow and a red-bricked Italianate monstrosity. Architecturally, this part of Hollywood, like most of "old" Los Angeles, boasted a style for every taste and need. In this part of town, nostalgia and ostentation always won out over aesthetic consistency.

Her father hadn't lived in the house in a couple of years but his handiwork was still very much in evidence throughout. A mechanical engineer, he had custom built closets, cubby holes and "spy windows," as he liked to call them, and had even fashioned a little photography studio in what had been her bedroom.

Her parents had divorced shortly after she had started business college, and her mother lived with Stanley in the house until his enlistment. Stanley had been gone only weeks when she married her father's former business partner, then followed him to Dayton after he was offered a lucrative War Department contract. Predictably, her father had thrown himself into his aircraft job, made essential by the war, and succumbed to a heart attack on the factory floor two months later. Neither parent had had the fortitude to inform Stanley of their marital situation, and by the time of their father's death, Stanley was back in the hospital.

Kit parked in the long driveway and headed for the side door. Following her habit of late, she glanced at the old pepper tree shading the front of the house. Sitting in the crook was an orange tabby, the same orange tabby that had perched there every evening for the past two weeks. He was stocky, with a short, bent tail. With his blockhead and chewed ears, he looked like the feline equivalent of a gone-to-seed pugilist. The crook was just wide enough to accommodate his frame, if not his striped tail, and the way he made the knotty tree his own was impressive.

After he greeted her with a gravely meow, Kit grinned and nodded. "Hello to you too, buddy. I suppose you want your dinner."

He responded with another meow, and Kit unlocked the door and immediately opened the icebox, where she had stored half of a meatloaf sandwich. So far she hadn't been able to pet or even touch him—on the few occasions she tried, he either hissed at her or scratched her—but he always took her meaty food offerings from her hand.

She had asked the neighbors about him, but no one admitted to knowing, let alone owning, him. One time, from her kitchen window, she saw him startle awake in the tree, then dive-bomb a white Persian who had wandered unsuspecting from the neighbor's yard. The Persian took off with a screech, launching himself up and over the neighbor's wooden fence a second ahead of the pursuing ginger. Satisfied that the intruder had been dealt with, the scruffy tabby returned to the tree and resumed his nap. Kit couldn't help but admire his bold style.

Armed with the meatloaf, Kit stood under the pepper tree and looked up at the waiting feline. "I think it's time we formally introduced ourselves," she said, waggling the leftover under his nose. "I'm Kit—yes it's short for Katherine. And you are . . .?"

A meow followed.

"Bomber? Short for the Orange Bomber." Would Henry approve? He was a fan of Joe Lewis, but less so of bombs. The tom apparently didn't care about Henry's feelings, because a second after he received his dubbing, he grabbed the sandwich half with a snap of his mouth, jumped from the tree and ran into the kitchen through the open door. "Bomber it is."

After devouring the meatloaf, Bomber then made himself comfortable on the living room couch, the tree crook already a distant memory.

"All right," she said to her new housemate, "dinner's over, it's picture-making time."

Armed with Dina's *Stars and Stripes* photo, Kit disappeared into her converted bedroom, now set up with lights, boards and a tripod with mounted camera. Gone were her pink, canopied twin bed and matching dresser (not missed) and her collection of Nancy Drew and Dana Girls books (missed). In between her bedroom and Stanley's was a small bathroom, which she had recently converted to a dark room.

She placed Dina's photo on the floor near the tripod, turned on one of the spotlights and aimed the camera lens down, widening the aperture and adjusting the focus. Satisfied with the set up, she started firing off close-ups of Peter Novak's face, grainy and gray-toned, until she had used up her shots.

She removed the spent roll, intending to develop it right then, then noticed the time on her old alarm clock: 7:30. The dark room would have to wait, she decided, until she had checked in with Henry. She headed back to the living room, passing by the still snoozing Bomber on the way.

At this hour, Henry would be at home with wife Bea, whose wellbeing was his constant worry. They had been married since forever, in some health and a lot of sickness. When she had first approached him about joining the company, he had made his needs clear, and made it clear that Bea was front and center.

"I'll need to be home by six," Henry had said, as though a PI's hours were the same as a banker's. She must have given him a blank look because he quickly added, "Except of course, when late hours are required."

"All right," Kit said. She knew she needed to be accommodating. He was in the catbird seat, after all. Talking him out of semi-retirement hadn't been hard, but getting him to commit to an office routine required finesse.

"I may need to take unplanned breaks, from time to time."

"What do you mean, breaks?" she said with concern. Memories of Terrence were still fresh.

"It's Bea. Her health is spotty and sometimes I have to take care of her."

Funny, she thought, though she knew he was married, he had never once mentioned his wife when they worked together at Empire. "Of course. That shouldn't be a problem."

And it hadn't been a problem, for her. Business had been slow. There were times when she and Henry would sit in the office together all day, waiting for the phone to ring or for some schmo to walk through the door. When neither happened, Henry would grab his hat and be out the door by 5:30.

Kit had only met Bea once in person. Early in the partnership, she had shown up at the office with Henry. She had been sharp-eyed and witty, tall and Mary Astor elegant, her voice a seductive alto. Her dress and walk, the way she sat and smoked her cigarette—all had suggested class. So, Henry had married up, was Kit's first thought. Or maybe Bea just had a thing for uniforms. But Kit had seen photos of Henry when he was a beat cop and quickly dismissed that notion. No, their chemistry must have been based on other, less obvious elements. Perhaps "less obvious" was how they stayed married, even in the absence of children.

As they had chatted, Kit had the distinct feeling Bea was sizing her up rather than getting to know her. She didn't seem motivated by jealousy, though. Bea had questioned her (casually, politely) on her detective training and past cases. In short, she wanted to know if her husband was in good hands, professionally speaking. Given all that Henry had gone through Kit understood her fear. She had never discussed the bombing with him, but she knew from news reports that he had been rattled by how close it had come to harming Bea.

As Bea was leaving, apparently satisfied with her husband's new partner, she noticed the ratty dartboard hanging next to the window. "So that's where my dartboard ended up."

"Your dartboard?" Kit said.

Bea laughed, full on. "He didn't tell you? I taught him everything he knows."

"It's true," Henry said. "She was the B'nai B'rith dartboard champion of 1914."

"1915," Bea said. "And 1916."

"You must have sharp eyes," Kit said.

"I had trained eyes," Bea said. "Trained by my father. That's how I found Henry."

Kit had liked Bea that day. She didn't know it then, but *that* Bea made only occasional appearances. And when she did, Henry would devour every moment like a fine five-course dinner.

Shortly after that, on the anniversary of the car bombing, Bea had called the office, desperate to find Henry. Her speech was slow and hesitant, as though she had just woken up, but at the same time, there was panic behind her words. Drunk, drugged, Kit never knew, but she soon came to realize that the Bea she had been introduced to in the office had been the exception, not the rule.

As she picked up the receiver to dial the number she now knew by heart, she wondered if she would ever hear that bright, clear Mary Astor voice again.

SEVEN
HENRY

Bea grimaced at the sound of the telephone. Henry knew she dreaded evening calls because they almost always came from Kit. When they had become partners, he and Kit had agreed that, whenever possible, his day would end before six so he and Bea could have a semblance of a routine. Bea needed routine to maintain her equilibrium, made tender by the bombing years before. Once he was at home, however, Kit thought nothing of interrupting him via the telephone. He debated ignoring the rings.

"Do you want me to get that?" Bea said.

"Nope. I'm going, I'm going." He shuffled to the hallway and picked up on the seventh ring. "Hello."

"How's it going with Movie Mook?" Kit said, repeating his nickname for Emerick. Their conversational shorthand involved no niceties.

"Case closed."

"Good. 'Cause I need your assistance on my new case," Kit said. "A missing vet."

"Shoot."

"Turns out it's a ticking clock."

A case with a hard deadline. "Something's happening tonight?" he said.

"No, no, not that soon. But soon. Can you come to the office in the morning so we can go over the details?"

"How early?"

"Can you make it by eight? I have to stop at Union Station first."

"Right. See you at eight then."

Henry returned to the table to find Bea smoking her post-dinner cigarette and teasing the last sip out of a highball. "That was quick," she said.

"Kit needs help on a missing persons case. A vet."

"Another lost hero?"

"Something like that. I may have to work extra hours."

Bea looked into her empty glass and sighed, but Henry couldn't tell if she was lamenting his schedule or her vanishing drink. By no standards was his wife beautiful, especially in middle age, but she had a graceful, almost dancer-like presence and her delicate skin and grey eyes seemed to defy her pugnacious nose and brow.

Before the bomb, Bea had been a drinker, but not a drunk, she had been delicate but not fragile, emotional but not manic. She could wake up sad, but like the L.A. sky in June, be sunny by noon. She could be hurt by the world but not broken. The future held possibilities, even if they often seemed far away.

Then in that moment of terror, wrapped inside a thousand bits of glass and metal, the wife he had known for twenty years had flown away. Caution had been replaced by paranoia, sensitivity by the jitters. Sunless days were many. Her friends sensed something was off but were too polite to mention it. Henry had taken her to multiple doctors, but they had no weapons to fight the creep of despair.

"Hey," he said, "I just remembered. You know what Saturday is?"

She looked at him with curious, unfocused eyes. "Saturday?"

"Chinese New Year." Watching the Golden Dragon parade had been a Richman family tradition in better times, for reasons he could no longer recall. "Why don't we go this year?"

"Hmm."

"We haven't had a night out in months."

"You haven't wanted a night out in months."

Technically Bea was right, although he had never admitted that her drinking was behind his refusals. "So I'm past due. The story of my life."

She laughed. "I can't remember the last time we went. Year of the Tiger? Rabbit? What is it this year?"

"Year of the Dog. You love dogs."

"I do love dogs," she said, finally warming to the suggestion.

"I can meet you there after work."

"What if Kit needs you?"

"I'll be there. Promise."

She stubbed her spent cigarette into her favorite green glass ashtray, as a look of relief passed over her face. "I'll be the one in the lucky red dress." She smiled tentatively at him, almost playful.

"Lucky for me," he said, gently squeezing her shoulder. "I'll finish up here."

EIGHT
STANLEY

Stanley stared at the pile of letters in his lap. They were bundled together with string and arranged in chronological postmark order, the oldest on top. He had promised Doc he would read them and "document his reactions" in his journal. Think of it like a homework assignment, Doc had said, as though that would somehow motivate him.

Stanley grabbed his cigarettes from the nightstand and tapped one out of the pack. He reached for his lighter and his eye fixed on the neat, even handwriting of the top letter's return address. He recognized the penmanship as Kit's and its familiarity made him uneasy. For some reason, he felt like a spy, snooping on her private life.

As he sparked up the Zippo, he considered tossing the letters and the journal under his bed and playing dumb with Doc. But he knew Doc was relentless and too smart to be fooled about such things. In that way, he was just like Coach. Like that time he had sworn to Coach he was practicing his curve and not sneaking off to drink beer. Coach had caught him red-handed at the latter and exposed his lie about the former by smacking every curve ball Stanley threw at him over the outfield fence.

Doc didn't humiliate like Coach, but his sighs and sad nods could be almost as unnerving. So with his pencil and journal at the ready, Stanley untied the string holding the letters together and slipped the first one from its envelope.

January 2, 1945

Dear Stanley,

Happy New Year! By the time you get this, 1945 will probably be old news already. It seems like a second ago that I kissed your dopey face goodbye. The folks and I had a pleasant if quiet Christmas. I won't tell you about my bacchanalian New Year's at the Canteen—you're still my little brother after all. But needless to say, with Margie and Annie serving up the punch, we were feeling no pain. I hope wherever you were, you were able to celebrate the holidays in some fashion.

And speaking of fashion! Guess who treated herself to a fancy new hat for Christmas? A little black satin number with dyed-to-match ostrich feathers—just like the one Tana Turner wore in "Slightly Dangerous." Mom says I have more hats than Hedda Hopper. That's the problem with working so close to Bullocks. Even with rationing, they manage to put up the most intoxicating window displays in the city. How can a career girl say no?

And speaking of career girls! Business at the agency is mercifully slow. I say mercifully because Terrence has been absent, and I'm doing everything, including the surveillance. Henry Richman, one of my mentors at Empire, has been a fount of advice, but the actual footwork is all me. And what tired feet they are!

Of course, I'm already missing you terribly. Saturdays at the house just aren't the same without you. I hate going to the matinees by myself, so I no longer know what "The Shadow" knows! I think of you every time I drive by the Cathedral field. (They repainted the stands and the scoreboard over the break.) Please be as safe as you can be out there. You're always in my thoughts. Mom is sending another care package, and you can expect one from me soon.

Lots of love,
Kit
P.S. I ran into Joan at the market the other day. She sends her best.

He made a note to ask Kit about the care packages. What exactly was in them? And possibly about Joan, his girlfriend from tenth grade.

February 12, 1945
Dear Stanley,

Looks like these letters are the 'Holiday Inn" of correspondence. Honest Abe would approve, as would Cupid. Of course, you know how I feel about the latter. (Raspberries.) But how are you? Safe and dry, I hope.

I was happy to hear my care package arrived intact. I figured I'd do a better job with recordings than cookies and candy. My cooking skills have not improved in your absence. And yes, that was Henry with me (in my Lana Turner hat) in front of the agency. He says a big hello!

And speaking of the agency! I have some news to report. Your sister is now the controlling partner in Comfort and Company Investigations! We lost Terrence, so I took over the lease. It was a big step, one I took only because Henry agreed to be my almost silent partner. Mom has reluctantly given her blessing to the operation. I think she's finally given up on making me the girl next door. You know I've always been more Veronica Lake than Alice Faye.

Well, that's all the news that's fit to print. I'll write again soon. Hearing from you is the highlight of my life right now. You're always in my thoughts.

Hugs and kisses,

Kit

Although he recognized Kit's tone—the words sounded just like her—nothing unmoored for him. Apparently, the contents of the care package had been lost. He wrote "care package?"

March 2, 1945

Dearest Stanley,

I hope you're feeling better and over your bout of dysentery (Mom filled me in). It's a relief to know you're safe and are being watched over by wonderful doctors.

Business is finally picking up at Comfort and Company, but that means I have less time to perfect my dart throwing! I'll never be as good as Henry, who I swear could hit the bulls-eye while blindfolded and handcuffed. (To answer your question—he doesn't bet the ponies anymore, although he does spend a lot of time reading the racing forms.)

And speaking of sports! You'll be happy to hear that Jim Sweeney has signed on to manage the Angels again. I guess the owners know a winner when they see one. It looks like half the players have been sent to Chicago to fill all the holes in the Cubs' lineup, though.

And speaking of holes! You asked about my love life and whether I had one. The answer is no, but I'm not complaining. I'm too busy with the business right now to make anyone a decent companion. I may take your suggestion and get a cat instead!

Look for another package or two from me and the folks. Thinking of you and hoping to see you again soon!

Love,

Sis

"Your bout of dysentery." He added that to his journal, thinking for once, he was grateful for his amnesia.

March 31, 1945

Dear Stanley,

I'm happy to hear you're back on your feet (and Mom's socks) and ready for action. I know you will do your duty and do it with courage and skill. You don't have to worry about making me or anyone else proud. I couldn't be any more proud of you if I tried.

Dad has been working long hours at the plant, which is probably why he hasn't written much. He's still adjusting to the new arrangements with Mom. And you know Dad . . . a man of few, but always choice, words.

It's inspiring to see how folks are coming together and doing their bit. Mom is following Mrs. Roosevelt's lead and knitting tons of socks. I'm still volunteering at the Canteen with Margie and Annie, taking photos of the boys with their dates. Last week, we sold over $100,000 in war bonds!

As always, take care and stay safe, little brother!

All My Love,
Kit

Finally, something was pricked. Not memories per se, but a feeling of unease. He moved on.

April 13, 1945

Dearest Stanley,

I guess our letters crossed last time. I'm so glad the care package arrived in one piece. I know Mom will be thrilled to hear the socks fit and were appreciated. Sometimes the little things really do make all the difference.

You asked about Comfort and Company and how I spend my time there. I'd like to tell you I catch bad guys like the Caped Crusader, but honestly, most of the 'criminals" we stop are of the naughty spouse variety. I tracked down my first missing person last week, but he turned out to be a naughty spouse too! Yes, I do take lots of photographs. Mom is not exactly thrilled having the old bathroom turned into a developing station, especially when the subjects are almost pornographic!

And speaking of naughty! Your pal Dewey sounds like quite the character. I sure hope I get to meet him some day.

I know you're on the move and may not receive this for a while, please know that I'm thinking of you and praying for your safe return. Please be careful.

All My Love,
Kit

Stanley dropped the letter. It was the last of the bunch and, though he couldn't say why, the most disquieting. He scribbled the word "socks" in his journal, then underlined it twice. Next, he wrote "Dewey." With a shaking hand, he drew a circle around the name. Dewey.

TAKE THE A TRAIN

Tuesday, February 5, 1946

NINE
KIT

Kit checked the Santa Fe board for the location of the Super Chief train, which was leaving on Track 2 in ten minutes. Union Station was overflowing with anxious passengers. The wind had suddenly picked up, and like precipitation, wind seemed to drain Angelinos of their confidence.

By the time she made her way to Track 2, the last of the Super Chief's passengers were boarding. Kit scanned the platform in search of a conductor, zeroing in on one who was helping an elderly man negotiate the train car steps. After the last of the passengers had filed in, she approached the conductor, armed with Dina's photo. His Santa Fe name badge identified him simply as "Frank."

"Excuse me, Frank," Kit said, flashing her warmest smile, "by any chance, were you working on this train this past Saturday morning?"

"Saturday? Sure was." Frank was short and slim, his boyish physique contrasting with his world-weary eyes. Kit put him in his late 40s.

"Did you see this man on that run?" she asked, handing him Peter's photo.

Frank studied the photo and frowned. "I might have. Can't say for sure. Sorry."

"Is there someone else on your crew who might have seen him?"

Frank thought for a second. "Sure. Roland might have. He's a steward."

Kit nodded. "A steward?"

"Stewards tend to notice things us conductors don't."

"Of course. And where can I find Roland?"

"He'll be coming along in a second," Frank said, turning to leave. "You can't miss him. He's only got one arm."

Before Kit had time to ponder the notion of a one-armed steward, Roland appeared on the platform. Kit scurried to catch up to him. Built like a palmetto tree perpetually bent by an ocean breeze, he loomed over her, his armless uniform sleeve pinned up as if to say, I dare you. "Excuse me. Roland"?

Roland stopped, silent for a bit while he appraised Kit. "How can I help you?"

Kit wasn't prepared for the gentleness of Roland's low and soft voice and stammered a reply. "Thank you. Frank said you might remember a passenger who took the train from Chicago on Friday." She offered him the photo. "This man."

Roland took the photo and glanced at Peter's image. "Yes, m'am. I remember him."

"You do?"

"I do. Fried eggs and bacon, black coffee, no toast. Corn beef hash for lunch. Dinner, fried chicken and potatoes, apple pie."

"And that would have been on Friday? After Kansas?" Kit asked, scrambling to extract her notebook and pencil from her bag.

"Yes, m'am."

"Do you recall when you last saw him?"

Roland paused to consider the question. "Dinner."

"So, you served him dinner, on Friday. What about breakfast the following morning?" Kit wrote the words "dinner" and "Friday" in her notebook, then underlined them.

"No, didn't see him at breakfast. Just dinner."

"Where was the train at dinner?"

"New Mexico. That's where it always is at dinner."

The platform had filled suddenly with exiting passengers, chattering and clacking their baggage, and Kit stepped back from the swirling crowd. "Do you recall anything else about him? Anything that stood out?"

"He ate dinner with a fellow."

"Someone he met on the train?"

"Must have been."

"Why do you say that?"

Roland paused. "He's a doctor? Your man?"

Already she was impressed with Roland. "That's right. A radiologist."

"The other fellow kept touching his chest. Your man . . .

"Dr. Novak."

"Right. I heard him offer to look at it after dinner."

"Was the other man touching his chest like he was having trouble breathing?"

"No, more like an injury. Like it was sore. But not an emergency."

"Did the two men leave the dining car together?"

"Don't think so," he said, pausing to take another glance at Kit's photo. "In fact, now that you mention it, the other fellow excused himself before dessert."

"Did you see the other fellow again? At breakfast?"

"Yes, ma'am. He showed up early. Only had black coffee, though."

"Is there anything else you can remember? About Dr. Novak or the other man."

Roland started to shake his head in the negative, then was seized by a memory. "This might be nothing, but he—the other man—had a funny way of writing his numbers."

"How so?"

"Mind?" He reached out for her pencil, and Kit held out her notebook. "We always ask the passenger to write their section and compartment number on their order. He wrote his like this." Carefully, Roland wrote two numbers and returned the pencil to Kit.

Kit glanced at the paper and recognized the numbers as 1 and 9, but the 1 resembled a cursive "T" and the 9 looked like a small "g."

"Never seen numbers written like that. Have you?" Roland said.

"No, I don't think I have." Kit's eye returned to the numerals. She knew their oddness could just be a quirk of the writer, but she made a note to check them out. "Thank you, Roland, you've been very helpful."

"So did he run out on you?" Roland asked, his curiosity finally getting the better of him. "The doctor?"

"Not on me. I'm a private investigator."

"For real?"

"You bet."

Roland threw his head back and laughed. "Well, knock me over with a feather. Who'd ever guess?"

She grinned. "Exactly. They never see me coming."

"Yeah, I know something about being invisible myself. You see some things, that's for sure."

She handed him a Comfort and Company business card. "If you happen to see Dr. Novak or the other man again, please call this number."

"Will do," he said, then looking at her card, added, "Miss Comfort."

As she made her way across the Mission style concourse, she picked up her pace.

She was in mid-throw when Henry slipped into the office and grunted loudly in greeting, distracting her. The dart barely kissed the outer band. "Hello to you too," she said. "I had six straight bullseyes going till you showed up."

Henry raised a graying eyebrow. "Six, huh? In a row?"

"Maybe not exactly in a row."

Henry chucked his hat at the mounted coat rack, flashing a self-satisfied grin when it landed squarely on a peg. Oblivious to the local fashion trend that had made hat-wearing for men optional,

Henry never went anywhere without his beloved fedora. "Six, huh?" he repeated.

"All right, two. Two not in a row."

"Double or single?" he said, removing his coat and hanging it below his hat.

Kit dropped the dart on the desk next to an open manila folder labeled "Dina Harris" and settled into the battered executive chair. "One of each."

"So what's the word?" Henry said, claiming the dart for himself and pushing his glasses firmly against the bridge of his nose. Just recently he had confessed to her that with his glasses on, he had 20/10 vision. He had insisted on the over-correction, which explained, in part, not only the extreme accuracy of his aim, but the ease with which he hustled unsuspecting challengers. "No one expects an old guy in glasses to have the vision of a hawk," he had boasted.

Kit showed him Dina's clipping and filled him in on the details provided by Roland and Manny, concluding with the kicker, "And she's pregnant."

"How far along?"

"Early days."

"Ah."

Kit didn't need to elaborate with Henry. Abortion was a fact of life in their world. "And there's this." Kit grabbed Roland's note and handed it to Henry, who adjusted his glasses and studied it for a beat.

"Huh," he said at last.

"Huh, what?"

Henry returned the paper to Kit and picked up the dart from the desk. "It's distinctive. The handwriting. Whose is it?"

"Technically, the train steward's. He said the injured man Novak was talking to wrote his numbers like that. Do they suggest anything to you?"

"Possibly that he was educated overseas, or by someone else who was educated overseas." After positioning himself in front of the board, he aimed and threw a double bullseye.

Kit paused to allow Henry another toss and another double. "Roland didn't pick up on an accent."

"Could have lost it, if he's been living here a while. But hand-writing? That's unlikely to change."

"So the doctor was chatting on the train with a stranger who might have been a foreigner—and likely injured, by Roland's account—but we have no idea who he is or if he was involved in any way with Novak's disappearance."

"That about sums it up," he said, punctuating the "up" with a bulls-eye toss.

"Are you going to keep doing that?" Kit asked, jutting her chin at the dartboard.

"Just one more." He threw the dart, just barely scoring a single bulls-eye. "Four's my lucky number."

"Four's no one's lucky number."

"Do you want me to tell you the story of why four's my lucky number?" he said, making no move to retrieve the dart.

"No," she said flatly. "What's our next move?"

"Hope Calvin comes up with something?" Calvin was Henry's longtime go-to guy, the most connected man in Los Angeles after Henry himself.

"And if he doesn't?"

"You'll think of something else."

"Me?" Kit said with more irritation than she intended.

"It's your case, Kit. I'm just lending a hand and a contact or two."

"I know." Kit glanced at her watch. "That's the problem." She adjusted her hat and reached for her gloves. Dina wasn't a big client, if such a thing existed in their line of work, but she was paying for that month's office rent.

"Leaving so soon?"

"I have to drop some photos off for Stanley. Should I just meet you at the park?" she said, suddenly recalling that it was the first Tuesday of the month, the day Henry had set aside for target practice and other tactical defense lessons.

He nodded. "Right. I'll go there from Calvin's." He walked to the door as Kit grabbed her bag and purse. "Did I mention we need a Girl Friday?"

"We can't afford a Girl Friday."

"We can't not afford one," Henry said, opening the door for Kit. "And it doesn't have to be a girl."

"Good luck with that," she said smiling as she passed by him. She caught a whiff of his favorite, bourbon, mixed with, what? Gasoline?

TEN
HENRY

Henry turned onto the boulevard that separated east Hollywood from its ritzier cousin, Los Feliz. Homes here were a mix of oversized California Spanish and East Coast columned wistfulness. Calvin Parsons lived north of the boulevard, in a curling warren of streets all named oak-something. The semi-wild Griffith Park was spitting distance. Henry had gotten lost up here more than once, but the route to Calvin's house was etched in his brain.

He parked behind the rambling Spanish stucco, complete with pool, fountain and foliage that seemed to draw a curtain on the ugliness lurking without. Henry pushed open the ornate wrought-iron gate festooned with a sign that never failed to make him both smile and cringe: Our Door's Open. Let He Who Enters Find Rest and Peace.

Calvin had lived more lives than a cat, from missionary to restaurateur to radio host to civic reformer. During the investigation into the city's corrupt police chief a few years before, he and Calvin had become unlikely partners, the rough ex-cop and the pious do-gooder. Their efforts led not only to the bombing attempt on Henry's life but the end of City Hall as they knew it. For a brief moment, Henry enjoyed celebrity status, and Calvin's reputation hit the stratosphere.

After his reformer activities, Calvin had done a stint in the Army, enlisting as a private and working his way up to corporal, Calvin-style. Of course, Henry knew that no matter how earnest and modest Calvin's actions were, his public persona had guaranteed special attention from the brass. Shamelessly, and with Calvin's endorsement, the Army had used him as a recruitment tool. Though it had been a while since Henry had last spoken with his former comrade-in-arms, he was counting on those connections to bear fruit for Kit's client.

The housekeeper, a petite brown-skinned woman he had never seen before, led the way, and even before Henry had reached the sunken living room, he was assaulted with the odor of burning incense. It was one of the many cultural oddities Calvin had indulged in since his missionary days in the Far East. With the exception of a pair of flags—the Stars and Stripes and the Union Jack -hanging crossways over the curved entry, the décor hadn't changed much since Henry's last visit. Mounted aboriginal masks and spears still competed with Chinese vases and framed calligraphy. A grand piano and music stand still crowded one corner, and the opposing wall of books still reminded Henry of his modest place in the intellectual hierarchy.

Calvin greeted him with a huge grin and an even bigger handshake. He was wearing his best gray wool suit and signature Chinese tie. Whether he was on his way out to work, or had just come home, Henry couldn't tell. He had always kept odd hours.

Physically, Calvin and Henry were polar opposites: Henry, stocky but paunchy, balding and near-sighted, with full lips and a round face, everything slightly puffy with lack of sleep. Calvin, as trim as a stretched rubber band, pointed nose and chin, thin lips and an eager, searching gaze. They made an odd pair. Henry, the seen-it-all detective and former unrepentant cop, and Calvin, the do-gooder restaurateur.

'You and Beanie are still together, aren't you, Henry?"

For reasons he could no longer recall, "Beanie" had become Calvin's nickname for Henry's wife, Bea. "We are. Why do you ask?"

"I'm starting a new business. Somewhat on the Q-T."

Calvin paused, and Henry stared expectantly at his sometime employer. "Have you ever heard the term "marital aids"?

"Feathers and dildos?"

'Yes, and other things."

Before Henry had time to process Calvin's question, a curvaceous, tanned woman walked into the room, smiling beatifically at his host. She was all bosom and hips, or at least that was all Henry could make out.

"Hi, darling. You've never met Henry, have you?"

"I've not had that pleasure, no." Her voice was soft but full, a bit on the high side.

'Henry, this is Marina, my girlfriend. Marina, Henry Richman, the investigator I was telling you about."

Henry took Marina's hot hand and pumped it gingerly. Marina beamed at him. "I'm sorry," Henry mumbled, "did you say. . .?" Without thinking, Henry glanced in the direction of the kitchen.

"Don't worry, Henry. Ellen's not here at the moment, but she knows about Mar. We're all one big happy family."

An image of the middle-aged Ellen—once a farm girl from Wisconsin—flashed through Henry's mind. They had met years before, when Calvin had first hired Henry to dig dirt on the police chief. A strain of the unconventional did run through her, but sharing her roof with her husband's mistress was a level of eccentric he would never have predicted. But then, he never would have pegged Calvin as a dildo man either.

Still smiling, Marina said, "Let me take your hat." Henry placed his fedora in Marina's outstretched hand and without missing a beat, she added, "And what can I get you to drink? Scotch?"

"Nothing for me, thanks."

"I was just telling Henry about our new business."

"Ah. Were you hoping to make a sale?" she said with a half-laugh as she poured herself two fingers worth.

"You never know. Henry's a very enlightened fellow. Aren't you, Henry?"

A younger man might have blushed but Henry only grunted. "Actually I was hoping to use your expertise on a different sort of delicate matter. If you have a moment." He shot Calvin a familiar look.

Calvin nodded and gestured toward the back of house. "Will you excuse us?" Calvin said to Marina.

"Of course," Marina said and smiled at Henry.

"Thank you. Uh, very nice meeting you."

"You too, Mr. Richman. And in case Calvin forgot to tell you, friends get a 20 percent discount on our entire inventory."

"That's very generous of you," Henry said with, he hoped, sincerity, as Calvin escorted him out of the living room and into his home office.

The game room boasted a regulation pool table with a mounted stick rack, an antique chessboard of unknown origins tucked into an alcove, an upright piano (another piano?) and a fully stocked oak bar with leather-padded stools. Henry was pleased to see the old dart-board he had bequeathed to Calvin years before still hanging next to the pool cues.

"Thanks for indulging me back there, Henry. I'm sure it wasn't what you were expecting." Calvin reached for a pool cue and began chalking it. Henry recalled Calvin had a solid technique, not as polished as his own, but with a chess-like studiousness. Every now and then he devised shots complex and clever enough for a break-and-run.

"You never fail to surprise me, Calvin. That's what I adore about you," Henry said, picking up his own stick. The table was racked and ready to go.

Calvin barked a laugh. "I know I'm going to regret this, but you go first."

"Stripes." Henry took the break shot, sending the 11 ball into a side pocket. The cue ball was exactly where he wanted it and he lined up another shot, tapping the 9 ball into a corner pocket.

"So, how can I help?" Calvin broke in.

Henry repositioned himself and another ball found its way into a pocket. "Are you still friends with that colonel back in Washington, the one who works at the War Department?"

"Earl Sheldon you mean? He's a general now."

"I'm trying to get information on an Army vet. Peter Novak. He was a doctor in the medical corps. He's gone missing, and our local contact doesn't have anything on him. "

"A doctor?"

"Radiologist."

"What sort of information do you need from Earl?"

"Anything that might lead us to his current whereabouts or condition." Henry didn't want to give Calvin any information that might prejudice his query. "All we know for sure is he boarded the Super Chief in Chicago on Friday and sent a telegram from Kansas City a few hours later. Our client went to Union Station on Saturday to meet him, but he never showed."

Calvin cocked his head, considering Henry's recitation. "May I ask, do you think he might be involved in anything?"

"No, not the criminal variety anyway." Henry winked and proceeded to hit three more winning shots.

"Ah, a woman. She must be very much in love to have hired you."

"Desperate might be more accurate."

"I see," Calvin said without a note of condemnation. "When did he get stateside?"

"A few weeks ago. Visited some family outside Chicago before heading here."

"It's not a lot to go on, but I'll telephone Earl in the morning, see what he says."

"It's a long shot . . ." Henry said, then tapped his last ball into the center pocket.

"But it's better than no shot." With a smile and a nod, Calvin acknowledged Henry's quick victory. "Glad to see you haven't lost your aim."

"Like riding a bicycle."

"A unicycle maybe."

"Thanks, Calvin, always a pleasure," Henry said, returning his stick to its stand. "I can see myself out."

"Thanks for stopping by. Really. Like old times. I'll call you after I talk to Earl."

"Appreciate it."

"And of course, give Beanie my best."

ELEVEN

KIT

Kit fought the urge to move closer to the good doctor as he examined the photo album she had brought for Stanley. The spontaneous smile he had greeted her with when she popped into his office unannounced could only be described as lusty, and his bedroom eyes were living up their nickname in a betrayal of professional decorum. When he had suggested they go over the photos on his couch, she didn't hesitate to plop down next to him.

"You're a talented photographer," he said after flipping through a few pages of family photos.

"Thank you. My dad taught me."

"Taught you? Not Stanley?"

"Stanley wasn't interested. Too busy playing ball."

Luca nodded. "Hopefully these will help flip the switch for him."

She pulled a thin stack of letters from her camera bag and held it out to him. "I also brought the letters he wrote to me. They aren't very detailed, but if you think they would be helpful, I'm happy to share."

Their arms touched as he reached for the stack. The sensation lasted only a moment, and Luca made no comment, but she could see a change in his expression. He's putting on his doctor face, she thought.

"Thanks. I'll take a look," he said, looking down at the letters. "You never know what might trigger a memory. It could be a smell, a song, an image, a phrase."

"What if he never remembers his service? Would that be such a tragedy? Wouldn't it be a blessing to forget, just pick up where his mind has left off and restart his life?" Like accepting that you're better off without your runaway bride, she thought, or your cheating boyfriend. Just let it go and forget it.

"It's a nice thought. Unfortunately he lost more than just a year of memories. A part of his personality is missing too. And I worry he won't be able to find peace and get on until we find it."

She sighed. Was nothing simple? "Of course. I get impatient sometimes. In fact, I'm notorious for my impatience."

"Impatience can be a good motivator in some situations."

"But not in this one."

"Maybe not in this one," Luca said with a gracious smile. He glanced at his wristwatch—it looked like real gold—and grimaced. "I'm very sorry, but I have an appointment coming in shortly."

"Of course," she said, standing. "I was lucky to have caught you at all." As she moved toward the door, the urge to linger strong, she took note of the framed licenses and certificates on the wall. One was written in what she assumed was German. "You went to school in Europe?" she said.

"University of Berlin. They had one of the best psychiatry schools in the world . . . before the war."

"Is that where you learned hypnosis?"

"That I learned at Yale, actually. But I got my foundational instruction in Germany."

Germany. That explained all the Freud and Jung on his shelves. The business of shrinks had always struck her as exotic. And foreign. But Yale was impressive. "Sorry. One more thing." Kit pulled Roland's note from her bag and offered it to Luca. "Do you recognize the writing style in this by any chance?"

Luca scanned the numbers and without hesitation said, "That's how Germans write their numbers."

"Germans?"

"Germans. Austrians. Most likely Hungarians too. Is that significant?" he said, his curiosity piqued.

"Could be." At that moment, a young man in jeans and a striped camp shirt came through the door. He reacted with surprise at Kit's presence, and Kit avoided looking at him as she reached for the doorknob. "Thank you, Dr. Moreno."

"Luca. Glad I could help," he said. Then after a pause, he added, "Stop by anytime."

Stop by anytime. As Kit strode toward the Recreation Area, she replayed Luca's parting words in her head. Had they been merely a polite afterthought? Or something more? Had she detected a note of hopefulness in his voice? Did she want him to be hopeful?

By most people's standards, Kit's love life was a pathetic affair, influenced unduly by her work. Her mother regarded her persistent singleness as a moral failing and was relentless in her disapproval. In her mind, being a "career bachelorette" was a million times worse than being a remarried divorcee.

Even her pals Margie and Annie had given up on her. Margie had recently married (to a pilot she met at the Canteen) and Annie had spent their last cocktail hour together showing off her big-rock engagement ring. Of the three of them, Kit had predicted Annie would be the last to marry. Starlet beautiful, Annie had her pick of men and dated constantly. But being surrounded by would-be lovers only seemed to bore and irritate her. "It's like eating chocolates," Annie whined at the Canteen one night, "you can't help but bite into them, but each time you do, you get nougat instead of marzipan."

The men came and went. Kit assumed Annie's Whitman's Sampler approach to romance would keep her single well into her twenties, but over their last gin and tonic together, she startled Kit when she slipped off her glove to reveal "the ring" before admitting to "the fiancé."

Kit asked Annie if her new fiancé was marzipan, but having conveniently forgotten her analogy, Annie responded that, no, he was a Hancock Park financier. "He loves marzipan, though." Kit couldn't imagine anything more deadly than a marzipan-loving money man, but smiled with approval. After all, now that the war was over, wasn't it every American girl's dream to have both a husband and a fur coat? If Money Man hadn't yet bought a mink for Annie, Kit thought, it was only a matter of short time.

For his part, Henry, being a man of learned discretion, had never questioned her on the subject of her love life. But at the start of their partnership, she felt compelled to explain herself by declaring, "I'm between beaus right now."

Romance had been on her mind as she had just wrapped an assignment involving a married Universal Studios executive and his ingénue girlfriend. The vice-president of production had hired Kit precisely because no one in the business would recognize her. Starlets were a staple of private investigators all over town, and many of their clients were repeat customers. Mr. Universal suspected his mistress of cheating on him with a recently discharged Marine, and Kit had acquired visual proof his instincts were on the mark. Kit marveled at the actress' self-destructive passion for the poor serviceman and briefly considered withholding the evidence.

"Worthless slut," the executive had mumbled upon seeing the photographs. His voice was soft, but Kit could see the rage in his face. An hour later, she knocked on the young woman's door and warned her to leave town and take her lover with her.

"I just wanted you to know there's no one in the picture," she had repeated to Henry, "in case you're curious about my state of affairs."

"Not my concern," Henry said, nonplussed. He was showing off his bulls-eye techniques on the office dartboard, warmed by a shot glass of bourbon.

"Right. It's no one's concern, because nothing's going on. But if something were going on, I'd tell you."

Henry turned and looked blankly at her. "Why?"

"In case I started acting different."

"Would you? Act different?"

"No. I don't think I would, but you never know. You've seen what love can do to a person."

"You want to succeed as a private investigator? Then keep your private life private and always separate. For your sake and his. Understood?"

"Understood," she had said firmly. "But just to be clear, there is no 'his,' at this time."

Truth was, she was enjoying her solo life. Her last affair with a vice-detective-turned-bomber-pilot had been so sapping that when it ended two years before, she felt liberated to the point of giddiness. He had wanted her to follow a conventional feminine path, and their passion crumbled under his prejudice and her stubbornness. And Terrence? There had never been a chance there. When it came to romance, she preferred men closer to her own age.

Juggling cases and lovers had proved exhausting and unfulfilling. So why was she still thinking about Luca and feeling like a class A dope?

TWELVE
STANLEY

Evidence. That's what Kit told him she was bringing—evidence of his recent past in the form of photo albums. Doc arranged for them to meet in the Rec Room, the big open room where patients could play cards or do giant jigsaw puzzles (like that actress in Citizen Kane) or read magazines. Or just sit and stare out the window, or sit and stare at the door, depending on your preferences. The tables and chairs were set up in a way to encourage chit-chat, even though many of the residents had lost the habit.

As he entered and spotted her sitting on a winged-back chair, she smiled and gave him a little wave. The sight of her made him both grin and recoil, like a bottle of bourbon that called your name while filling you with dread of next day's hangover. He nodded back and walked over. Across from Kit's chair was another winged-back chair, with a little bistro-style table between them.

He didn't sit down but said, "Do you mind switching seats? I like to keep my eye on things."

"Sure," she said and stood up. If she found his request weird, she didn't let on.

He settled into the vacated chair and saw a Coca-Cola and glass of ice waiting for him.

"I took the liberty of buying you a drink," Kit said, with a lopsided grin.

"Thanks," he said, staring at the drink he loved but not touching it.

Kit plucked several small photo albums from her camera bag and placed them side by side on the little table.

"Whoa, you weren't kidding when you said you had a lot of photos."

"And these are just from the last few years." She pointed to a dark green album labeled "Stanley Pfc." and said, "That one is your enlistment album. Doctor Romero wanted you to look at that in particular."

Stanley picked up that green album and slowly turned the pages, registering each snapshot before moving on. Most were just of him, wearing his Army uniform. He was grinning and smirking in most, waving at Kit or mock saluting. His mother was in some, sporting awkward smiles of pride and dread. These frozen-in-time smiles left him slightly off-kilter.

If he was unnerved seeing himself in uniform, the soldier in the last photograph of the album, pictured standing next to Stanley, his arm draped casually around his shoulder, merely perplexed him. "Where did you get this?"

'You sent it with one of your letters. You wanted me to have it for safekeeping."

He stared at it. "Do you know who he is?"

"You wrote his name on the back. Dewey."

"Oh, Dewey." Now he had a face to go with that name.

"Do you want to take it?"

"No," he said hesitantly. "That's all right."

He moved on to the next album, titled simply "1944." Theoretically he remembered most of this year, and indeed, the images—a mix of family, friends and places—were recognizable. On one page, he stopped, riveted by a photo showing him with his arm around a pretty girl. She was blonde, with a shy smile and bold eyes. He pressed his lips together in deep concentration. "What's her name?"

"Judy, I think. You had just started going out with her."

Judy. He had only a vague memory of her. "Where was this taken?"

"Outside the house. You had just gotten back from a matinee at Grauman's."

Stanley nodded as though memories of Judy at Grauman's were flooding back. He took in his own wide grin—the boy without a care. Would Judy recognize him if she saw him today? Would she want to go to a matinee with him? Unlikely, he mused.

In high school, he had been too busy with sports to spend a lot of time dating. And as an all-boy school, Cathedral had made it easy to hang on to his virginity. But was he? A virgin? If he wasn't, Judy wasn't giving it away in this photo.

On the next page, he stopped at a photo of an older man in a nice suit, and pointed. "What was his name?"

Kit glanced at the shot. "That's Terrence. From the agency."

He sensed tightness in her voice and suddenly recalled a letter. "The one who died. Did you ever date?"

"No," she said, emphatically. "He was practically dad's age."

"Yeah, that would have been weird. How did he die?"

She paused and looked down at his untouched glass. "Accident."

Not the whole story, he figured, but he didn't push it. It reminded him of another matter, however. "Why didn't you or mom tell me about her getting married and moving?"

She shifted and sighed. "Mom and I wanted to tell you, but the Army was always telling us that short of a death in the family, not to bring up particularly sad or distressing news. Ignorance was bliss, I guess."

"I can't believe she married that guy."

"He treats her well enough."

"If you say so." Suddenly, he found he couldn't resist the Coca Cola a second longer and grabbed the bottle and poured. "So why are you so interested in missing persons?"

Once again, she paused, then returned her gaze to the photo of Terrence. "When mom told me you were MIA, honestly, it was like a part of my life had gone dark. Like I was talking on the phone with someone and suddenly the line got disconnected. Not gone, just . . . not there. When someone goes missing, everything becomes a question. It's paralyzing in a way."

"You think it's easier when you know they're dead?"

"In some ways, yes," she said after a thoughtful beat. "There wasn't anything I could do to find you in Japan, but I thought that maybe if I could help others find their loved ones, I'd feel a little better about the world."

"What if they can't be found?"

"It happens," she said, settling back in the chair, her mouth set firm. "But I don't give up easy."

THIRTEEN

HENRY

The shooting range in Griffith Park was a short drive from Calvin's house, giving Henry plenty of time to practice on his own before Kit arrived. Located near the temporary veterans' quarters, the range was modest, with only a half-dozen rows of targets, but it was free for ex-servicemen and former cops like himself, so he couldn't complain. In fact, he had to grudgingly admit that it was a lovely day for an outdoor activity involving firearms.

Henry took his time loading his revolver and shot only the farthest targets in each row, striking them solidly each time. Although he owned three guns, including a Remington derringer he kept strapped to his ankle, he had forgotten about the standing date (remembering appointments was Kit's department) and only had spare bullets for his Colt with him. He and Kit would have to take turns firing it, as Kit didn't own any firearms.

When they had first started working together, she had refused even to carry one of his until Henry insisted that she learn how to shoot as a condition of their partnership. He also demanded she take judo lessons and practice various knife-wielding techniques. She was no Annie Oakley, but she could now handle a gun well enough to fend off, if not kill, an attacker. Her confidence had grown even to the point that she made fun of the derringer.

Henry couldn't deny his obsession with warding off danger, accepting it as an after effect of his recent past. After the bombing, his interest in life and his willingness to gamble on its outcomes, had taken a hit. A few months after the trial, he retired from private investigation and accepted a lucrative position as a fraud inspector at Empire Insurance. Work at Empire was as boring as he and Bea had hoped it would be—safe, predictable and routine. Investigating for a large company had provided a layer of protection he never enjoyed as a private detective or even as a cop, and for years, he reveled in the security of his anonymity.

Inevitably, of course, the boredom became deadly in its own right. Consequently, when Empire's secretary-turned-detective started her own agency and asked Henry to partner with her, he jumped at the chance. Although he had never confessed his ennui to Bea, she didn't seem surprised when he quit Empire, and she took his return to private eyeing in stride. For all he knew, she may have even welcomed it.

If Bea suspected he had a romantic interest in Kit, she hadn't let on. Even when young, she hadn't been the jealous type. No, she probably had figured out that Kit, albeit attractive and appealing, stirred only paternal feelings in him. He and Bea had never had kids, and while their childlessness was by choice, the urge to pass on his knowledge, father-style, intensified with each year.

As he fired his final round, he saw Kit striding over from the parking lot and smiled. She hated target practice, but you'd never know it from the energy of her walk. If such a thing existed, she was a natural investigator, blending curiosity with smarts. Unlike Henry, she could extract information from people with little effort. While Henry tended to intimidate, Kit inspired mutual trust. Her weakness lay there as well. Too often she would give away the game. She didn't always know when to hold back, or to wait and watch. But like shooting a gun, she would learn.

"They're German," she announced the moment she was within earshot.

Henry was reloading the Colt and looked up. "Who's German?"

"Not who, what. The numbers. The weird ones the man on the train wrote." She took the revolver from Henry and positioned herself in front of the first target. "Traffic was terrible, by the way. Highway construction."

"Who told you about the numbers?"

"Dr. Moreno. Stanley's shrink."

"You were discussing the case with Stanley's shrink?" Henry said, trying to keep his tone even.

"He said he went to school there, so I showed him the note. And he recognized them as German right off."

"That's all?"

"That's all." She fired and scored a hit, grinning in spite of herself. "So we now know the other guy was German, or was raised in Germany at least."

"And was injured," Henry added.

"That certainly narrows it down," Kit said, as she squinted at the next target. She took a deep breath and squeezed the trigger. "Bulls-eye."

FOURTEEN
STANLEY

He was about to grab the letters Kit had left him and retreat from the Recreation Room when the power of inertia overwhelmed him. Inertia had become a real problem for him, and fighting it took all his strength, even on his best days. Doc insisted his mental paralysis was a symptom of depression, and claimed that getting rid of his depression was the main goal of his therapy. Remembering your past was the method, according to Doc, but a sense of fulfillment was the objective.

Today fulfillment felt a long way off. His strength was in short supply, especially as he had suspected that Dewey, whose homely face was now fixed in his mind, would be a star player in his letters to Kit. Mindlessly he fingered his drained Coke glass and stole a glance around the room. Several members of his community were studying him, perhaps wondering why he continued to sit there like an idiot, alone and not moving. At the very least, he imagined them thinking, he should be enjoying a cigarette.

With shaky fingers, he pulled his Chesterfields and Zippo from his front pocket and lit up. Between drags, he sorted his letters to Kit according to their postmarks and gently slipped the oldest one from its envelope to read.

January 29, 1945

Somewhere in the Philippines

Dear Kit,

Happy New Year to you, too! Getting your letter and the pictures really made my day. One thing we can't get enough around here are letters. Believe me, mail call is the highlight of every G.I.'s week.

That said, you know I'm a lousy letter writer, so sorry if this is short and not so sweet. My mind just goes blank whenever my hand has a pen in it. Not to mention all the stuff we're not supposed to talk about!

Our days are a mix of busy and boring. Sometimes we're hurrying up just to wait. I prefer keeping busy, as there's less time to worry and get homesick. Everyone in my squad is anxious to get going. The faster we start, we figure, the sooner we'll get home!

I hope Terrence returns soon, though I'm sure you're doing a great job of holding down the fort. Just stay away from those shadows and nameless terrors, all right? And definitely no whistling!

Your loving brother,

Stanley

February 18, 1945

Somewhere in the Philippines

Dear Sis,

Well, I'm sitting here, writing this on my knee, hoping the mail comes through today. It's already been three days since the last delivery, so I figured I should just write to you now and not wait any longer.

Now that the novelty of army life has worn off, I find myself missing you all the more. I sure wish I was back home. Me and a few million other guys!

It's hard to believe it's only February. It sure is hot and sticky. And it rains a lot too. Today, though, it's not too bad. And we're safe here. I'm eating well, you'll be happy to hear. When I can, I play pickup ball with some of the other guys. A couple of them are really good (not as good as yours truly of course).

One of the better players is a kid named Dewey. He's from Stockton and is an Angels fan. He just turned 18 and is crazy about chickens. He saw the picture of you in your "Slightly Dangerous" hat, and I promised to introduce him to you someday. Hope you don t mind!

And speaking of fashion (as you would say), you'd get a kick out of what I saw the other day. A native gal had found an abandoned parachute somewhere and made a silk dress out of it. It looked great from the front. Running across the back, though, were the words

"Inspected and passed by U.S. Army quartermaster inspector." How's that for a designer label?

How's the business going? Is Henry still betting (and losing) on the ponies? Are you seeing anyone? Have you considered getting a pet?

Well, my "dinner bell" is ringing, so until we meet again, happy trails to you!

Your loving brother,

Stanley

March 14, 1945

Somewhere in Japan

Dear Kit,

Thanks for the thoughtful care package! You don't know how much it means to me to see your face, even in a picture. Your photos remind me of why we're fighting, beyond just staying alive. Mom sent more socks, which my dogs and boondockers do appreciate.

You probably heard I was in the hospital for a while. It was just dysentery, but once that bug's got you, you're not good for nothing. Fortunately, the docs here know how to treat it and they get you back in action as soon as they can.

Mom told me about Terrence (not directly, but I read between the lines). I'm awfully sorry, Kit. I guess knowing is better than not knowing, but it's still tough news for anyone to get. Out here, you never know what's coming next—you just keep your eyes open, duck, and pray you make it.

How is Dad? Mom tells me he spends all his time at the plant now. Is he still mad at me for enlisting? I got one letter from him, weeks ago, and haven't heard anything since. I know we weren't exactly getting along before I left, but I'd still like to hear from him.

I'll fill you in on the team in my next letter. They're a great bunch of guys. Thanks for asking.

Your loving brother,

Stanley

March 31, 1945
Somewhere in Japan
Dear Sis,

How are you? We had an unexpected delay this morning, no (April Fool's) joke, so I decided to use the time to write. Lucky you!

How are things going at Comfort and Company? Is it keeping you busy? I said I'd tell you about the fire team, so here goes:

There are four of us. Sergeant McGee is our leader. A real tough guy, inside and out. He reminds me of Coach in some ways. Perhaps to make him seem less scary, the guys call him "Fibber" and, when we're really annoyed with him, "Molly." I can't tell if his nickname annoys or amuses him, which pretty much sums up the guy. Right under McGee is a guy named Corporal Briton Early. Really, that's his name! He's a crack shot and was the Ohio state champion target shooter in high school. What more could you ask for in a teammate?

Dewey and I are the new recruits, also known as the fresh meat. Dewey has stick-out ears like you'd expect a guy from Stockton to have. Other than the ears, though, he's not at all what you'd expect from a farm kid. He's kinda quiet and shy, except when he's had a beer or two. Then he likes to play 'You Are My Sunshine" by tapping his head and opening and closing his mouth. You have to see it, or hear it, to believe it! He says he's a good guitar player, too. He's a pretty accurate shot, and as I said before, a real good infielder. It turns out, our birthdays are only three days apart! I'm sure Henry would have something to say about that coincidence.

Looks like we're finally taking off. Word is, the next stop will be the real thing.

Love,
Stanley

April 2, 1945
Somewhere in Japan
Dear Kit,

This may be the last letter you get from me for a while. Or at least that's what the S.O. has been hinting at.

It's getting hotter here by the minute. And steamy. It reminds me of the locker room at Cathedral, and not at all in a good way. At least it hasn t rained much. The "old timers" say marching in the rain and mud is the worst. Your boots and socks never dry out. One thing I know, I'll never complain about California weather, ever again!

Thanks for sending the newspaper clippings. We get the "Stars and Stripes" sometimes, but the news is always weeks old. We have to do our own detective work just to figure out what's going on in the world.

Sounds like you're keeping busy too, doing your part. Still haven't heard from Dad. I guess it could be worse. Dewey rarely gets any mail. (Did I mention he's an orphan?) He tries to act like he doesn't care, but I know it makes him sad. If you could find time to write him, I know it would cheer him up. You can just send it care of me, and I'll pass it on.

Thanks for everything. I love you, sis!

Stanley

In a lame effort to fool inertia, Stanley reread the last few lines of the last letter, twice. To satisfy Doc's inevitable curiosity about the letters, he tried to think of a reaction to add to his journal later. Would he note that he hadn't mentioned the girl Judy anywhere? He hadn't mentioned Judy to Doc, or as far as he know, any girl, but maybe he should. Just to let him know he liked girls, and maybe one or two liked him back.

In the end, he couldn't say for sure that any memories had been stirred, not specific ones anyway. Reading his own words had felt like watching bits and pieces of his life swirling by him in an undercurrent. A few had bumped against him—mainly the Dewey parts—but when he tried to reach out and grab one, it had slipped from his fingertips and floated away, unremembered.

Was this progress toward fulfillment? He wondered.

FIFTEEN
LUCA

Stanley's letters to Kit had been eye-openers for Luca. They may not have unlocked anything for Stanley, but for Luca, they had been like torches in pitch darkness. He now could see that Dewey had been a central figure in Stanley's Army days—his best pal. What combat friendships lacked in longevity, Luca knew, they more than made up for with in intensity. A mere two weeks of shared terror could cement a bond for life. The specifics of Dewey's relationship with Stanley, Luca guessed, would be at the heart of his psychic injury. Reuniting the two in Stanley's memory would now be Luca's mission.

Luca flipped on the reel-to-reel and slid his chair next to the couch, where Stanley had already settled, eyes closed. Calmed by Luca's induction instructions and his soft, deep voice, Stanley slipped into a relaxed state with little effort. Within seconds, Luca was guiding him down the stairs and into the library.

"On the left are books about the war, your war. I want you to go there, to the left side. Are you there?"

"Yes."

"Good. Now I want you to look for a book titled Okinawa."

Stanley's fingers tensed at the mention of the place, but his face remained relaxed as he scanned the shelves of his mental library.

"Remember, you are safe in the library. Nothing can harm you. You can leave at any time. But I want you to keep looking for the book titled Okinawa. When you find it, raise your right arm."

Stanley's fingers twitched for a few seconds, then finally he lifted his right arm a few inches.

"Good. Now I want you to open the book." He waited a few beats, looking for signs of stress in Stanley's face. "Where are you?"

"Cactus Ridge."

"Near the Shuri Line?"

"Yes. Sergeant says we have to take it tonight, but first we need to do a sweep to make sure we haven't missed any infiltrators."

"What are you doing?"

"Checking dead Japs for booby traps. Trying to."

"What's it like there?"

"It's raining. It's always raining."

"What else?"

"Smells like shit. It always smells like shit. And rot. Even in the rain, we stink."

"What do you see?"

"Bodies. In the mud. Where the bombs fell. Arms. Legs."

"Yes. What else?" Luca said after a pause.

'Heads. We try not to look, but we do."

"Who's we?

"Dewey and me."

"Dewey's next to you?"

"Dewey's always next to me." Stanley's voice fell to a harsh whisper. "Hey, Dewey, that head is grinning at me. Like it knows something we don't. Like it knows we're fucked."

Suddenly Stanley's head snapped to the right and he grimaced. His breathing became quick and shallow, as though he were running.

"What's happening? Where are you now?"

Stanley answered with a soft, steady moan.

"Can you tell me where you are?

Stanley shook his head. Tears streaked his face. The moaning grew louder.

"All right, Stanley. You're safe. Nothing can hurt you. You can close the book. Go ahead and close the book."

At that, Stanley's breathing slowed and deepened. He straightened his head.

"You've done a good job, Stanley. You can leave the library now."

In the few minutes he had between appointments, Luca replayed Stanley's tape. In his session notes, he wrote, "strong sensory recall, esp. olfactory, and awareness of environment." For Luca, sensory cues were a double-edged sword. They could be used to trigger memories or drive a patient like Stanley deeper into oblivion. Cactus Ridge was the 7th Infantry's first objective, and Luca assumed, Stanley's introduction to combat. The worst of Okinawa was yet to come, but Luca could hear in Stanley's voice that, for all intents and purposes, he had already lost himself.

And then there was Dewey. What had happened to him? Luca flipped back a few pages in his notebook, looking for clues about the man. He was an orphan from Stockton. Not much to go on, but perhaps it was a starting point?

SIXTEEN

KIT

This time Dina declined to sit, pacing and worrying her gloves as Kit fussed with the window blinds and Henry buried himself in his racing forms. Although it was only mid-afternoon, the hour at the shooting range had sapped much of Kit's mental energy. She hadn't expected to see Dina back so soon, and Henry's presence, under the circumstances, felt intrusive. He must have sensed it too, because after a minute or two, he announced he was taking a cigarette break downstairs, even though he had stopped smoking years before.

Kit stole glances at Dina's belly, looking for visual confirmation of her predicament. "I'm sorry to say I have nothing to report yet. We're working some angles, but it will take a few days to see if they lead anywhere."

"I understand. It's just . . . I really don't have a lot of time."

Kit paused, debating how far to probe. "Are you thinking about leaving town?"

"No, it's not that. I just need to make some decisions."

"How soon do you need to make these decisions?"

"Ideally no more than a week or two," Dina half-whispered.

Kit flexed her bruised toes inside her new shoes, recalling her mother's platitudinous advice on clothes buying: Pay less today, pay more tomorrow. "Do you have time for some shopping?"

"Shopping?" Dina said, thrown by the change of topic.

"There's a Bullocks not too far from here. They're having a Valentine's Day sale on hose and shoes."

"Hose?"

Kit thought she saw Dina's eyes brighten a little. Even an unwed pregnant woman could appreciate discounted hose. "Better cheap hose than cheap booze I always say. Although honestly, I have nothing against cheap booze."

Dina gave a sweet, light laugh and followed Kit out the door.

Sale notwithstanding, Bullocks was practically empty. It was still a little early for the lunch crowd. After a few minutes of browsing, Kit had suggested they head for the in-store café.

"You must get this question all the time, but I'm curious to know," Dina said, "how did you come to be a private investigator?"

When asked about her work, Kit would respond by saying she had just fallen into it. One thing had led to another. I didn't grow up dreaming of being a private detective, she'd insist with a laugh. But do people fall into jobs, really? Had she? It's true when she took the secretarial pool job at Empire Insurance, she had no idea she would be typing up investigative reports and taking dictation for the company's lead detectives, including the notorious Henry Richman. It was just a job—her first and the first one offered—one that paid the rent on her downtown bedsit.

But everything after that? Her willingness to be taught and to offer ideas, the extra hours she put in, sometimes without pay? Irwin had exploited her, but did he push her, or just get out of her way? When she heard through the grapevine that Terrence Hennessy was looking for an assistant, that it was a job that might require more than just answering phones and typing, she applied without consulting Irwin and said yes to the offer.

She had never once thought about starting her own detective business—that much she could honestly say—but when the opportunity arose, albeit through war and personal misfortune, did she hesitate to act on it, even knowing the finances would be dicey?

As a photographer she had always been attracted to people. Her dad, the engineer, preferred the lines and shapes of city landscapes. He felt at home capturing the artifices of manmade objects. Not Kit. In landscape art, she told her dad, there were too many creative possibilities, the framing was too wide and open, whereas the canvas for portraits was limited and simpler. She had argued that, but did she mean it? Was her preference for shooting faces about stylistic choices or subject choices? In the end, was it that she found people and their intimate details more stimulating than places, no matter how beautiful or varied?

"Maybe you're just nosy," Stanley once said about her choice of jobs. She had bristled at the insult, but now, contemplating a bank account that had been depleted by a Yellow Pages ad featuring an imaginary dog, she understood that Stanley was right. If she didn't exactly crave the personal, she didn't shy away from it either, even in its most corrupted forms.

"I was a Girl Friday to the PI who used to own the place," Kit told Dina. "Photo processing, secretarial work, bookkeeping. Sometimes he would ask me to help with a surveillance or to get information out of someone. Men usually. When he died suddenly, I just took over the business. By that point, I knew all the tricks of the trade." Kit stirred some cream into her coffee. "Not exactly an inspiring tale."

"I disagree," Dina said, pouring an alarming dose of cream into her tea. Five lumps of sugar followed. She must have noticed Kit's reaction because she added, "I've had such a sweet tooth lately."

"When did you say you met Peter?"

"Early '44."

"'44? That long ago?"

"We were stationed together in Wilmington."

"Wilmington? Here?"

"Yes, that's where we first met. A few of us WACS went to a couple of canteens with him and his buddies. Nothing serious. We ended up in different places in Europe, until we ran into each other again in Germany. The way people did over there. That's when things. . ."

"Got serious?"

"Yes."

"What changed?"

"I suppose it was the war's end. It seemed to have the opposite effect on me than on most folks."

"How do you mean?"

"Most people were throwing caution to the wind and getting hitched during the war. But I couldn't think even about dating then. Maybe because I never feared for my own life, the weight of others weighed me down more. I felt personally responsible for them somehow. Does that make any sense?

"Yes," Kit said, debating whether to tell Dina about Stanley but deciding now was not the time.

"When it was finally over, it was like I could see everyone around me as just people again. Including Peter."

Kit gave Dina a pointed look over her teacup. "And caution was thrown to the wind?"

Dina nodded. "How could I have known that Peter would disappear?"

Dina looked away, her eyes shining with sudden tears. Kit said, "Look, my partner, Henry, and I will do what we can to find Peter, but we can't guarantee the results." Kit reached across the teacups and touched Dina's hand. "I need you understand that."

"Yes, I understand. Thank you."

SEVENTEEN

Excerpt from "My Escape: A Confession" (submitted to O.P.M.G., February 1946)

Hunger finally overcame me. I had skipped the breakfast and lunch service, preferring instead to sleep, but I couldn't ignore the gnawing in my stomach any longer. After all, I was used to eating three sizable meals a day. I had managed to steal some loose bills and a pack of cigarettes from an unwatched handbag, but neither would last me as far as California.

In the dining car, a man in a dark blue suit and matching tie, crisp and tidy despite the travel, sat across from me. The fullness of his wavy dark hair was undercut by a slightly receding hairline. His dress shoes looked new, their maple brown leather shining and creaseless. Nicely tailored, I thought, though after years in the camp, I hardly knew what gentlemen were wearing these days.

The stranger smiled and nodded at me, then turned his attention to the daily menu lying atop his dinner plate.

A second later, the train braked as it rounded a curve. The sudden slowing tossed the stranger backward a bit, while I pitched forward. My chest struck the edge of the table, and I groaned. Unbidden, my hand flew up to my sore ribs.

"Are you alright?" said the stranger as he righted himself.

"Yeah, thanks," I answered, trying to smile.

"Are you sure?" The stranger tilted his clean-shaven chin toward my chest. "It looks painful."

"No, it's nothing." I willed my hand down. "I had a stupid fall the other day, that's all."

"I'm a doctor," the stranger said after a pause. "I'd be happy to take a look. Rib injuries can be tricky."

A doctor? "Thank you. That's very generous of you." I didn't detect any suspicion behind the doctor's words. "Maybe later." With as much brightness as I could muster, I pointed to the man's suit pocket and said, "Can I bum a cigarette, though?"

"Of course." The doctor extracted a single cigarette from his pack and offered it to me. "Light?" he asked, a silver lighter in hand.

"Please." I leaned forward to meet the flame, sucked in a deep breath, and savored the smooth, sweet taste of the American tobacco. I resisted the urge to turn the cigarette inward, as we had been instructed to do in training so many years ago.

Up ahead, I saw the steward approaching. The left arm of his uniform shirt was empty and pinned up. A war injury? Not from the recent conflict, I thought, the gray-haired Negro was too old for that. And the smooth and easy way he carried himself suggested years of adaptation.

As I watched the amputee deftly handing out menus, I thought about the colored soldiers I had encountered at the camp. They lived in separate quarters and performed the foulest duties. The white soldiers treated them like shit, as did a lot of the prisoners. I had no fondness for the Negros myself, but it rankled me that my captors would crow about the moral superiority of their system, their "freedoms," while blindly practicing their own repressions. Hell held a special place for such hypocrites, I thought. I could feel my anger rising.

"Can't find anything you like?"

The doctor's question, spoken softly with an edge of confusion, brought me back to the here-and-now with a jolt. I refocused and forced a smile. "Coffee, please. Black."

It had taken me a few minutes to fully grasp what had happened with the doctor. I had run into him outside the toilet nearest my berth, and once again, he offered to inspect my injury. "Only take a second," he assured me with a grin.

I had accepted the doctor's offer, unable in that second to assess all the possible risks in doing so. I hadn't thought about the tattoo, those tiny letters AB high on my shoulder, in years. They had been required for the early recruits, a safeguard against blood transfusion mishaps. The practice had since been abandoned—or so I had heard.

I was sure the doctor had noticed the tattoo and had understood what it was, what it meant. His fingers had been probing my chest, checking for sore spots, when suddenly his face clouded over and his professional smile disappeared into a twitch of alarm. He had been looking at my shoulder.

"Is something wrong?" I had said, my gaze on the doctor's chin and mouth.

In an instant, the doctor's relaxed smile returned. "You've got some pretty bad bruising, but it doesn't feel like anything's cracked. I have some bandages in my bag we can use as a chest wrap. That and some stiff drinks will help with the pain." The doctor sounded as cheerful now as he had in the dining car.

"Thanks, Doc. I'm sure glad it's nothing serious." I forced my tone to match the doctor's. "I just might take your advice about that drink."

"Do that. I'll go get the bandages."

"Please don't bother yourself. I'll be fine."

"No bother," he said, his voice firm but still friendly. "I never introduced myself," he said, extending his hand. "Peter Novak."

I took Peter Novak's hand and gave it a firm shake. "I'm Abe," I said at last. AB. It was the best I could do.

EIGHTEEN
HENRY

Henry made his way past the neon palm tree, up the faux forest steps and behind the waterfall that made the Calson's cafeteria a set designer's fever dream. He and Bea, who ate here often, had stopped noticing the theatrical décor many harvest moons ago, but it still had the power to dazzle the tourists and westsiders. It was mid-afternoon and, live organ music aside, the place was as quiet as it ever got on a week day. After Henry had returned to the office from his "cigarette break," he found Kit and Dina gone, and the phone ringing with an urgent summons from Calvin.

Calvin's office was tucked in the back of the second floor, at the end of a long corridor. The place had started life as a department store, and the wall still bore the words "Little Boys Department" over a west-pointing painted arrow. Henry was halfway down the hall when a trim middle-aged man in a brown tweed suit exited the office. He looked down as he passed, avoiding eye contact, but Henry noted the prominent upturned nose and thinning chestnut hair.

Calvin stuck his head into the hallway and said, "Henry, perfect timing. Come on in."

Inside the already cramped office Henry encountered boxes of different sizes, stacked and scattered across the floor. "More marital aids?"

Calvin chuckled. "No, no, no. I'm starting a foundation with a Caltech professor, Barzan. He's created a low-cost Multi-Purpose Food using a soy-based protein. We're going to produce and distribute it around the world. We're calling it Meals for Many." He pointed to a random pile of boxes. "These samples were just delivered."

"You never cease to amaze me, Calvin."

"Oh, no. Barzan's doing all the hard work. I'm just providing a platform. And floor space." Calvin motioned to Henry to sit on the loveseat next to his oversized desk, and Henry complied with a tired plunk. "As I mentioned on the phone," Calvin said, his voice suddenly quiet, "the message I received from the general is best shared face-to-face."

Calvin parked himself on the edge of his executive-sized desk while Henry leaned forward on the overstuffed yet too small love-seat. "Fire away," he said.

After one of his signature dramatic pauses, Calvin said, "Here's the skinny. In short, the general didn't recognize the name Peter Novak when I first mentioned it and he claimed he was unaware of any recent Army business he might have been involved in."

"Did you believe him?"

Calvin paused again, thinking. "Yes. I don't think he knew anything about Novak. But when I mentioned in passing that the doctor had sent a telegram from the train station in Kansas City, he made a comment about strange coincidences."

"Coincidences?"

"He said a German POW had escaped the day before from a camp around there, and, exact quote, 'wasn't that a strange coincidence?'"

"I take it he didn't think it was a coincidence?"

"I don't believe so."

"Did he mention anything else about the German?"

"No. In fact, he started asking a lot of questions about your part in all of it."

"My part?"

"Who hired you and why. I said I didn't know all the details and was just doing an old friend a favor."

"So, you think he's not telling you everything."

"That would be my assumption, yes."

"And now I'm on the Army's radar."

"That's why I wanted to see you. To tell you and maybe your client to be careful."

For a moment, Henry was speechless. A simple AWOL lover case had suddenly acquired many wrinkles. He didn't like wrinkles. Gracelessly, he rose to leave. "Thanks, Calvin. I hope you're not in the soup now too."

Calvin shrugged. "Soup's my specialty. In or out."

"Amen to that, brother," Henry said over his shoulder.

"Give Beanie my best."

For the second time in as many days, Henry found himself in the periodical room of the Central Library. He was playing another long shot, but a cheap one. In the corner where newspapers were housed, he gathered up dailies from the Midwest—Detroit, Milwaukee, Chicago, Kansas City, Dodge City—and took them to the same table he had shared two days before with Emerick. With a grumpy sigh, he started going through each page of the previous day's reporting.

From the *Chicago Daily Tribune,* he learned that a firebug had set four fires at the Congress Hotel, killing one guest and injuring a dozen others. And the *Detroit Evening Times* reported that an elderly flower seller had been robbed of her $100 savings, which mysteriously became $1,850 after she had spied a stack of unclaimed cash at the police station. And so it went, from Wisconsin to Illinois.

Finally, in *The Kansas City Star* he hit pay dirt. A headline on the second page read: "Wily German POW escapes, eludes capture."

Klaus Fischer, 32, a captain in the 9th Panzer Division, escaped early Monday from his Camp Crowder barracks. Guards say he slipped away from a work site during afire emergency. A $25 reward is being offered for information leading to his apprehension.

There was no photo or physical description, but at least now he had a name: Klaus Fischer. But was Klaus Fischer, escaped POW, also the German on the train with the doctor? And why was the Army concerned about keeping his existence to themselves? Calvin wasn't prone to over-reaction, so Henry felt compelled to take his warning seriously. If Calvin sensed danger, especially danger of the official sort, Henry knew to be on his guard. He trusted the oddball like no one else.

Eight years before, Henry had been just the man that Calvin needed. Calvin's enemies wore the badge, and he figured Henry, the disgruntled ex-cop, would be both motivated and flexible in his approach to them. Like most of his contemporaries at the LAPD, Henry had been happy to enforce the law as long as the law didn't get in the way of maintaining order. During Prohibition, good guys and bad guys were as fungible as starlets on Louis B. Mayer's couch so it hardly paid to be a stickler for morality. Some laws just weren't worth their upkeep, especially knowing, as he did, the men who made and unmade them. As far as he could tell, law enforcement was just another tool in the corrupt man's toolbox.

Back then, the trick for Henry had been staying on the right side of that tool, of knowing his place and sticking to the script. More than once, however, he had gone off script, and it had finally cost him his livelihood. His fellow cops had turned on him and framed him in an extortion scheme. His expulsion had been pro forma but permanent.

If Henry's LAPD experience had taught him anything, it was to trust no one, especially not your fellow law enforcers. Going forward, he knew, he would have to keep one eye on the investigation and one eye on the rearview mirror. The case was taking off, and the next step was as clear as an L.A. sky in July.

On the library's ground floor, he slipped into a phone booth and dialed the number he knew by heart. After many rings, he was about to hang up when he heard a familiar voice say hello.

"Calvin. It's Henry," he said into the receiver.

"Did you find something already?" Calvin's voice, while always polite and measured, had a hint of distraction in it.

"Don't know, yet, but I could use your help."

"All right. Shoot."

"That fellow you know at Paramount. The screenwriter with the Nazi hunting side gig."

"Rudi Schmidt?"

"Schmidt, right. Call him and let him know I'd like to talk to him, will you? As soon as possible?"

YOU ARE MY SUNSHINE

Wednesday, February 6, 1946

NINETEEN

HENRY

At Paramount, Henry caught Rudi Schmidt on his lunch break. A studio guard had directed him to a bench in the courtyard outside the writers' building, where Schmidt routinely took his mid-morning meal. The Austrian émigré enjoyed all the perks that came with being an A list screenwriter, including his own bungalow and personal secretary. He had met Calvin while researching one of his scripts, and in typical Calvin fashion, a lifelong friendship soon developed.

Even from a distance Henry could see that Schmidt was an all-around large man, the bench barely accommodating his suited bulk. He was bent over, elbows on his knees, sandwich clutched in one hand, a large napkin in the other, long legs spread. Henry approached from the side with instinctive caution.

"Mr. Schmidt?" Henry said.

Without looking up from what appeared to be roast pork and onions between slices of rye, Schmidt raised a finger in acknowledgement, then wiped his mouth with the oversized napkin. Finally, he acknowledged Henry, his round face flush with sun and good food.

"The guard always knows where to find me." His voice was as deep and thick as his body was wide, the Viennese accent unmistakable. "You're Mr. Richman?"

"Henry."

"Pleasure to meet you, Henry." Schmidt gestured for Henry to join him on the bench. "I've heard of you, of course, from the bombing trial. I followed that case closely. Calvin has mentioned you many times."

"Likewise," Henry said. "He's a big fan of your work."

"Calvin's very kind." The pleasantries done, Schmidt got to the point. "What can I help you with?"

"I understand you might have some information about local Nazis. Fifth columnists."

"Nazis?" Schmidt said with a soft chuckle. "I don't know if you heard, but the war is over. The Nazis—thank God—were crushed."

Henry returned the smile. "Maybe not all of them."

"Maybe not, probably not. But our operation shut down years ago. Most of the leaders were arrested or deported." Then without missing a beat, he added, gesturing to a soggy white bag nestled next to him, "Pickle?"

"No, thank you. But what about their followers?"

"What about them?"

"Did they go their merry way?"

"Some did."

"And the others?"

He shrugged. "Officially it's no longer my business."

Henry waited for the "but" and when it didn't come, he said, "How about unofficially?"

Schmidt leaned in and whispered, "Unofficially we try to keep an eye on them."

"How?"

"We still have connections we use. Those connections let us know when there's any notable activity or movement."

"Movement?"

"You'd be surprised how many Nazis have ended up in Los Angeles, either permanently or as a stop on their way south. Sometimes illegally, but sometimes with the blessing of our government."

Henry was aware of Washington's strategic embrace of any Nazi with political or technological potential. "My guy's an escapee from an Army POW camp in Missouri."

Schmidt raised an eyebrow. "A German POW?"

"Klaus Fischer. He was a captain in the 2nd Panzer Division."

"The 2nd?" Schmidt said, his concern and interest now fully piqued. "They were SS Waffen. The worst of the worst. Real fanatics. If this POW was with the 2nd Panzer, he's a Nazi for sure." Schmidt paused. "The FBI, they aren't looking for him?"

"Sure. In Missouri."

"You said his name is Fischer?"

"That's right, Klaus Fischer. Heard of him?"

"I've never heard of a Klaus Fischer, but I know about a William, formerly Wilhelm, Fisher," Schmidt said, stressing the "v" sound in Wilhelm. "That's Fisher with no 'c.' He dropped it when he emigrated, like a lot of Germans. He owns a furniture store near downtown. He used to be quite active in the group, but lately, not so much. Of course, Fischer is a fairly common German name, like Schmidt, so we could be talking about a completely different family."

"How organized is this local group?"

"It's a loose network of cells. Some are like family associations, more about cultural identity than politics. Others are deeply ideological and prone to violence. The more violent groups tend to be the most controlled and disciplined."

"And if I were looking for the latter group, where would I go?"

The hand clutching the last of the sandwich paused in midair while Schmidt considered Henry's question. "I can tell you this much—it might be helpful, or not," he said, taking the final bite. "You sure you don't want a pickle? It's kosher."

"No thanks. I'm not a big pickle eater."

"Shame. I could eat them all day. And they are very good for the digestion." As if to punctuate that claim, Schmidt burped softly and brushed sandwich crumbs from his lap with his napkin. "Are you familiar with downtown?"

"I am."

"Figueroa and 7th, there's a bookshop, The Continental Traveler."

"I've seen it."

"Yes. It's owned by an old fifth columnist, Bert Bitenburg. He lives in San Marino now, but he used to be in Anaheim—lots of Germans down there you know. During the war he was very careful, very discreet, so we never had enough evidence to arrest him. Now he's helping escapees get to Mexico and South America. Or so I've been told."

"Helping how exactly?"

"Fake passports, work documents, connections—things he can make money from. Apparently he has a fondness for money."

"There's a lot of that going around."

"Indeed. It's a very old story." Schmidt gathered his trash. "You'll need an introduction . . . if you want to meet Mr. Bitenburg."

"Where can I get one of those?"

"We had a mole in his group. He's not active now, but he's still in good standing with them. His name is Christian Zimmer. He's down in Anaheim now. If you mention him at the shop, they'll be more likely to believe your story."

"Christian Zimmer," Henry repeated. "What if they check on my story?"

"Oh, they will definitely check on your story. I'll contact Christian, let him know to expect a phone call from his old friends. What name will you be using?"

"How about Tom Kurzbach?" It was the name of his high school baseball coach, and the first German one that popped into his head.

"Tom Kurzbach. Good." Trash in hand, Schmidt rose. "And speaking of stories, I have a comedy and a drama I need to get back to."

"Of course," Henry said, standing. "Thanks." He offered his hand for a parting shake, and the writer reciprocated with a firm grasp.

"My pleasure," said Schmidt. Then as Henry was turning to leave, he added, "One last thing. Bitenburg . . . please be careful, yes?"

"Careful is my middle name."

From his Studebaker, Henry studied the front of Fisher's Fine Furniture through a pair of compact binoculars. Compared to its business neighbors—Kress's lively five-and-dime and SQR's palatial shoe emporium—it was a modest affair. According to the posted hours, the store was about to close for the day, and if Henry's assumptions were correct, William Fisher would then be heading home. As Schmidt had warned him, Fisher was a common name, and the phone book contained at least fifteen listings for "W. Fisher." He debated calling all of them in the hope that a man with a German accent—assuming Wilhelm/William Fisher still had one—answered, but decided that staking out the furniture store would be the quicker approach.

At the stroke of five, a bald, thickset man Henry assumed was Fisher stepped out of the shop and locked the door behind him. With a lumbering gait, he made his way to a Plymouth parked in the alley behind the shop. Henry folded his binoculars and turned on his ignition, waiting for Fisher's car to pull out in front of him so he could discreetly tail him.

A few turns later, Henry was following Fisher onto the north entrance of the Arroyo Seco Parkway, towards Mt. Washington and Cypress Park. Mt. Washington, he recalled, was the home of one of the phone book Fishers. Fisher drove carefully at the speed limit for a few miles, then signaled his intention to exit the parkway.

As Henry did the same, allowing another coupe to ease into the lane in front of him, he glanced in the rearview mirror and saw a dark blue Ford sedan make an abrupt move into the exit lane. His pulse quickened as he focused on the Ford's two male occupants. Years of experience told him he, too, was being followed.

TWENTY

KIT

Henry had just walked through the office door when the phone began to ring. Kit acknowledged him with a nod and grabbed the receiver. "Comfort Investigations."

"Miss Comfort?"

Kit immediately recognized the deep, honeyed voice. "Speaking."

"Hello, ma'am. It's Roland. From the train. Roland Chestnutt."

"Roland," she said, and it struck her that she had never asked for his last name. "Hello."

"I'm about to clock in. I'm at a pay phone. Had to borrow a nickel from my buddy to make the call."

"How can I help you?"

"I was just wondering. Have you found that doctor fellow you were asking about?"

"No, why, have you seen him?"

"No." He paused, and she could hear a shouted hello in the background. "But I've been hearing things."

"Things?"

"I don't have any of the particulars and it might be nothing at all, but what I heard was . . . interesting, given what you asked me about."

"Shoot."

"I was headed for the train back to Chicago and ran into Jimmy, who was just pulling in from Pasadena. We used to work the run together, but now he's coming when I'm going. We don't usually see each other anymore but today his run was late getting in."

Kit had her notebook out. "Jimmy's a steward too?"

"That's right. He said yesterday's train was late because of a body being found in some brush next to the tracks, just before Barstow. They had to wait 'cause the police were investigating."

"Any information on the body?"

'He—the dead man—didn't have any identification on him, but on account of his nice clothes, they guessed he was a businessman of some sort. Not like the bums they usually come across."

Kit's mind raced with the possibilities. "Barstow. So, after dinner . . ."

"But before breakfast. That's right, ma'am. That's exactly what I was thinking."

For a moment Kit let the assumption hang in the air. "We'll check it out. Thanks, Roland. I owe you one."

She hung up and turned to Henry, who was pouring over the *Times* sports section, stub pencil in hand. "Got any friends in Barstow?"

"Bad news, huh?" he said without looking up.

"Maybe. They found a dead man next to the tracks."

"And we have reason to think he's our man?"

"Location and general description fit, but the timing hasn't been confirmed. But something tells me the police there won't be forthcoming with any details. Not without some encouragement anyway."

Henry raised his head and nodded slowly. "I think there's at least one old head there who still remembers me." He dropped his pencil and reached for his hat. "I'll call Bea and tell her I'll be late for dinner."

TWENTY-ONE

HENRY

Henry slid out of the Commander and glanced around what passed for a parking lot at the Barstow Sheriff's Department. He had talked to a clerk on the phone to make sure the sheriff would be in, and the clerk had laughingly assured him that Sheriff Judson would be there, most likely tinkering with his squad car.

Decades before, Henry and Jack Judson had been partners in the LAPD's vice unit. While it wasn't an oil-and-water sort of relationship, it wasn't sweetness and light either. Henry had trouble with Judson's tendency to cut corners and drinking on duty, often to the detriment of both the victim and the law. One instance in particular had gotten under Henry's skin. Over many months, Henry had cultivated a confidential informant in one of the bootlegging gangs, a young hophead named Lonnie who had grown up in orphanages and foster homes. The boy was tender, despite his rough upbringing, and ripe for exploitation. Henry knew the fear of jail would motivate him to cooperate, but if pushed too hard, it could also send him spiraling.

Henry had mentioned all this to Judson—even pointing Lonnie out during one of their drive-by patrols. One night, though, Judson, with no heads up to Henry, had ordered a raid, during which Lonnie was arrested and tossed in jail. By the time Henry learned Lonnie's plight, the informant, in the throes of withdrawal, had already hanged himself.

Guilt and fury had consumed Henry, but Judson insisted his mistake was unintentional. Judson's sloppiness had indeed been the cause of Lonnie's incarceration, not malice, but it took Henry a long time to accept his partner's apology.

Whatever animosity had lingered; Henry was forced to bury it when a corruption scandal engulfed their vice unit. At the time, Prohibition was the law of the land, and from it flowed all sorts of illicit behavior. Where there were bootleggers, there were prostitutes, gamblers, drug dealers and racketeers. Where there were racketeers, there were politicians and cops on the take. And where there were politicians and cops on the take, there were politicians and cops looking to bring the takers down.

And that's where Henry and Judson entered the picture. Higher-ups in the department would instruct them to surveil a particular elected official or his campaign challenger to assess their vulnerabilities. Then, depending on the higher-up's motives, they would be told either to warn the target to cool it and, if necessary, destroy evidence, or to stage a frameup for blackmail based on the target's known weakness.

It was the latter scenario that had landed Henry and Judson in hot water. They had been ordered to trail Oswald Reginald, a lawyer in the prosecutor's office who had his sights on the district attorney's job. The DA was "protected property," meaning, corrupt as hell, and the police chief was his biggest supporter. Rumors had been circulating that Reginald had a thing for young girls, and the hope was that Henry and Judson could catch him in the act with one.

Judson recruited a girl he had busted for prostitution, a twen-ty-year-old who could pass for fourteen, but when Henry joined Judson at the Ambassador Hotel where the rendezvous was to take place, the lawyer was nowhere to be found. As they were the only ones who knew the details of the frameup, the police chief accused Henry and Judson of tipping off the target.

In the end, both he and Judson lost their badges and their LAPD careers. For Henry, getting fired was just the kick he needed to wash the stink off and recalibrate what was left of his life. Of course, with the recalibration came a fair amount of lubrication of the bourbon kind. And it was during this time, that Henry had perfected his dart throwing.

Henry had concluded that, denials aside, Judson had tipped off Reginald, and Judson had come to the same conclusion about Henry. Many years later, Reginald's former secretary cornered him at Calson's and, under the influence of a few daiquiris, revealed that the lawyer had skedaddled after seeing Judson flash his badge in the Ambassador lobby. Judson, of course, had been careless (and probably half-drunk).

Fortunately for Judson, soon after the DA won reelection without the benefit of blackmail, Henry found work at the insurance company, and Judson reinvented himself in Barstow. Henry could only guess how much the Barstow force knew about Judson's past, but since he had managed to work his way up to sheriff, he assumed it was limited. Or maybe the good folks of Barstow just valued experience more than reputation.

Judson's nickname at the LAPD had been JJ, but privately, Henry called him Jugs on account of his drinking. During their time together, Henry had never seen him without his flask, which he would fill with his favorite cheap gin and draw from all day.

On the far side of the parking lot, Henry spotted the squad car. Its hood was up, and a tall older man in a brown sheriff's uniform was peering at the engine, his hands straddling the frame. Henry strolled over, scuffling his feet a bit so as to not startled his former partner. "Still getting your hands dirty, I see," Henry said.

Judson snaked his head out from under the hood and squinted to take in Henry's face. Apparently, the clerk hadn't warned him to expect visitors. His stare softened into a full-on grin. "Henry Richman?"

"The one and only."

"I almost didn't recognize you."

"Come on, JJ. I've been fat and bald since you were in diapers."

Judson laughed. "Got rid of the bowties, I see."

Without thinking, Henry touched his unassuming dark blue tie. Back in his LAPD days, Henry always wore bowties, the flashier the better. "Gotta keep up with the fashion."

'You still in the PI business?"

"Pay my license fees every year. Got a partner now."

"Partner? Henry Richman? I find that hard to believe."

"She's a lot better looking than me. And smarter. But I know people."

"She?" Judson's eyebrow shot up. "How did that happen?"

"The war, what else?"

"Unmarried I take it."

"It's complicated."

"Naturally." Judson wiped his hands on an old rag. "Why don't we head over there."

Judson led Henry to an ancient oak tree standing lonely on the edge of the station and sat on one of the sunbaked lawn chairs scattered underneath it. Things truly were slow in Barstow, Henry thought, as he grabbed an empty chair next to Judson's. As soon as he was settled, Judson offered him his flask.

"Thanks, I got my own," Henry said, bringing his flask out. He had no intention of drinking from it, but figured it would keep Judson focused on his own.

"So what can I do you for?" Judson said at last. "I'm assuming it's of a business nature."

"I heard you picked up a body by the train tracks the other day."

Judson's flask hand paused halfway to his mouth. "Could be. And you're asking 'cause . . .?"

"I'm looking for a man who got on the Super Chief in Chicago but never got off. At least not where he was supposed to."

"Really, now."

"He's a doctor, 32. Dark hair, average build, average height. Last seen before Barstow, due in Los Angeles Saturday morning."

"Saturday, eh?"

"How old is your body?" Henry slipped a copy of Dina's photograph out of his suit pocket and offered it to Judson.

"Hard to say for sure, but more than a day." Judson took the photo with a greasy hand but barely glanced at it. "The problem we have right now is . . ."

"I know there wasn't any identification on the body."

"Yep. That much was reported in the paper," Judson said, returning the photo to Henry. "But as of right now, we don't have any way to identify him. We ran his fingerprints, but they aren't on file. Not that we expected they would be, considering he was traveling through."

"But does he look like the fellow in the photo?"

"Can't say." Judson took a long swallow from his flask. "There's a problem with the head."

"Damaged?"

Judson hesitated. "If I tell you, it's strictly between us. I can't afford it getting out in the press."

"You know me, JJ; I put the 'private' in 'private detective.'"

"Yeah, you always was a cagey fucker," Judson said with a snort.

Henry forced a smile. "So, was it damaged?"

"More like missing."

"Missing? Was it an accident?"

"Jury's still out on that, but the coroner's leaning towards no."

"Why's that?"

"There was a slash mark on the throat, 'inconsistent with natural breakage' as the coroner put it. He thinks the throat might have been slit before the body was tossed. Probably facing outward. The head might have hit a post or something on the way down." He made a broad flinging gesture with his free hand.

"Any chance of finding it . . . the head?"

"Maybe," said Judson with a shrug. "We'll get the dogs on it. But even if we find it, there's no telling what condition it'll be in. Did your man have any identifying scars, or what-have-yous?"

"He was circumcised."

Judson winced. "Not much left there. Nothing else?"

"Nope."

"What's your client's connection to him?"

"Fiancée," Henry said, hoping his promotion of Dina's status would stir extra sympathy in the old drunk.

"Fiancée? That's rough."

"Mind if I check out the dump site?"

"Old habits die hard, eh?"

"Something like that."

"Not much to see, but you're welcome to go out there. Just ask the girl inside for directions."

Henry rose slowly, his knees creaking from the strain.

"You staying in town?" Judson said.

Henry shook his head. "Bea's expecting me," he said.

"Bea," said Judson, as memories appeared to cascade over him. "How's she doing?"

"Not too bad, all things considered," Henry lied.

"Glad to hear it. I always liked Bea." Judson said. He placed his knobby hands on the chair's arms to push himself up, straining at the effort. "Leave the picture inside with the girl. In case we find it."

"Sure thing," Henry said, tugging on his hat brim in preparation for his own departure. Then he stopped, mulling, before saying, "By the way, I ran into Reginald's secretary at Calson's a few years back."

Judson's features stiffened. "Reginald?"

"The lawyer from the Ambassador. The secretary told me he made you in the lobby that night."

Judson let the statement drop into the desert air before turning in the direction of the idle squad car. "Goodbye, Henry. Drive carefully."

If he had to look for a head in the Mojave Desert, February was the time to do it. Not only were the harsh creosote bushes flush with yellow blooms, the lilies and verbena were also blossoming. When they were first married, he and Bea would sometimes drive out here because Brooklyn-born Bea loved the desert blooms. She would talk about them in philosophical terms that meant little to Henry, who preferred the mountains, but he appreciated anything that could make her so contented, even briefly. It had been many years since their last visit.

Henry looked down at the spot near the rail line where, according to the girl in the office, the body had been found. In the grayish soil on the west side of the track, a large brown stain, where the body must have landed, still was visible. Scattered about were remnants of police activity—cigarette ends, gum wrappers, and tire tracks coming and going.

After inspecting the nearby telegraph pole the body had apparently struck on the way down, Henry adjusted his hat and started walking north, counting each step as he went. As a former insurance investigator, he had learned a few things about physics, such as how far an object might go after being tossed from a moving vehicle or striking a pole. There were variables of course, but the possible radius wasn't that wide. And the low, stark vegetation wasn't capable of hiding much.

Henry pulled his hat even lower on his forehead and scanned the nearly cloudless sky. The air was still and barely warm. A lone crow was circling a little way off, and Henry started off in that direction. He hadn't gotten very far when he saw several more crows feasting on something atop a creosote bush. He didn't need to get much closer to make out what they were enjoying. There'd be no facial recognition.

He turned and plodded back to the tracks. When he reached the pole, he stopped and scanned the desert canvas while debating his next move. He sighed, then began walking south. It was a hunch, but one he felt compelled to act on. The coroner had speculated a knife had been used, and any killer with a lick of sense would have disposed of the weapon along with the body. Henry assumed the body would go first, followed closely by the knife.

After he'd gone about a tenth of a mile or so, Henry's steps became slow and measured again. He paused to wipe his glasses, then inspected the ground around him.

And there, lying between a creosote bush and a desert lily was a switchblade.

Judson had been skeptical about the switchblade and its provenance—"Could be anybody's"—but agreed to hang on to it for fingerprinting. Henry imagined his old friend, never one for thoroughness, tossing it into a junk drawer in the station kitchen. On the other hand, he took Henry's news about the fate of the head hard. He hadn't given up on the idea of retrieving it, but conceded its usefulness would be limited to dental records, if that. They would try for a fingerprint comparison. For the time being, the body would remain in the morgue.

The sun was slinking west as Henry steered the Studebaker back onto the highway. Up ahead a bank of clouds shimmered a soft yellow, while Venus was just starting to show itself. He had performed his inspection and now had the road to himself. Although he had promised Bea he'd wouldn't be too late, he felt no hurry to get home. The desert had that enervating effect on him.

On the radio, he found nothing but static, so to fill the silence, he launched into the first verse of "You Are My Sunshine," the only song he knew by heart. He once had a decent bass voice, but time had turned it craggy and unpredictable. He had gotten as far as Jimmy Davis' "shattered dreams" when he saw a roadside vegetable stand advertising fresh artichokes. Without a thought, he pulled over.

TWENTY-TWO

Excerpt from "My Escape: A Confession" (submitted to O.P.M.G., February 1946)

Later, I found myself alone on the train's observation deck, enjoying both a cigarette and the passing darkness. The cigarette, my third in a row, came from a pack I had swiped off an unattended lounge chair. Thanks to the camp, my thieving and money-earning skills had improved immensely. I had discovered that with a little effort, cash could be acquired in any number of ways. For example, although our camp salaries had been paid in scrip only, I had managed to convert some into dollars by selling my chocolate and cigarette rations to the guards. I used my English skills to earn money writing love letters for a prisoner who had taken to slipping out at night to rendezvous with a mill foreman's daughter. And I had found a five-dollar bill tucked under the blotter on the commander's desk, which he often left unattended while consulting with his secretary.

As the stinging winter air kept reminding me, however, I had yet to get my hands on a suitable overcoat. I took a last drag of my cigarette and crushed the butt under foot. I had vowed to stop after three, but just then, the deck door slid open, and the doctor stepped out. With a conspiratorial nod, he moved next to me and said, "Pretty chilly out here without a coat."

"The cold dulls the pain," I said, and then slid a fourth cigarette from the pack. This time Novak made no move to light it for me and watched silently as I struck my stolen match.

"So, tell me Abe, were you in the service?"

I knew this part by heart. If Novak (a Jewish name he assumed) thought he could throw me off here, he'd be disappointed. "1st Infantry. Armored Division."

"The 1st. That's a tough one. I treated some of you in France. Army Medical Corps. I'm a radiologist."

"Radiologist? Glad I didn't end up meeting you over there. I guess I was lucky."

"Indeed you were," he said. "Are you headed home?"

"Naw, just looking for a fresh start. I've always dreamed about moving West." That much was true.

He chuckled. "Me, too. I guess that makes about a million of us. Funny how peacetime does that to you."

"Does what?" I asked.

"Makes you want to move on to the next thing as fast as you can."

"What else can you do?" My question was sincere.

"Nothing I suppose. But what happens when you realize you can't move on because, like it or not, you and the world have unfinished business. You have scars that can't be erased. Sins that can't be forgotten. So that even when you find a new place, the memories are still there with you, and you're right back where you started."

I didn't know what to make of Novak's sudden opining. Was it just the tepid musings of a bored intellectual, or was it a trap? Was he self-reflecting or speculating about me, his reluctant patient? In the next second, the doctor seemed to give me his answer.

"Where are you from, Abe? I detect a bit of an accent in your voice. Almost like German," he said flatly. "Are you German?" The doctor's right hand had slipped inside his coat, and with that, the game had shifted.

"And if I am German? Is that a problem?" I maintained a careful eye on the doctor's right hand.

"Depends on which side you're on."

"The fighting's over, as you just said."

"The fighting's over, but the reckoning's just beginning."

"For some, yes," I agreed. I dropped my cigarette and gave a deep sigh. In my pants pocket, my fingers wrapped around the rusty switchblade I had found at the bottom of the toolbox. I hadn't intended to use the blade, but took it in case of emergency. In an emergency, I thought, even a rusty knife will get the job done.

The doctor's overcoat proved a perfect fit. I would have preferred to have acquired it by less violent means, but Novak had given me no choice. As a precaution, I had also taken the watch and the wallet, the only item in the doctor's trousers, before tossing the body from the back of the train. In the wallet, I discovered a driver's license, military identification, a few snaps—his family I presumed—four dollar bills, two fives, a ten and a twenty dollar bill. Not a fortune, but enough for a down payment on my travel expenses.

I had taken a chance with the doctor, even in the freezing darkness, and gotten lucky. As far as I was aware, no one had seen our confrontation, and no one was aware of his absence. I didn't like relying on luck, though, and vowed to be more careful, starting with the note. In searching the overcoat pockets, I had found not the weapon I had feared, but an orange, the silver lighter and a slip of paper with a Los Angeles address and phone number on it. And underneath the phone number, the words "Send D WU alert" were scrawled.

Back in my roomette, I rolled onto the foldout bed (it reminded me unpleasantly of my camp cot) and spent the last two hours of the trip debating the meaning of WU. My first, despairing thought had been that it was a person, a friend or relative whose identity I could never guess. Then I convinced myself it was a type of message or code, but overwhelmed with drowsiness, I got no further than that.

The train was hustling toward Los Angeles and the Pacific Ocean, the farthest point west I had ever been. I could sense morning approaching by the slight shift in the light that snuck in beneath the roomette's window blind. Novak's orange was resting on my chest, near my heart, its sharp, sweet scent filling my nostrils and reminding me of Christmas back home. We always had oranges at Christmas. In bad years, that was all we had. Now I was headed for a place where an orange might literally fall into your hand from above, or be stuffed into a coat pocket for casual consumption.

Did the orange connect to the note? I didn't think so. My mind wandered back to the westerns I watched every Saturday afternoon as a boy in Dresden, and my fantasy of becoming a cowboy like Tom Mix, riding free under a perpetual sun. And out of this cinematic daydream, the meaning of WU hit me. Western Union, the American telegram company. Send D Western Union alert.

The question was, what was the alert and when was it to be sent? And who or what was D? Had Novak written the note after his discovery? Did he intend to notify authorities in Los Angeles? Or did it relate to something different?

Just then, another memory bubbled up, this one more recent. I was in the camp's crew office, having been summoned to translate for Joe, the manager, a large lump of a man who always wore bowties and suspenders. Joe was trying to convey to one of the German workers that he needed him to complete several small tasks before going back to the camp. "Tie up the loose ends," he had said. The meaning of the phrase had eluded me at first, but when Joe, seeing my confusion, mimicked doing up his bowtie, I understood.

I knew now that to be in control of my future and not at the mercy of luck, I would need to "tie up the loose ends." Starting with the note.

During the final, and slowest, leg of the trip, I mentally prepared for various contingencies, though it seemed unlikely the doctor's disappearance would raise alarms before Los Angeles. I now had cash and a coat, but no knife, as I had discarded it on the train tracks out of caution. If suspicion fell on me, I could no longer fight my way out but would have to rely on talking my way out. Fortunately, as it turned out, no fast-talking was required.

When the train pulled into Union Station, I waited until the other passengers in Chimayo had exited, then slipped into Novak's roomette and removed his valise and medical kit. I decided against checking for any stored luggage, as the risk of discovery seemed greater than the reward of possession. If there were additional bags, I would be long gone before they were identified.

With Novak's cash in hand, I hailed a cab, giving the driver my uncle's address, which I had memorized, in an exaggerated French accent. When he attempted a conversation, I apologized for not speaking English and that was the end of that.

Anticipating the jolt of relief that first pull on my cigarette would give, my hands started to shake. They were shaking so much I could barely get the lighter's flame to the cigarette's end. With the first inhale, my body relaxed into the enormous armchair that was currently serving as my bed. My uncle had made it clear I wasn't welcomed at his place, but being family and generally sympathetic to the cause, he had agreed to hide me in his garage—at least until they could figure out how to get me to Mexico.

I had awoken to find some fresh, if threadbare, clothes in a neat pile atop an old suitcase. My uncle must have slipped in after I had fallen asleep and left them there. Though for years I had been getting up with the sun, willingly and not, I had slept until 7:00 that morning, an hour past the time my uncle would be leaving for his shop.

I would need to find an outside telephone to call the number on Novak's note. I had decided phoning would be safer than just showing up at the address. On the telephone, I would have more control and be better able to assess the situation without risk of exposure. If Novak had alerted anyone about me, I thought, my passage south might require extra vigilance and maneuvering. The network would want to know the details sooner rather than later.

Along with the telephone, I would have to find a bathroom. As a precaution, my uncle had forbidden me from going in the house during the day. His neighbors' hours were unpredictable he said, and it would be easier to present me as an evening visitor than a daytime intruder. It was an inconvenience, but nothing my camp experiences hadn't prepared me for.

I took another drag on my cigarette. My uncle only smoked hand-rolled tobacco, but had left me a carton of Lucky Strikes, the brand I had become addicted to in the camps, on the floor next to the chair. Under those, was a newspaper, dated the previous day. I grabbed it.

A front-page article about a pack of women storming the Los Angeles port to protest the return of their Italian POW sweethearts, who they claimed had done "more for the war than the G.I.s ever had," made me snicker. In some ways, you could say, this was true. Along with tens of thousands of others, I had been taken prisoner in Tunisia, after the Germans surrendered. Our defeat was due in no small measure to the weakness of the Italians who were fighting with us. If only the Italians' military skills had matched their talent for fucking, I thought, the Axis nations might have won Africa and the war.

As part of the Nuremberg proceedings, I then read, Uruguay had asked the United Nations to spare Hermann Goering and other top Nazi leaders from the death penalty. I grunted. "Victor's justice," as the Germans called the trials, had certainly produced some odd alliances. I wondered what life was going to be like "south of the border." It would take some getting used to—I didn't speak Spanish—but I figured I would worry about that when I got there.

Reading about the lost war depressed me, so I paged my way to the funny pages and my favorite strip, *Dick Tracy.* I had missed a few days, but knew I could easily catch up with the story. Only small bits of action unfolded each day—just enough to keep you engaged and reading. Though I suspected its author, Charles Gould, was a Jew, *Dick Tracy* was the only comic that consistently held my interest. At the camps, American newspapers were everywhere—a not so subtle stab at propaganda—but the comic section had proved the most popular among the prisoners. I had learned much of my American slang reading *Dick Tracy* and *Lil Abner* (which I loathed).

I knew the commander at Crowder would have waited a day before alarming the public with news of my escape, and that his hesitation would have kept my picture out of the newspapers. From my years of confinement in American camps, I had gleaned that communications of any sort rarely extended beyond a state line. In practice, the Americans suffered from acute regionalism, with each area declaring itself a fiefdom, separate and superior to the rest.

Security at Crowder had been practically non-existent, even for the "problem" prisoners. Guards permitted the men to stroll away from the sites to smoke or eat, and the locals treated them with odd deference. I didn't know what was more outrageous—the trust of the Americans, or the complacency of the Germans. When working outside, which we did six days a week, we wore regular canvas coats over our prison uniforms, with only a ribbon sewn onto the front pocket to identify us as captives.

Of course, if things had gone differently in the war, if the Russians weren't laying claim to my hometown, it's unlikely I would have bothered to escape, duty or no duty. I was a dedicated Nazi, but not a particularly dedicated soldier. Yes, I still believed in the Party's ideological mission and most of its 25-point program—I was still committed to achieving Aryan purity in my homeland. But I would be the first to admit that the war, while well executed, had been ill planned. What had I learned in my engineering course? Make sure each part of the design works before moving on to the next. Or in the Fuhrer's case, defeat one enemy before moving on to the next. Thanks to that miscalculation, I no longer had a home to return to, only a Communist deathtrap.

Thinking about it now, my decision to help Josef, a POW at Camp Meade, with a "problem" had had unforeseen but happy results. If I had kept my mouth shut and my hands, and blade, to myself, I never would have been transferred to Crowder. If I had stayed at Meade, I never would have considered escaping—security was much tighter there, and the final destinations limited.

At Meade, Josef had discovered that fellow prisoner Heinz Luedicke was not, as he had advertised himself, a committed Nazi, but a Jewish pretender. Josef thought Luedicke an actual spy, but I suspected he was just a self-loather, a Jew whose self-contempt had driven him to first join the Party and then to enlist in the Navy. Either way, he was a liar and marked in Josef's eyes. A lesson must be taught, and Josef and I were the ones to do it.

I hadn't intended to use the blade I had fashioned from a discarded metal sander and hidden in one of the latrines, but when Luedicke tried to fight back rather than accepting his beating, my anger was roused. I had always been quick with a blade, much more so than with a gun, and Luedicke was on the ground before the surprise could hit his eyes. The wound proved fatal.

Thinking fast, I hid the bloody blade under Josef's mattress, and when questioned by the camp's security troops, I mentioned that Josef and Luedicke had fought over their work assignments. The knife was recovered, and a week later, Josef and I had been put on separate trains: Josef as punishment, I for protection.

The switchblade I had stumbled on in the barn had, like the camp knife, served its purpose and been discarded. I would have to find another someday.

AFTER THE BLUE, BLUE RAIN

On the busy street at the bottom of the hill, I found a phone booth inside a drugstore. The store was all but empty, save for one older customer who was busy chatting with the chemist about her various ailments. They paused briefly to take in my presence then returned to their conservation as soon as I reached for the phone booth door.

In the booth I fumbled in my pocket for a nickel and dialed the number on the note from memory. After ten rings, I hung up and reclaimed my nickel. I would return tomorrow and try again.

TWENTY-THREE

HENRY

If Henry had a weakness for cheap bourbon, Kit had a weakness for artichokes. "Hats and artichokes, my two vices," she would quip. She would purchase the delicacies by the dozens from Grand Central Market and drag them home for late-night steaming. When Henry had shown up at the kitchen door with a box of artichokes, she had been about to sit down for dinner. Needless to say, all thoughts of meat and potatoes went out the window at the sight of his fresh-picked produce. She had grabbed them from his outstretched hand, almost stumbling over an enormous orange cat, skittering in a panic, on her way to the stove.

"Bomber! Be careful!" Kit had yelled at the disappearing feline.

"Where did he come from?"

"My tree. He was a stray."

"And you adopted him?"

"More like he adopted me," Kit said. "He just made himself at home."

Later, when Kit brought the steaming artichokes to the table, Henry noticed the cat—Bomber?—glaring at him from the hallway. Would he have to make friends with the new addition? He glanced at the feeding bowl on the floor, which appeared to have the remains of a steak in it. Who wouldn't make himself at home, he thought, with fresh beef on the menu?

Kit dipped a leaf into a bowl of melted butter, then plopped it into her mouth and scraped the warm flesh off with her front teeth. "Hmmm. First one of the season. Always the best."

Henry pulled a leaf off his and dipped it in the butter. When in Rome, he thought. "Did you know one of my first collars was part of an artichoke gang based in Castroville?" Henry enjoyed sharing stories from his distant past, before he had gone rogue, and Kit seemed to like hearing them.

"Artichoke gang?"

"Before your time, I guess, but back then, the mob used to control the artichoke trade up north. Gangsters back East would literally kill for them. Worse than hooch in some ways."

"And you arrested one of them?"

"Their enforcer. He had come down to L.A. to take care of a truck driver who had inconveniently gotten lost on his way to deliver a shipment. Guess what his nickname was."

"Artie?"

He chuckled. "The Choke. Sal 'The Choke' Sabatini."

"Because he really liked artichokes?"

"Because he really liked to strangle people."

"'Choke chiselers?" she said with a laugh.

"More like 'choke mopes."

"Pull the other one," she said, pointing to Henry's artichoke. Henry dutifully tugged off another leaf and doused it with butter. "So what happened in Barstow? Did Judson cooperate?"

"After a fashion. The coroner's convinced it wasn't an accident. But there's no chance of the head turning up. The crows saw to that. They'll have to get a fingerprint for comparison. And for what it's worth, I think I found the murder weapon. A switchblade."

"You were busy. I hope the sheriff appreciated your efforts."

Henry smiled wryly. "The only thing Jugs Judson appreciates is a free drink."

Kit scraped the meat off the last leaf of her artichoke and contemplated its fuzzy center. "What are the chances that our guy is last seen on a train in New Mexico, and a headless body shows up the next day on the Barstow tracks, and they're not the same?"

"A trifecta box with seven horses chance," said Henry.

Kit grimaced as she worked the heart from its nest. "That's what I thought."

"Do you want me to fill Dina in?" he asked. "Judson may want to question her."

"No, thanks. She should hear it from me." She chewed the final morsel slowly, savoring the last burst of flavor while debating her options.

Although death was a common enough outcome for missing persons, she had never investigated a case involving one, and he guessed she wasn't looking forward to her initiation. "Better she hear it from one of us than Judson."

"I suppose," she said flatly before changing subjects. "So, how's Bea? It's been a while since she came by the office."

Henry pushed his plate away. He understood what she was really asking—why was he here instead of at home with his wife. Since they'd become partners, Kit had uncovered the dark parts of his life—some of them at any rate. She'd seen Bea drunk and angry, or so drained of life she couldn't get out of bed to say hello. If Bea called the office in the middle of the day, upset, Kit knew that Henry would stop work to tend to her. She never questioned him about any of it, which of course made him want to tell her everything.

"She's been better."

"Sorry to hear that."

"Something about seeing Judson today made me . . ." He looked away. In the sea of bullshit that had been much of his life, he knew there was one island of truth: his love for Bea. He couldn't explain it, but whatever beguiling spell she had cast on him thirty years before still had a hold on him. He was clinging to more than a shared life, or a sense of decency, or a vow made decades ago, he was hanging on to her, all of her. He just hoped, in the final act, they didn't go down together. "It's just tough to remember sometimes."

INTO EACH LIFE SOME RAIN MUST FALL

Thursday, February 7, 1946

TWENTY-FOUR
STANLEY

Stanley was seated in his usual spot near Doc's window. He listened to the rain as it clattered against the hospital's metal drain pipes, sharp pings alternating with muffled clunks. It was quite firm and steady, mesmerizing him with its unexpected rhythms.

The urge to get out his chair and move overcame him, but Doc didn't seem to mind his quiet restlessness. "Do you want to smoke?"

Stanley considered the offer. "No, thanks."

"Does the rain remind you of something?" Doc said.

"Should it?"

"I don't know. You seem a little agitated. What are you thinking about right now?"

"Now? The rain. The fact that it's raining. Rain is a big deal in L.A., isn't it?"

"Is it a big deal to you?"

Stanley shrugged. He knew he wasn't giving Doc what he wanted, but it couldn't be helped. The few memories he had managed to scare up were just sparks and flashes, not enough content for catch and release. Doc had never asked him about his dreams, and he had never brought them up, mostly because they made no sense, even to him. The night before he had dreamed about the girl in the parachute. He was fondling her breasts and she was kissing his neck. He had been aroused, but was it a memory? Had he made love to the local girl he had described in his letter? Or was it wishful thinking? He had no idea.

He walked over to the book shelves and let his gaze wander over the many-colored spines of Doc's medical texts. His eyes came to rest on a slim volume by Sigmund Freud, *Civilization and Its Discontents.* "Now I'm thinking about this book."

"Are you familiar with Freud?"

"Never met the guy, but the title's catchy."

Doc smiled. "Intentional or not, it's curious that you stopped on that book. Freud wrote it in 1929, in the aftermath of the Great War. It explores the tension between civilized man and natural man. I believe, like Freud did, that much of what we're coping with today goes back to that fundamental clash between learned behavior -what we're taught in Sunday school and civics class and such—and basic survival, what survival sometimes requires us to do. The greater the divide between those two, Freud says, the deeper the psychic wounds. *Homo homini lupus.* Man is wolf to man."

"You think I'm wounded . . . psychically?"

"I think it's safe to say the war upended your unique sense of humanity. You experienced things very few of us ever experience. Or imagine experiencing."

"But I can't remember what I experienced."

"Forgetfulness is your hideout. And in its own way, it has protected you. But like all hideouts, it's not designed for the long haul."

"Nec praeterita nec future"' Stanley said, the Latin coming to him in a disarming rush.

"Exactly. Without the past, there's no future."

Stanley snorted. "It's weird I can remember my Latin. I stopped taking it after 10th grade."

"At your high school?" Doc consulted his notes. "Cathedral?"

"Cathedral," Stanley repeated without inflection.

"According to your school records, you excelled at Latin, math, history and baseball."

"Baseball." Without thinking, Stanley curved his fingers around an invisible baseball and flexed his wrist, as though revving up to toss a splitter.

"You're a southpaw"

Stanley lowered his arm and returned to the window and the rain. "I don't think I've ever liked rain."

"Never? Why not?"

He pictured a baseball sailing into a catcher's mitt. "Because, you can't be a phantom in the rain."

"A phantom? What do you mean?"

And just like that, the curtain fell. He shrugged and turned to face the window. Down below he saw an imposing man in civilian clothes in the yard, oblivious to the rain, looking up at him. They exchanged glances, and an instant later, the man bowed his head and strode away.

TWENTY-FIVE

LUCA

Rain. Dewey. Baseball. Socks. Father. Looking at his Stanley notes for the past week, these were the nouns that appeared most. In the correspondence, the chats and the sessions. Somehow, Luca knew, they were each significant and all connected. They were all objects -people and things—that bound one key memory to another and led to the moment of forgetting.

Even if unconscious, Stanley's choice of "library books"—where he was and what he was doing under hypnosis—had always been his. Through his choices, he'd been telling Luca where to help him look for his lost experiences. Or rather, where to find that one experience that undid all the others. And somehow, in the heart of that terrible experience lay rain, Dewey, baseball, socks and his father.

Luca recalled that Stanley had been reported missing on April 2 and been found miles away on April 10. He knew that at some point during that period, Stanley had suffered a concussion and experienced a moment of forgetting. Hoping to find some detail he had overlooked or dismissed as unimportant, Luca rechecked the Army's formal incident report. Scribbled in the margin was the notation: "Comfort last seen with Pfc. Dewey Barton, M.I.A. same date."

He had been thinking about Kit in a non-professional way, and he sensed that these non-professional feelings went both ways. It had been over a year since he last dated—a doomed affair with an out-of-his-league Vassar coed he had met at a Yale mixer. The military's guidelines regarding the mixing of personal and professional relations were vague, though, especially when the link was once-removed. Under ordinary circumstances, he wouldn't have felt restrained pursuing a romance with Kit, but given the precariousness of his situation here, he felt caution was in order.

And the truth was, he needed her professional help with Dewey Barton. Dead or alive, Stanley would need to know his friend's fate. In the confusion of battle, the two had become separated, and as far as the Army was concerned, their connection had been lost. Going through official channels would take time and might raise questions that Stanley wouldn't be prepared to confront.

When he finally reached her by phone, Kit had been startled by his request but agreeable. She had contacts at the Veterans Center, she said, and would be happy to meet for coffee the next morning. Anything for Stanley, she repeated. And, he hoped in a moment of optimistic immodesty, anything for Luca.

TWENTY-SIX

Excerpt from "My Escape: A Confession" (submitted to O.P.M.G., February 1946)

It had started to rain. It had rained a lot in Maryland, and there was snow in Missouri, but I hadn't expected rain in Los Angeles. Among the clothes my uncle had left me was an oversized yellow raincoat, the kind I associated with whale hunters. I wondered why my uncle would have such a thing, but it had a hood, which I appreciated.

The walk back to the drugstore seemed longer than it had the day before, made worse by the puddles and rivulets that were forming in the steadily increasing rainfall.

This time, my call was answered almost immediately. Not knowing who or what to expect, I had prepared various scenarios, hoping one would click.

"Hello?" The voice was high and rather thin.

"Good evening. To whom am I speaking?"

"I'm sorry. Who's this?"

"I'm a friend of Dr. Novak." A gasp exploded on the other end of the line.

"Peter? Have you heard from him?" she said with obvious excitement.

"No. I was hoping you had." In contrast to the woman, I struck a note of mild concern. "He was supposed to call me after his arrival."

"In Los Angeles?"

"Los Angeles, yes," I said. "When did you last hear from him?"

"A few days ago. He sent a telegram."

"A telegram. When did he send it?"

"On Friday."

Sent from the train, I calculated, but when? "Morning or evening?"

"Morning. What difference does that make?"

"Probably none."

After a pause she said, "Who are you? How did you get my number? Are you with the Army?" The questions shot out; her tone had suddenly grown tense.

"No, I'm a friend," I said, with as much lightness as I could muster. "From long ago. Like I said, he was supposed to call me. I'm worried I haven't heard from him." A long silence followed, annoying me. "Hello? Are you there?"

Finally she responded. "Why don't you leave your name and number and I'll call you when I hear from him."

Now it was my turn to pause. "I'm afraid I don't have a number at the moment. Perhaps I'll call you again later. Thank you for your time." I hung up before she could react and stared at the telephone, replaying the conversation. She had mentioned the telegram without prompting and confirmed it had been sent prior to my encounter with the doctor. She might have made inquiries, even gone to the police, but nothing in her comments suggested she knew anything about me.

Out of the corner of my eye, I noticed a fat woman who had been talking to the chemist walking in my direction. I turned away from her, pulling the hood of the raincoat over my head. When I saw her pass the booth, apparently on her way somewhere else, I made a quick exit.

Was it expecting too much to assume this loose end had been tied?

TWENTY-SEVEN

KIT

Kit pulled up the office blinds to confirm that it was indeed raining. Not the lazy, soft rain of spring, or the scattered, spitting rain of late summer, but the mad tempest of winter. The sidewalk was empty, and save for a taxi or two, the street was deserted.

Despite the biblical nature of the weather, Kit yearned for the comfort of a lunchtime coupe of gin. It was time to give Dina a full update, and while bad news went with the territory, headless bodies didn't. No matter how she practiced it in her mind, Kit knew the conversation was going to be brutal. She needed some Dutch courage.

Complicating matters further, she had promised Luca she would try to dig up some information on Dewey's fate, which meant asking Manny for another favor.

As she was reaching for her rain gear, the phone rang, and after a silent curse, she answered it. "Comfort and Company Investigations?" she said in her best secretarial voice.

"Kit? It's Dina."

"I was about to call you," Kit said, a wave of dread passing through her. 'How are you?"

"A man called asking about Peter," Dina blurted.

"What? What man?"

"I don't know, he didn't identify himself. He said he was a friend of Peter's. He said so little, I wasn't sure if I should even tell you about him. But, I don't know. . ."

"Dina?"

"There was something about his voice that spooked me. I think he knows something."

"What did he say?"

"I don't remember exactly." She paused, apparently trying to recall the details. "He said Peter was supposed to call him when he got to town. He asked me about the telegram Peter sent."

"What about it?"

"He wanted to know when I got it. Morning or evening."

The telegram sent from the train. "Did he have an accent?"

"Maybe a slight Brooklyn accent? Nothing pronounced," Dina said. Then sensing something in Kit's silence, she added, "Do you know who it was?"

"No," Kit said. It was only a half a lie. She didn't know anything for sure, but if her instincts were to be trusted, Dina had just spoken to her lover's killer. And if he had Dina's phone number, he probably knew where she lived too. "Are you at work?"

"Yes, but I was thinking of leaving early."

"Can you meet me at Cole's in a half-hour?"

Cole's attracted a smaller, quieter crowd at lunchtime than it did at cocktail hour. Even the ones who ordered martinis with their Salisbury steaks ate with purpose, with one eye on the clock. Add downpours to the mix, and only the most diehard, or desperate, customers crossed the threshold.

Nursing her gin and tonic in a back booth, Kit took notes as Dina, her hair damp from the rain, went over the fine points of the phone call. Afterward, she shifted on the booth bench and looked at Kit with a mix of apprehension and impatience. She had declined alcohol, ordering only a pot of tea and a slice of dry toast. Morning sickness, Kit assumed.

Dina's phone call had put a twist in the plan. Finally Kit looked up from her notepad and said, "We think Peter might have had an altercation on the train with someone. Most likely an escaped

German POW. We don't know exactly what happened, but we know Peter and this man were together."

"What's his name? The POW?"

"Klaus Fischer."

"Klaus Fischer." Dina paused. "Is he the man who called me?"

"Maybe. He has an uncle in Mt. Washington. He might be hiding out there."

"Are they Nazis?" Dina asked softly, as she rubbed a spot on her breastbone. She seemed to be hovering between terror and rage. Before Kit could respond, she said, "What's the uncle's name?"

"We'll deal with him," said Kit, before taking a generous sip of her gin. "There's something else I have to tell you."

"Yes?"

"The police in Barstow are going to be calling you."

"Barstow?"

"They found a body near the train tracks."

"A body? Whose?"

"They think . . . it might be Peter's."

"Oh!" Dina blurted. She blinked, as the color drained from her already pale face. "They *think* it might be Peter?" Her breathing had become shallow. "What does that mean?"

"They can't identify the body as it is, but they could do a fingerprint comparison, if they had a comparison sample."

"So it might not be Peter," Dina said. Suddenly, her eyes brightened with hope.

"It might not be," Kit mumbled, not wanting to add any fuel to the desperate thinking. "If they had Peter's fingerprints, they would know for sure." Kit paused, allowing reality to catch up to Dina's thoughts. "Do you have something of his that might have his fingerprints on it? A book or a letter perhaps?"

Dina spoke in a monotone. "A letter, I have letters he wrote."

"Good. We can arrange for someone from Barstow to pick it up."

Dina nodded her consent and sipped her tea, but Kit could see her thoughts were running on a different track altogether. Kit hoped she hadn't given away too much by mentioning the uncle. Dina was clever but vulnerable.

"It's best if you stick as close to home as possible for the next few days. If you notice anything or anybody out of the ordinary, call me or Henry immediately."

"All right," said Dina as she took a grudging bite of her toast.

"We'll take care of it, don't worry," Kit said with more force than she had intended. "I'll call you."

Kit caught Manny typing reports in one of the Veterans Center's administrative offices. She had scurried over from Cole's, doing her best to dodge raindrops and feelings of despair. At the end of their conversation, she had seen something in Dina's eyes that worried her. It was a look she recognized from some of her other clients—vengeance.

As Kit walked through the open door, her hair dripping, Manny glanced up from his Underwood and whistled. "Lordy, look what the proverbial cat dragged in." He gestured to the chair on the other side of the desk. "Take a load off."

"Thanks," Kit said as she peeled off her drenched raincoat.

Manny jumped up to take it from her. "Does the name Mr. Bell ring any bells? He invented this thing called the telephone."

Kit blew out her cheeks. "I had a tough meeting with my client. I just needed to clear my head and stop thinking for a second."

"I believe I've just been insulted, but after my behavior last time . . ." He let the thought hang, then said, "Who are we trying to find today?"

Kit slid a slip of paper across Manny's desk. "Dewey Barton. He served with Stanley."

At the mention of Stanley's name, Manny grew quiet. "How is Stanley?"

She shrugged, trying to push down a rising wave of sadness. "They got him a decent doctor, at least. He's a civilian."

"That's good to hear. There are some genuine quacks around here." Manny said in a half-whisper. Then he sighed and said, "Last time I saw Stanley, he shot me with a pop gun. Just missed the family jewels. He must have been eleven, twelve?"

Kit's face broke into a grin. "I remember that. Seems like forever ago."

"The Dinosaur Age." Manny studied Kit's note. "What do you need to know about Dewey Barton of Stockton?"

"Did he make it out of Okinawa? And if he did, where did he end up?"

"That's it? Piece of cake."

"How soon?"

"I'll call you in the morning."

TWENTY-EIGHT

HENRY

Henry detested disguises, but fearful he might be recognized from newspaper photos taken during the bombing trial, he had returned home to apply his "not Henry" makeup and attire. He had found that people were less attentive to a particular facial feature than to the more obvious qualities—sex, size, age, hair and clothes—so to be "not Henry," he focused his efforts on the latter three.

Hoping to take off a few years, he had already dabbed some of Bea's foundation into the lines of his cheeks and was now focused on his hair and eyebrows. From their unmade bed, the pajama-clad Bea, highball glass in hand, watched him at her vanity darken what was left of his locks with a swipe of carbon paper. It was a beauty trick she had taught him, and she happily kibitzed him.

"Start from the roots and work out. Slowly," she instructed him.

"I have roots?" he said, changing his application technique.

"Everyone has roots. Even you."

Bea seemed to be enjoying herself, propped up on pillows, her bedside radio broadcasting her favorite big band tunes. Henry couldn't help but notice she was in the same pajamas she had been wearing that morning, and all day the day before as well. He knew not to call attention to them, even though they signaled that she was sinking into one of her "melancholies," as she called them, those long periods of sadness that sapped her strength and initiative. There was little he could do to prevent them—and she had begged him not to try—but his impotence gnawed at him.

Satisfied with his more youthful hair and cheeks, Henry dragged a brown pinstripe double-breasted suit out of the wardrobe, a hand-me-down from Bea's deceased brother. He had been much heavier than Henry when they were younger, but thanks to his semi-retirement, Henry had recently caught up in the weight department. He hoped the suit, together with his homburg, screamed East Coast, where he had decided his "Tom Kurzbach" would hail from. Finally, he tucked his glasses into the interior pocket of the pinstripe. Tom Kurzbach, he figured, was too vain for glasses.

"So who am I?" he said, initiating a game he and Bea first played when they were dating.

Having spent her youth in the fashion and jewelry district, Bea was extra sensitive to the cultural subtleties of attire. Just by studying their hair and clothes, she could tell a Chicago musician from a Boston banker, or an Italian gangster from a Jewish one. "You're a New York businessman," she said after a quick appraisal of his clothes. "Perhaps Italian. Not Jewish."

"I need to be German. Definitely not Jewish."

"German?" She pursed her lips and squinted in concentration. "Silk pocket square and suspenders."

"Suspenders? Are you sure?" He had a pair but loathed wearing them.

"Nothing says German like suspenders."

"I wasn't planning to strip." He had found his red silk pocket square and tucked it into his front pocket.

"That's a relief. But you still need suspenders," Bea said, slipping out of bed and going to the closet, where his one pair of suspenders hung. She pulled them out and sauntered over to him. "Here," she said, dangling the black suspenders in her hand.

At that moment he became aware that Benny Goodman's "Memories of You" was playing on the radio. The sweet sounds of Goodman's clarinet soon lulled him into a strange state of complacency, and he didn't resist when Bea dropped the suspenders and started to remove his jacket. She dropped that too, and sidled up to him. She smelled earthy and unwashed, but as her long tapered fingers groped for his belt buckle, his nostrils filled with the scent of her favorite jasmine perfume. It was a perfume she hadn't used in years.

Sometimes memories were an amazing thing, he thought, as he drew his wife close and swayed with the beat.

The bookshop would be closing soon, but momentum was telling Henry not to wait. What exactly he was investigating at this point, though, he couldn't say. The missing person was almost certainly a corpse, and catching killers was not in the Comfort and Company charter. But the knowledge that he had triggered something in Washington, something big enough to warrant his surveillance, had changed the calculus for him. Whatever was going on, he didn't want to be even more behind the eight ball than he already was.

"Are you looking for something in particular?" Her voice was low and clipped, and Henry detected a hint of an accent—buried German with a twist of Brooklyn. For a middle-aged bookstore clerk, she dressed quite stylishly. Kit, he thought, would approve of the blue bolero jacket and matching skirt that hugged her generous curves. Her name tag said "Senta."

"I'm headed for South America and was looking for some background reading," he said, while working the band of his homburg with his hands. "I was told you had a good collection of travel books."

Her perfectly plucked eyebrows, the same mahogany brown as her hair, rose just slightly. "We do as a matter of fact. Business or pleasure?"

"Both, I hope."

"Any place in particular? South America's a big continent."

"Brazil. Chile. Argentina."

"So below the equator?"

"Sounds right."

She led him to a bookcase labeled, appropriately, South America. "It's arranged in alphabetical order, by country, or region. Books on southern South America are down there," she said pointing to the bottom row. "I recommend this one, for an overview." She bent to pull *Latin Style, Below the Equato*r from the shelf and offered it to Henry.

"The author is British but has lived all over Latin America and knows his stuff. The photographs are quite good."

Henry turned the oversized pages, feigning interest in their contents. "Great photos, but I might be looking for something less about travel and more about living. Something with information about business and emigration."

"More encyclopedic?" she asked, returning *Latin Style, Below the Equator* to its spot.

"Yes, if you have it."

She reached up to pull a book from the top shelf and Henry got a good whiff of her perfume, recognizing it immediately as Caron's Alpona. The odd but enticing citrusy scent was a popular item, brought back from Paris at the end of the previous war. "Alpona," he mumbled in spite of himself.

She gave him another smile, this one genuine and full. "That's right. Alpona. It's my favorite. I'm surprised you recognized it."

"I spent some time in Paris," he said, as though that would explain it all.

"The French do know their perfume."

"Must be hard to get here."

"It is, but I have my sources," she said with a wink. She pressed the second book into Henry's hands, flesh touching flesh for the briefest of moments. "I'm told this book on Argentina is helpful. Very up-to-date and comprehensive."

Henry read the title out loud. "*Argentina in the Twentieth Century*. So there are good opportunities there?"

"From what I've heard, it's very welcoming. If you can afford to get there, of course."

"Getting there. Yes, that's the challenge."

"Is it just you who's traveling?"

"Just me. Does that make a difference?"

"Some ways are better suited to families than others, that's all."

"Ah. No, I'm a solo act."

"I'm curious. Who told you about us?"

"Sorry?" he said.

"You said you were told about our travel books. Who told you, if you don't mind me asking?" She gave him her best sales smile, showing off an unexpected pair of dimples and perfectly even teeth.

Casually he returned his gaze to the book and flipped its glossy pages. "A friend."

"Someone from the community?"

He paused. "That's right. Christian Zimmer."

"Christian, of course. He used to come by quite regularly on his lunch breaks."

"He's in Anaheim now."

"Anaheim? Yes, we have a few customers from there. Not as many as we used to, unfortunately." Her professional smile returned as she gestured to the book in his hand. "May I ring that up for you, or do you want to keep looking?"

"I'm through looking," he said following her to the sales desk, "but I still have a question."

"Go ahead."

"What are you doing after six?"

The question disarmed her momentarily. "I'm having dinner with friends."

"What about before dinner?"

"Before dinner?"

"We could talk about Argentina over an aperitif."

She hesitated. No doubt being invited out by a customer, or any male with a pulse, wasn't an everyday occurrence for the overripe Senta. "I'd prefer to talk about Paris."

"All right," he said with a half-laugh. "I'm Tom Kurzbach, by the way."

"Nice to meet you, Herr Kurzbach."

He wasn't sure if it was contrariness that led him to suggest that he and Senta continue their conversation at the lounge at nearby Calson's, but she was game. Calvin didn't hang out at the business after dark, and the likelihood that one of the other lunch regulars would be here now was low, he thought. He had ordered schnapps for them both, but only she was drinking.

Henry gestured toward the nametag that was still pinned to her jacket. "You're the first Senta I've ever met. Is it a family name?"

"My maternal grandmother," she replied while discreetly removing the badge.

"Was she German?"

"Yes, as am I, by birth." She reached into her clutch and extracted a cigarette.

Though he had stopped smoking after his hospital stint, he still carried a lighter and flicked it into life as Senta leaned in. "I thought I detected an accent."

"It's not something I advertise," she mumbled after inhaling. "Especially now"

"Understandable. I heard some in the community were targeted."

"Not me, but yes, a few were arrested and deported."

"Another casualty of war."

"To be honest," she sighed, "they weren't the best and brightest. Circumstances demanded discretion, and they were hardly discreet. The community suffered. And you? Where are your people from?"

"Solingen," he said. "Both sides, although my mother's side emigrated a long time ago." A little bit of truth to wrap around the lies, he thought.

"I understand the Old Town was completely destroyed there."

"Yes, there's not much left."

"When were you in France?"

"Years ago, during the first war."

"You were stationed there?"

"Briefly. Then they sent me to Berlin."

"I have an aunt and young cousin in Berlin."

"Which sector?"

"Soviet."

He winced. "That's rough. Not that the others are much better. What we did to the German people . . . What we're still doing to them." He let that sink in through a cloud of cigarette smoke.

"I don't know how they're getting by. My aunt's husband was killed in Tunisia. My older cousin died in France."

"Tough luck."

The subject spent, Senta finished off her schnapps, then asked, "Why is it you need to go to South America?"

He narrowed his eyes. "Did I say I needed to go?"

"You didn't. I just thought maybe . . ."

"Maybe what?" he said sharply.

"Nothing." She flashed a calming smile.

He paused, then leaning in, spoke in a low, conspiratorial voice. "Last year the War Department sent me to Berlin as a transportation expert. It was a civilian posting, but I had access to our German counterparts. I was pursuing business connections with some of them—not strictly legal—and got on the Constabulary's radar. I don't know how seriously they're pursuing the matter but I don't want to stick around to find out or leave any clues as to my whereabouts."

"I see." She seemed to be weighing his words, trying to decide whether to pry more meaning out of them.

"Really, I'm just looking for a place to retire. Some place cheap and . . . welcoming."

"For like-minded folks?"

"Exactly. A safe place for like-minded folks."

"It will cost you."

"Naturally."

"Do you have a number I can reach you at?" she said.

Henry pulled a pen from his jacket and gently took Senta's hand. "Where would you like it?" he said.

Senta turned her hand palm-up. "A real Biro," she said approvingly.

"Bought it in Germany," he lied. He then wrote a number on her hand. It was for his "spy phone," as Bea liked to call it. The unlisted number was a leftover from his dealings with the LAPD, when he and Calvin needed to communicate without worry of eavesdropping. If someone from the German Family Association tried to track it down, they would be sent into a bureaucratic labyrinth that would go through Calson's but ring at his house. "You can reach me there after eight."

TWENTY-NINE

KIT

Kit struggled to see through the swishes of her wipers. The narrow road that wound around the Mt. Washington hillside where William Fisher lived had become, in places, a lake. Her high-beams were on, but visibility was limited, and she gripped the wheel tightly while maneuvering around each bend. Houses big and small, some with lights on, some dark, were scattered along the drenched landscape. She had taken at least one wrong turn, which was leading her downhill instead of up.

For a change, she was playing a hunch. For Henry, hunches came as easily as breathing, but for Kit, they were as rare as snow in the desert. A gut grip, as Henry liked to call them, had overwhelmed her. She had been unable to reach Dina since their meeting, and her only thought was that she had looked up Fisher's address and had gone to confront him. Had she taken the bus and then walked up?

Static overtook the car radio, drowning out Betty Hutton's musical tribute to doctors, lawyers and Indian chiefs. She turned the song off and kept an anxious eye out for road signs. Although lots of Angelinos loved hillside living, she found it too removed. If you're going to be in a city, she thought, be in a city. Especially on a stormy night in February.

As Kit inched the car toward the last bend, she was startled by a fierce cracking sound and flinched instinctively. Just above her, she saw a full-sized fir tree topple over and start to tumble towards the road. Unsure of its trajectory, she floored the gas in a vain attempt at a getaway. The car lurch forwards a few feet before being swept up by a rush of water racing down the road like a newly formed river.

She tried to steer but the rain had turned the car into a rudderless boat. She gave herself over to the water's power, and as it carried her down the twisting road, she calmly said to herself, well, this probably won't end well. A random comment by Stanley—life is heavenly, living is hell—popped into her head, followed by Henry's favorite truism—what can't be cured, must be endured. What was she supposed to do with that thought?

She felt the water's momentum ease up and tested the wheel, hoping to avoid two abandoned cars blocking the bottom of the street. With a couple of taps of the brake, she was able to bring the car to a stop, just feet away from the others. She gave herself a second to breathe before cutting the engine and climbing out.

She slid and stumbled down the dark street, heading for the lights of police cars and a fire truck. She was halfway there when a terrible bellow shook the air, followed by a gasp of silence. A wave of mud and debris then came tearing down the hill, carrying with it snapped tree limbs and a house, now in pieces big and small. As Kit ran, it plowed into the cars, turning them sideways and upside-down before finally losing steam and thudding to a stop.

At the fire station, Kit dialed Henry's home number, having once again, failed to reach Dina. She had hitched a ride down the remainder of the hill in an ambulance called to the disaster. No one on the scene appeared injured, but a swamp's worth of muck had engulfed her car, and the rain continued to soak the ground.

"Hello?" came Henry's reassuring voice.

She took a slow breath, determined to be calm, though her heart was still pounding. "I have an insurance question for you." Henry knew more about catastrophes, natural and manmade, than anyone who had ever worked in insurance.

"Kit?" Henry said into the ensuing silence. "You there?"

"Acts of God," Kit exhaled. "Does that include mudslides?"

"Mudslides? Are you all right?"

"I'm fine, but my car is buried under a hillside of mud, trees and iceboxes. Kaput. And I left my handbag on the seat." Suddenly panicked, she patted her raincoat pocket, feeling for her notebook. It was still there. Small mercies.

"So you need a ride home?"

"You should be a detective."

"Where are you?"

"Cypress fire station."

"Give me fifteen minutes. And yes, mud is an act of God."

THIRTY

HENRY

As Henry drove west from the fire station, steering around monstrous puddles of rainwater, the wild downpour eased to a steady but civil shower. Kit sat shivering next to him, trying to explain how she had ended up rafting down a Mt. Washington hillside in her now abandoned car. She had gotten as far as needing to track down Dina, when Henry interrupted.

"How would she have known about Fisher? Or where to find him?"

Kit paused, and for a moment, the sound of the windshield wipers, frantically whooshing away the rain, filled the car. "I guess I told her. Sort of."

Henry sighed his disapproval. Apparently his words about the importance of keeping details close to the vest hadn't penetrated. His fingers tensed around the steering wheel. "You told her where he lived?"

"Only that he lived in Mt. Washington. She must have looked him up in the phone book."

"How did she react when you told her about the body?"

"Sad. Angry. Desperate. Just what you'd expect." Glumly changing the subject, Kit said, "What's going on with your hair, by the way?"

Henry glanced in the rearview mirror. "My disguise for Senta. I didn't have time to remove it."

"Senta? Is that her perfume I smell?"

"Alpona," he said with a half-smile.

Kit sneered. "Did she buy your story?"

"We'll find out soon enough. The trap's been set."

"Should we be focusing on finding Dina instead?"

"Unfortunately, if your hunch is right," he said, "that's exactly what we'll be focusing on."

THIRTY-ONE

KIT

Kit could hear the phone ringing as she unlocked her front door. Part of her wanted to ignore it, but she forced herself to make a dash to the hallway. She grabbed the receiver on what must been the tenth or eleventh ring.

"Hello?" She thought she heard a sigh followed by a second of silence. "Hello."

"Miss Comfort?"

She recognized the voice. "Luca? It's Kit."

"Kit. I've been trying to reach you."

"I've been . . ." She wanted to say nearly drowning and suffocating, watching my life flash before my eyes, but composed herself. "I've been working. Is Stanley all right?"

"He's safe, don't worry."

"Safe? From what?"

"He became very agitated. We had to sedate him."

Kit stiffened. "Why?"

"The rain seems to have set him off."

"The rain?"

"As soon as it started, he became upset," Luca said. "It's a sensory trigger and not uncommon with combat stress." "But he's not in danger?"

"No, but he seems to think you are."

"Me?"

"He needs to see you. Can you come?"

She pictured her sedan, abandoned in a sea of mud, and felt a wave of fatigue wash over her. "Of course."

The cabbie dropped her off at Birmingham, where they had moved Stanley to the emergency ward. She found him sitting on a chair facing the window, calm but vacant. He didn't acknowledge her arrival, but leaned closer to the glass instead.

"Hi, Stanley," she said, her voice steady and clear. When she got no reaction, she added, "Dr. Moreno said you wanted to see me."

Stanley slowly turned his head. "Kit?"

"The one and only."

"Are you all right?" he croaked.

"Of course. How are you? Dr. Moreno said the rain was bothering you."

Stanley nodded. "I had a feeling about you. A bad feeling."

"About what?"

His face contorted with pained confusion. "I don't know. I woke up, thinking about my session with Doc, and suddenly this feeling of . . . danger went through my whole body."

"That must have been scary."

"And this thing Coach used to say, 'you can't be a phantom in the rain,' kept repeating in my head. And then I had to know if you were all right."

"I'm fine. And I'm here," she said, daring to move a little closer. "And I'm really happy to see you."

"I'm just glad you're safe," he murmured.

She fought the urge to wrap her arms around him. Stanley had resisted hugs and kisses, even as a little boy. From the start, he had been subjected to their father's expectation of tough independence. "No comfort from Comfort" had been their father's parental motto. In Kit's case, though, enforcement of the motto had been delayed until her tenth birthday. Prior to that, she had been a daddy's girl through and through.

Unlike her, Stanley had never known the pleasure of being swept up in strong arms or held tight during a mournful or frightened moment. Yet Stanley had never resented her for it. Between them, there had always been a deep, unexpressed connection. "Do you mean Mr. Fowler? Coach Fowler?"

He furrowed his brows. "Fowler?"

"That was Coach's last name."

He shrugged. "I'm very tired. I'd like to go back to sleep."

"Of course." She forced a smile. "I'll try to come back tomorrow."

As he turned back to the window, he repeated, "I'm glad you're safe, Kit."

She couldn't sleep. As exhausted and wrung out as she felt, she could not fall asleep. Something was tugging at her mind, a thought or memory in need of retrieval. She flung herself out of bed and stumbled into Stanley's bedroom. She groped for the light switch, momentarily forgetting it was on the wall behind the door. When illuminated, the room radiated an odd stillness, like a painting capturing a moment in time. The airplane models lined up on his dresser, the shelf of baseball trophies, the beat-up street sign, the felt dart board, the "severed hand" reaching toward a pinup of Veronica Lake, and on his nightstand, a pack of playing cards and a copy of *I Saw It Happen,* bookmarked with a nail file, the ending still waiting to be revealed.

Kit hadn't spent time in this room since Stanley's deployment, and looking at it now, she realized just how much of him had been taken in the war. Like many, Stanley had still been a boy when he had enlisted. It made no sense, she thought, to force the young to participate in mankind's most terrible activities, to witness its most atrocious behaviors. Experience was the only effective armor against human horrors, and how much experience could an eighteen year old like Stanley have? She sat down on the narrow bed, pressed her hand into the chenille bedspread and let a few tears slide down her cheek.

After a few moments, she forced herself to stand and was heading for the door when she saw it. There in Stanley's closet was his letter jacket from high school. The letter "C" was stitched onto the leather front, for Cathedral, and on the back, in fancy script, was the name of the school's mascot: "The Phantoms."

She slept fitfully after that, anxious for morning. At five, she gave up and rolled out of bed. Her mental to-do list was growing by the second, and she wanted to jump on it as soon as the sun came up. Problem was, when she got impatient, she got sloppy. Both her father and Henry had cautioned her against impetuous action. She knew she couldn't afford to be careless again with Dina's case, or with Dina.

MOONLIGHT COCKTAIL

Friday, February 8, 1946

THIRTY-TWO

KIT

The morning had started off on a hopeful note, as Manny had called with some preliminaries about Dewey. When she pulled up at Sarno's in a taxi, Luca, already seated, waved a greeting through the large plate glass window that fronted the street. The exterior was festooned in the colors of the Italian flag and perched on the bright green awning was a life-size plaster statue of a fat, mustached chef holding a tray of baked goodies.

Immediately upon entering, Kit was hit with the hot-from-the-oven scent that was wafting from the industrial oven. The interior décor echoed that of the outside—Italian kitsch throughout. Beaming with pleasure, his somber professional demeanor tucked away, Luca motioned her to join him at his café table.

"They just opened," he said. "Straight from Italy via Chicago."

She took another deep breath, savoring the sweet, yeasty odor of the oven. "Can't beat that smell."

"I took the liberty of ordering some pastries," he said, nodding at a plate of assorted goodies on the table. "And some coffee."

Kit sat down and ogled the coffee. It was darker than any joe she had ever seen.

"It's Italian," Luca explained. "Very strong."

"Strong is exactly what I need right now." To show she meant it, she lifted the demitasse to her lips and took a healthy sip. It was as intense as advertised and delicious.

"I guess it was a rough night all around," Luca said.

Kit nodded, then said, "How is Stanley?"

'He's better now. Your visit seems to have calmed him. Thank you for showing up."

"He was worried that something had happened to me."

"Yes, because of the rain."

"Funny thing is, I did . . . have an accident last night. Because of the rain."

A long silence followed. "Curious," Luca said at last. Then he added, "You're all right?

"I'm fine. My car got the worst of it."

"Sorry to hear it."

"He also said he couldn't be a phantom in the rain."

"He said that to me too. During one of our sessions."

"I think he's referring to his high school baseball team. They were called the Cathedral Phantoms."

"Curious," he repeated. "It's not unusual for pieces of memories recalled in hypnosis to surface when fully conscious. In fact, it can be a valuable problem-solving tool."

She noticed that Luca's brow would furrow whenever he was talking about his work, a quirk she found strangely attractive. "How so?"

"The answers to problems often lie right under the surface of our conscious thinking. We don't always know what we know. But if you relax your mind, as you would in hypnosis, the connections between ideas and memories can grow sharper."

"Relaxing anything right now would be a blessing," Kit said, and Luca took up the challenge.

"All right, close your eyes."

Kit shut her eyes lightly.

"Good. Now take a few deep, slow breaths and say, in your head, the letters of the alphabet, from A to Z. Tell yourself, that by the time you reach Z, you'll be completely relaxed."

With eyes still shut, Kit began her silent alphabet countdown, making it as far as "L" when she heard Luca talking in Italian. She opened her eyes to see the bakery's proprietor at their table. Just like his plaster likeness, a pristine white apron covered his ample belly and a chef's hat hid his balding head. He was chatting with Luca like an old friend. Luca offered his compliments (she could make out that much of their Italian) and the baker sauntered off, well pleased.

"I guess you really are Italian," she said, then flushed at her inartful observation. "Not that there's anything wrong with that. Italians are great. Like this coffee." As proof, she finished off her coffee in one gulp.

Luca leaned in and spoke in a low voice. The "good doctor" had returned. "So, Dewey Barton?"

Kit, too, reverted to business mode, placing both palms on the table. "He's alive. He was given a medical discharge in early June 1945 and sent home. I'm still working on his current whereabouts."

Luca's face lit up. "Excellent news. Thank you, Kit." He reached for her hand and squeezed.

Kit grinned, surprised by the sense of relief she was sharing. Until this moment, she hadn't thought about who, besides Stanley, might mourn the death of the jugged-eared orphan from Stockton.

THIRTY-THREE

STANLEY

More evidence, more clues. His brain was filling up with both. Scenes and moments from his combat days were playing out in his head like coming attractions at the Saturday matinee. Some were replays of his hypnosis sessions, bits and pieces he described for Doc while under. A few were spontaneous recollections, triggered by something his sister or Doc had told him. Others are more like reconstructions, created from information gleaned from his family's letters—memories of memories, projected through a screen of artificiality.

But one thing he was sure of now—Dewey was real. Dewey existed, or had existed—he wasn't sure which—and details of their history together were taking shape in his mind. Doc had determined that Dewey was important "to his recovery" and under hypnosis had prodded him to recall his earliest memory of their time together.

"Where were you, what were you doing?" Doc said from his chair. Stanley closed his eyes, but now his thoughts were sharp and concentrated as he zeroed in on the moment:

"We're on guard duty together. It's night and raining and we've taken cover under an empty water tower."

"Panay?" Doc asked.

"Sure, it might have been Panay."

"Is there anything else you remember about that night?"

Stanley thought. "Dewey started talking about his life BA. To pass the time."

"BA?"

"Before the Army," Stanley said.

Doc nodded and memories of the conversation flooded Stanley's thoughts. "Dewey's from Stockton," he told Doc. His parents had run an egg farm there. Dustbowl Okies. He remembered Dewey describing them that way, daring him to make fun of them. Stanley never did. He had no opinions on family businesses or geographic origins. He didn't prejudge. His imagination and experience didn't stretch that far. Dewey's dad had drunk himself to death, and his mother had died from a brain aneurism a few months before Dewey enlisted. "I guess that makes me an orphan," he recalled Dewey saying.

Doc asked him what he remembered most about Dewey, and just like that, Stanley said, the way he loved animals. He had names for all the laying hens on the farm and took pride in their productivity, which he claimed was due to his diligent coaxing and flattery. "Folks think hens are stupid, but they like sweet talk, just like everyone else," Dewey had insisted to Stanley.

Dewey could talk about hens all day and with such authority that if he had said they could speak fluent French, Stanley would have believed it. He'd talk your ear off about dogs too. His favorite was Blackout, a bomb-sniffing Belgian Malinois who had been killed on a battlefield in France. He had been shot by a German tank sniper while alerting his squad to the presence of a buried mine. Blackout was so beloved, Dewey claimed, he had been buried with full honors at the big military hospital in Los Angeles. "Some day, I'll show it to you," Dewey had vowed.

He didn't recall seeing Dewey get angry, except once. And that was a doosey of an outburst. Dewey had caught another G.I. beating one of their pack mules and had wrestled him to the ground in a fury. He got extra latrine duty for that, but said he had no regrets and would do it again. "There's no excuse for being cruel to an animal," he had explained to Stanley, "not in my book."

There was a softness about Dewey that had worried Stanley, he told Doc. Though they were the same age and size, Stanley felt protective of him. And Dewey accepted Stanley's guidance. "I guess I was more experienced in the ways of the world," he explained, "being from the city. At any rate, he always followed me."

"Except for that one time," Doc said quietly. Then his voice changed and he said, "All right. It's time to leave the library. You'll remember everything we talked about today."

Stanley opened his eyes and reoriented himself. There was a knock on the door and a tall man stuck his head in. Stanley recognized him immediately as the man he had seen in the yard the day before. He was wearing the same blue suit and brown fedora.

"Can I help you?" Doc said.

"My apologies, wrong office," the man muttered and backed out with a smooth smile.

"Curious," Doc said after he exited. The interruption seemed to have thrown him and he checked his watch. "It's almost two," he continued, "so we may as well stop for the day."

Stanley felt himself stiffen. He wanted to ask about Dewey, to confirm what he suspected, but instead he said, "That guy was standing in the yard yesterday, like a phantom in the rain."

THIRTY-FOUR

KIT

Kit exited the cab next to an enormous boulder squatting in the middle of the street. The rock and a police barricade marked the end of the drivable road. Her car had been towed and was now sitting in a Cypress Park garage, where its fate was still being determined.

After carefully sinking her boot-clad feet into a bed of muck, she started up the hill, her camera and bag slung across her chest. A dry winter wind blew across the concrete that just the night before had been a bed to an impromptu river. The air smelled of musk mixed with motor oil. Mud smeared every surface, low and high, and tree limbs and other debris sat in rough piles on lawns and, where they still stood, porches.

As she picked her way up to the house, she debated how best to approach the uncle. City work crews, busy with restoring power, watched her with curiosity.

Aside from a few broken palm tree fronds littering the front yard, the tidy cottage-like house, perched on its own small hill in the middle of the block, looked to be unscathed by the flood. On the edge of the driveway, she pulled her camera around and snapped a couple of photos that included the house's address.

She knocked on the door and immediately heard movement inside. Then many seconds of silence. She knocked again.

"Hello."

"Who is it?" The voice sounded thick with age and too many cigarettes.

"Mr. Fisher?"

"Who is it?"

"Sorry to bother you. My name's Marjorie. I'm a reporter for the *Citizen News.* I was hoping I could ask you a few questions about last night." The door opened the width of a chain lock, and a narrow face, ringed by a mane of thick gray hair, peered out at her. "Mr. Fisher?"

"What do you want?" he said, the words betraying the lightest of German accent.

"We're doing a story on the flooding." Kit gestured behind her. "You were lucky to have escaped unscathed."

"It wasn't luck. I built on the highest point and made sure the foundation was solid," he said, his righteous pride punctuated by a barking cough.

"That was smart of you." She raised her camera. "Do you mind if I take a few shots of the exterior?"

"I prefer that you do not."

"May I come in then? As I said, I just have a few questions." She flashed him what she hoped was a warm smile.

He stared at her for a moment, his dark sunken eyes taking in the details of her face. Apparently satisfied, he unhooked the lock, opened the door and silently retreated inside. Kit followed, taking in the oddly rustic décor, accented by Bavarian knick-knacks and old German books. His thin wool cardigan hung loosely on his frame, the sagging shoulders hinting at a formerly robust body.

Fisher took his seat at a small oak breakfast table, decorated with two country-style placemats. A folded newspaper sat next to a cheap glass ashtray, where a cup of coffee and a smoldering hand-rolled cigarette lay waiting for him. He grabbed it and took a long drag. "The coffee pot's over there," he said with a half-hearted wave toward the stove, "and there's a clean cup in the rack."

"Thank you. It smells wonderful." She picked up a cup sitting in the wooden dish rack over the sink, where a second dirty cup lay, and filled hers halfway with jet-black coffee from the percolator.

"There might be some cream in the icebox."

"No worries. I take mine black." She took a modest sip and smiled with approval.

"I use a special brand. Ethiopian. It's a bit stronger than most American coffee." He yanked the second chair from the table, angling it toward Kit.

"It does pack a punch. But I like that," she lied as she took the chair. Unlike the espresso at Sarno's, this coffee had a bitter aftertaste. As soon as she sat down, Fisher pointed to a pile of his homemade cigarettes. "No, thank you," she said, "I don't smoke."

"That's good."

"You roll your own?" She eyed the ashtray, which was reaching maximum capacity. Some of the butts were bunched on one side and were Lucky Strikes.

"Better flavor. Cheaper too," he said with another round of coughs.

She extracted her notepad from her handbag. "Mind if I take notes? For accuracy."

He shrugged. "I don't have anything to say, as I wasn't here that night."

"Not here? They aren't letting any cars in. How did you get back up?"

"Walked."

"That's a long haul by foot."

"I'm used to it."

"How long have you lived here?"

"I moved here in 1926."

"From Germany?"

He narrowed his eyes, inhaling deeply. His cigarette was nearly gone. Kit studied his fingers as he tapped it gently on the ashtray. His hands were big and looked strong, despite the arthritic knuckles.

"That's right."

"Any family in the area?"

"Why are you asking about my family?"

"Just making conversation."

"I didn't know reporters made conversation."

"That's where we get some of our best scoops," she said with a wink. "So, do you? Have family here?"

"No, as a matter of fact I don't. I'm a widower. Five years."

"Sorry to hear that. I imagine it wasn't easy, being alone here. As a German."

"I didn't have any problems. Everyone knows me."

"That's good. The Japanese weren't so lucky." He snorted and Kit sensed he was holding his tongue. "Do you still have family back in Germany?"

"Who knows? We haven't been in touch."

Under Fisher's stare, Kit took a last sip of coffee. "So you really missed the whole shebang? The mudslide, I mean."

"That's what I said. I wasn't here."

"What about your neighbors?"

"You'd have to ask them."

"All right," she said, snapping her notebook shut and rising from the chair. "Thank you for your time and the delicious coffee."

"Of course. I'm sorry I couldn't be of more help." Fisher stood, hands on hips.

"Please. I'll see myself out."

On the porch, Kit noticed two pairs of muddy rubber boots, one slightly smaller than the other. Surreptitiously she snapped a photo of them before heading out. Halfway down the mud-smeared driveway, her eye was caught by a glint of silver and she bent over to investigate. It appeared to be a necklace chain with an odd-shaped metal piece attached at one end. Without thinking, she slipped it into her coat pocket and resumed walking. When she looked back at the house from the street, Fisher was watching her through the front window.

"He was lying," Kit declared to Henry the second her bottom hit the desk chair. She unpinned her hat and sighed with relief. Some hats you could wear all day and barely notice them, but this hat, with its lovely felt, seemed determined to suffocate her head.

Henry was fussing with the window blinds, but Kit knew he must have vacated the chair just before she walked in because its leather seat was still warm.

"About his nephew?" he said.

"About everything. His family, his whereabouts, his visitors. Someone besides him was there recently. Someone who was walking around in the mud, drinking coffee and smoking with him. Maybe driving."

Suddenly remembering it, Kit pulled the necklace from her coat pocket for inspection. The clasp on the delicate chain looked like it had been ripped open and the ring that held the pendant was bent. The pendant itself was also silver, an odd rectangular shape with M-shaped short ends.

"What's that?" Henry said, leaning in to peer at her hand.

"I found it in the mud on Fisher's driveway. Looks like it might have been run over or stepped on." She handed him the necklace. "I don't remember seeing anything like it on Dina, but who knows."

Henry turned the metal piece over. "It's rough on one side, like it might have been attached to something. Or something was attached to it."

"Attached? Like a jewel?"

"Maybe. Mind if I keep it? I'll show it to Bea. She used to work in a jewelry store."

"I didn't know that."

"Her dad was a jeweler in the district; she helped out on the weekends. That's where I met her."

"After a jewelry heist?"

"Yep. I was still a beat cop then. Ever heard of Downtown Diamond Dick?"

Kit shook her head. "Did he like diamonds and live downtown?"

"He was Bea's father, the biggest diamond merchant in Los Angeles."

"And she fell for you."

"Amazing, huh?" Henry said as he pocketed the busted necklace.

THIRTY-FIVE

HENRY

When Henry came through the door, he was surprised to find Bea sitting in the wingback chair facing the big front window. As usual, she wore her pajamas and had her favorite drink in hand, a tumbler of iced bourbon, and appeared to be lost in a memory or a waking dream.

"I've got something for your eagle eye," Henry said, without a hello. He placed the battered necklace in front of her.

She raised her eyebrows, peered quizzically at the pendant and took a sip of her highball. "Does it have a name?"

"Possible clue found at the possible scene of the crime," he said. "What do you think? Ringing any bells?"

Bea picked up the necklace, gave it a quick sniff, then felt it tenderly with her fingertips. "Good quality silver. Definitely not costume. But obviously it's missing a piece." For what seemed like a full minute, she stared at the pendant, turning it over in her hands. After another big sip of bourbon, she pointed to a side table and said, "Paper and pencil, please."

It had been a long while since he had seen her so focused. She traced the outline of the partial pendant onto the paper, stared at it, turned the image sideways and then traced the pendant again, at a slightly different angle to the first. She nodded appreciatively at her handiwork. "That's what I thought."

"What?"

Bea turned the paper so her husband could see her rendering and slumped back in her chair. Combined on paper with its shadow shape, the odd rectangle had transformed into a six-sided star. "I'll be damned," he said.

"It's one way to make a Star of David. You solder one piece onto the back of another. It gives the star a simple elegance. But it also makes it delicate."

"Anything else?"

"The chain is pretty long. The star probably hung at breast level."

"So not necessarily visible."

"I'm guessing it was very personal."

The phoned invitation had come sooner than he had anticipated, and that worried him. The German Family Association was meeting that night at a home in San Marino, Senta had informed him. "Get there at 7:00." After she gave him the address, no-nonsense like, she wished him a good evening and hung up. He had sensed a shift in her tone—subtle and maybe alarming.

By that evening, the rain had returned, blown in by another, if weaker, storm front. Torrents had been replaced by gently expanding puddles. Undeterred by the weather, the German Family Association gathering on Lorain Avenue was in full swing by the time Henry, in full "not Henry" disguise, arrived shortly after 7:00.

A stern-faced housekeeper waved him in to the foyer, which was bigger than his entire Boyle Heights living room. "I will take your coat and hat, please," she said with an almost comically thick German accent. Tall and ramrod straight in her gray uniform, with ink black hair, blank eyes, and a long, aquiline nose, she looked about 40, but could have been younger. Before Henry could react to her request, she moved behind him and placed large, rough hands on his shoulders. Henry shrugged to release his coat to her waiting mitts.

"It's a little wet," he said apologetically.

"Yes, it is raining," she said, draping his damp coat over her left arm. "Hat?"

"It's wet too." He shook it off a bit before handing it to her. "Apologies."

She regarded the homburg with mild curiosity. "It is German?"

"As German as you are. Though not as good looking."

A small smile broke over her face. "I have never been mistaken for a hat."

She started to lead him through the spacious Dutch Colonial. Henry wondered whether the neighbors were aware they were living amongst Nazis. Maybe they were and didn't care. For all he knew, they could have been Nazis too.

"Where's the boss from?"

She regarded him with a mixture of curiosity and suspicion. "If you mean Herr Bitenburg, he is from Cleveland I believe."

"Nice town, Cleveland."

"If you say so."

"Where are you from, if you don't mind my asking?"

"Berlin."

"Too bad about how things ended over there."

"I never cry about it."

"No, I don't imagine you do."

She stopped on the edge of the large, enclosed sun porch, where the gathering was in full swing. "Herr Bitenburg wishes to speak to you," she said, indicating a rotund, balding man in a navy blue pinstripe suit. He acknowledged Henry's arrival with a nod and motioned him to approach.

"Herr Kurzbach I presume?" The nasal, high-pitched voice was unexpected, but not the reserved smile and piercing, blue-eyed gaze that accompanied it.

Henry extended his hand. "Pleasure to meet you, Herr Bitenburg."

Bitenburg's grasp was firm and cold. "Senta has told me a little about you."

"She's been very helpful." A server floated by with a tray of cocktails, and Henry helped himself.

"Indeed. What do you know about our organization?" Despite being American-born, Bitenburg affected a kind of German-accented English.

"Christian filled me in."

"Yes, he mentioned you had crossed paths. He said you were interested in going to South America. Is that correct?"

"That was the plan."

"We do offer special travel deals through the association. But you have to be a member. Are you willing to become a member?"

"If it gets me to South America."

"There are dues."

"Of course. I have money."

Bitenburg gave a wan smile. "Our dues are modest, but donations are always welcome."

"Then I'm willing."

"There's a waiting period for applicants. I hope you're not in a hurry."

"How long?"

"Just long enough to process and approve your application."

"I understand."

"All of our travel specials leave from Anaheim."

"Senta mentioned something about Anaheim. Land of Germans and oranges."

"Indeed. I have a little citrus operation down there," Bitenburg said with a polite chuckle. "Senta will telephone you with the particulars. In the meantime, we expect you to be discreet."

"It's my middle name."

Bitenburg regarded him for a moment. "It was nice meeting you, Herr Kurzbach. Perhaps we'll see each other again soon." With that, he pivoted to greet another eager guest. Then over his shoulder, he said to Henry, "Please, stick around. There will be a special presentation very soon."

Henry would have liked nothing more than to go, to return to his Jewish wife, but he knew this particular lily needed more gilding. "Wouldn't miss it," he told Bitenburg.

It could have been worse, he thought, but considering Hitler had been dead for months and the Nazis ground into inglorious defeat, its unquestioning optimism was disturbing.

All the guests had gathered in the living room, forming a loose circle around Bitenburg, who was attempting to silence them by tapping his coupe with a cocktail fork. "Please, if I may have your attention." Within seconds, all chatter ceased. "Thank you all for coming. I know it has been some time since our last gathering and much has occurred—very little of it good, of course, either for Germany or the GFA. But we persevere. We always persevere."

"Here, here," called out one of the guests.

"Our core mission, to promote Aryan virtues in our community, continues. Germany lives on in our hearts. Our pride hasn't diminished in defeat."

"Amen," murmured an older woman standing next to him.

"We must continue to support our Nazi brothers abroad. As you know, they are being hunted, imprisoned and even killed as we speak. Some of our sister groups have reported being harassed. The GFA has set up a fund to help. We know it will be a drop in the bucket, but if you can spare a dime, or even a penny, Lina will be collecting them."

At that, the housekeeper entered with a green crystal bowl. Henry couldn't tell if this duty was a pleasant one for her or if he should make anything of the fact that she approached him first. "Every penny will count, so please, give what you can," Bitenburg repeated while Henry scrambled to place a few bills in the bowl. Without a thank you, Lina moved on.

Bitenburg smiled and raised his glass. "Deutschland, Über alles in der Welt."

The group repeated the phrase in unison, three times, like an incantation. In a high but powerful voice, Bitenburg then began singing the SA favorite, "Horst-Wessel-Lied." As the opening words "Die Fahne hoch! Die Reihen fest geschlossen!" spilled out, the lights dimmed, and the housekeeper carried in a Nazi flag with pomp and circumstance. Bitenburg's guests raised their arms in the Nazi salute and somberly joined him belting out their anthem. Henry slipped to the back of the crowd and pretended to sing, hoping all attention was on Bitenburg and the flag.

Near the conclusion of the final verse, Bitenburg looked up, aiming his salute toward the ceiling. Henry and the others followed suit, and as the old woman in front of him warbled "wenn Heil und Sieg durchs Vaterland erschallt," a giant swastika affixed to the ceiling greeted Henry's gaze. A chorus of "Seig heils!" filled the room.

The rain had not let up and Henry could see a bathtub-sized puddle forming around a nearby sewer drain. Before heading down the slate-tiled path, he detoured to the detached garage, where he assumed Bitenburg kept his car. A bare-bulb light had been left on, illuminating the interior just enough for Henry to make out the Nazi's fawn-colored Maybach. The fucker must have had it shipped from Germany before the war, Henry thought. He wondered how often he drove it, if at all.

Hustling down the driveway, Henry made mental notes about the cars parked directly in front of the house. As he neared the Studebaker, he tried to excise the Nazi spectacle from his thoughts and focus instead on the car. Tonight, rain or not, he needed the reassurance of a solid inspection. He opened the passenger door and grabbed both his eyeglasses and a flashlight from the glove compartment. He opened the hood and passed the light around the starter mechanism. Satisfied all was clear there, he bent down and scanned the undercarriage with its beam. All looked normal.

He lowered the hood and let out a soft sigh. As he drew the ignition key from his pocket, he noticed the dark blue Ford sedan parked a half-block down the street. It was as far from the streetlamp as it could be, but even in the dark and rain, Henry could make out two male silhouettes in the front seat. He debated approaching the pair but, as raindrops streaked his lenses, he slid into the warmth and dryness of the Studebaker instead. It was time to go home to Bea.

When he finally made it home, his head full of Nazis and blue sedans, Henry dashed upstairs to greet Bea. He had a long-standing agreement with her that no matter how late or how tired he was, he would alert her to his safe return.

He found her lying on the bed at a diagonal, her left arm dangling over the side. Instinct told him to check for a pulse. It was steady but slow.

"Bea," he whispered inches from her ear. When she didn't react, not even with a twitch, he raised his voice and repeated, "Bea. Bea." She half-groaned but didn't wake. He stroked her arm gently. Finally her eyes fluttered opened.

"Henry?" she croaked, struggling to focus.

"What happened?"

"Happened?"

"What did you take?" Henry said, unable to keep the anxiety out of his voice.

"What the doctor gave me."

"The doctor? What doctor?"

Before Bea could answer, Henry grabbed a prescription bottle off the nightstand and read the label. Pentobarbital—also known as goofballs—prescribed by Dr. Richard Reynel. He let a wave of fury wash over him before returning bedside.

"Was it a house call?"

"It's all right," she said with growing awareness. "I couldn't fall asleep."

"Did he come to the house?"

She nodded. "I just wanted to get some sleep. You know I have trouble sleeping. Don't be upset."

He stroked her arm again, willing his anger to dissipate. "Come on. I'll make some coffee."

"Henry. You don't have to do this. You don't have to keep doing this."

He rose and turned away. "I'm making coffee."

GONG LI, GONG LI

Saturday, February 9, 1946

THIRTY-SIX

STANLEY

When Doc asked him right off the bat if he was "up for" more hypnosis, Stanley shrugged his consent. Doc seemed different today. More energetic? Or focused, like Stanley used to get just before a big game?

Stanley settled on the couch and a minute later, Doc was leading him to the library.

He guided him to the book shelf, back to the place and time they last visited. Stanley quickly fell into his patterned responses, a mixture of direct dialogue and remembered interactions with Dewey.

"We're back on Cactus Hill. You're on the hill. With Dewey. He's come back for you." Anticipating a reaction, Doc paused, but Stanley was still and silent. "Do you see Dewey?"

"He's come back. So I follow him."

"Does your sergeant see you go?"

"No."

"What happens when you reach the other side?"

"They start shooting at us. We keep running."

"Where to?"

"Nowhere. We're just running down the hill." He stopped his narration and his breathing grew erratic. He twitched and jerked his legs, like a dog dreaming of chasing rabbits.

Doc allowed this to go on for a minute before asking, "What's going on now, Stanley?"

"Dewey trips on some rocks and falls. His knee hurts. He's holding it. I'm going to help him up, but he gets shot. His leg. It's bleeding. 'Dewey, we gotta keep moving. C'mon.'" Stanley mimed bending over.

"What are you doing?"

"Picking him up. I'm carrying him." His voice was strained.

"Carrying him where?"

Stanley didn't answer, keeping his focus on Dewey. "'C'mon. We can hide in the cave,'" he croaked. His face contorted with remembered effort as he pretended to drag Dewey into the cave. "'It'll be okay, Dewey. It'll be okay.'"

Stanley continued to murmur "It'll be okay" over and over until it became unintelligible. "'It'll be okay. It'll be okay. It'll be okay. It'll be okay.'"

"Stanley," Doc said, almost sharply. At the sound of his name, Stanley suddenly quieted. "Private Comfort?" Stanley remained silent, but his breathing was loud and ragged. "All right Stanley. It's time to leave the library. You'll remember everything."

And he did.

THIRTY-SEVEN

KIT

From the office, Kit tried Dina's roommate a second time only to learn that Dina had not come home the night before, nor had she called the roommate to say where she was. The roommate agreed, this was not like Dina.

Bea had identified the broken necklace she had found outside Fisher's house as a Star of David. A damning piece of jewelry to have been dropped in front of a Nazi's house, she thought. But was it Dina's?

The bigger question was, were they in over their heads? Henry had experience with the rougher side of PI work—he had survived a bomb blast after all—but beyond a few verbal threats from her clients' unfaithful spouses, she had never dealt with danger. Now her client was apparently missing, and the missing person, apparently murdered. The war was over, but here they were, still fighting Nazis.

Dina had stated she worked at a medical office down the block, but had she mentioned a name? Kit checked her notes on the case. No name, but there in her tiny, neat print, was the word "neurologist." Kit shot up and went to the window. She replayed the moment when she first saw Dina walking down Spring Street. She had been heading north.

Kit scanned the building directory for a Dr. Levy and found a listing for Dr. Clara Levy, Neurologist, on the fifth floor. The office was at the end of the hall, tucked in like an afterthought. Inside, a plump, red-haired receptionist greeted her, flashing a perfunctory smile with coral painted lips.

"Can I help you?"

"I hope so, Miss . . ."

"Steinman."

Kit placed her PI license on the receptionist's desk. "My name is Katherine Comfort. I'm a private investigator. I'm looking for Dina Harris."

"Oh" was all Miss Steinman could say. She glanced toward the inner office door to her right.

"I understand she works here?"

"Yes. She's Dr. Levy's transcriptionist. But she's not in today."
"Have you heard from her today?"

"No, actually."

"Do you know her well?"

"Me? Not really." Nervousness had crept into her voice. "She works in the back with Dr. Levy," she said, now pointing at the inner office door.

"Is there anyone else in the office she might have called?"

"I don't think so."

Kit weighed whether to question her about the necklace. In a typical office, the secretary types would band together, but that dynamic didn't seem to apply here. "Could I speak with Dr. Levy?"

"She only sees people by appointment."

"I just have a few questions. If she has a few moments, I would greatly appreciate her time."

With a sigh, Miss Steinman disappeared through the inner office door. While waiting, Kit studied the décor, which included, oddly, a framed poster of the Ingrid Bergman movie *Gaslight* and the Cary Grant picture Suspicion.

Finally, Miss Steinman returned and said with a stiff smile, "Dr. Levy has five minutes for your questions. Her office is the on the left."

"Thank you."

Kit found Dr. Levy seated behind an oversized mahogany desk, flanked on either side by overstuffed bookcases. Stacks of manila folders, some several inches thick, formed wobbly pillars at each end of the desk, and loose papers were scattered across the rest. Dr. Levy made a show of tidying up, but the gesture only seemed to increase the chaos.

Kit offered her hand, which the doctor accepted with a quick squeeze. She was petite and forceful, with a tangled crown of auburn hair that made her look like a terrier in a windstorm. "Katherine Comfort. Thank you for seeing me, Dr. Levy."

"Of course. Please, sit." Dr. Levy motioned to a chair on the other side of the desk. "You're inquiring about Dina?"

"I'm trying to locate her. Her roommate hasn't seen her since yesterday morning, and I can't reach her by phone."

"May I ask how you know her?"

"She hired me. About a week ago. She wanted me to find a man she'd met in the Army."

"Is that unusual?"

"Sadly no. A lot of our recent cases involve missing veterans." Kit reached into her handbag. "Do you recognize this as Dina's?" she asked, extending first the necklace, then Bea's drawing towards her. "It probably looked like this."

"A Star of David?" Dr. Levy said. "I don't recall seeing one on her, no."

Kit returned the jewelry and picture to her bag. "If you don't mind me asking, is Dina Jewish?"

"On her mother's side. But I never got the impression she was religious. Her mother's family emigrated to America three generations ago. She's from the Midwest. Milwaukee I think."

"Did she ever show you this photo?"

Dr. Levy repositioned her reading glasses and studied the photo. "No, sorry. But she's never talked about her personal life with me. Our relationship is strictly professional."

"I see."

"Are you really worried about her?" the doctor asked softly.

"Yes, I'm afraid I am."

On her way out, Kit was stopped by the sound of Miss Steinman's voice, now softer and almost conspiratorial. "Dina told me about her boyfriend."

"Oh?"

"We went out for drinks a couple of times. Last time, she mentioned he was missing. I felt terrible for her."

Kit produced the mangled pendant and drawing. "Did you ever see her wearing this?"

Miss Steinman nodded. "That looks like the Star of David her boyfriend gave her. She showed it to me."

Kit said thank you and, out in the hallway, cursed both the confirmation of her worst fears and her own misreading of the secretary. It was another "live and learn" moment all around.

THIRTY-EIGHT

HENRY

It took Henry about two seconds to size up Dr. Reynel's operation. His office was located above a liquor store in the sleaziest corner of Boyle Heights. Henry had parked a block away and was approaching the building when a barrel-chested man carrying a medical bag exited. Henry followed as he turned down the neighboring alleyway, heading for a parked sedan.

When he was a few feet behind him, Henry said, "Dr. Reynel?"

The man stopped, his body visibly tensing. He turned toward Henry and squinted. He looked about forty, somewhere between youth and middle age. His Clark Gable mustache and tailored wool coat did nothing to hide his menace. "Yes," he finally said. "Who are you?"

"Mr. Richman." Henry showed no emotion, but his hands were in fists at his side. "Bea Richman's husband."

At the sound of Bea's name, Reynel pressed his lips into a tight line and glared. "What do you want?"

"No more house calls, for a start." Henry lunged forward and his right hand shot out, but the doctor deflected the blow with his medical bag and pushed Henry back against the alley's brick wall. His eyes blazed with rage as he pressed the bag hard into Henry's torso. Henry gasped.

In one swift motion, Reynel drew back and dropped the bag. Then his fists went to work on Henry's gut, three quick blows that doubled him over.

"Next time, old man, I'll kill you." Reynel retrieved his bag and strode toward his car.

Henry righted himself and stumbled back to the wall, watching as Reynel's red Cadillac glided away.

Rumor had it that the new Chinatown had been designed by Hollywood art directors. With its curling, pointed roofs and shops with names like Forbidden Palace, Central Plaza in particular looked like an artifact from a Cecil B. DeMille set. The sky sparkled with crisp, post-storm freshness, producing the sort of sunshine postcards were made of.

Despite the swarming crowd, Henry had no trouble spotting Bea standing on the corner. As promised, she was wearing a scarlet dress that flattered her straight, lean physique. Her hands were full. One held a half-full champagne glass, the other, a bottle. She waved the glass at him, then took a sip. Henry maneuvered around a many-headed dragon puppet, hoisted on poles controlled by young men in traditional costume. It undulated down Broadway to the beat of ceremonial drums being played on a red-festooned platform. The longer the dragon, the better the luck, the legend went.

"Gong hei fat choy," a very drunk stranger shouted at him as he passed. Henry repeated the New Year's greeting in response.

When Henry joined Bea, she wiggled her glass at him and said, "Do you want some? You look like you could use it."

Henry could see it wasn't her first, or even her second. Reynel and his goofballs were already a distant memory for her. "No, thanks," he said, "brought my own." He pulled a dented flask out of his coat, trying not to wince from the pain even that small move generated.

Bea pulled a face. "That rotgut? I swear, sometimes you act like Prohibition never ended."

He took a quick swig. "They don't make it like they used to."

"Lethal, you mean?"

"I prefer 'frisky.'" They watched as a troupe of dancers in intense red, yellow and white costumes glided by. "Did I miss anything?"

"Just a show-stopping speech by the president of the Chinatown Business Improvement Society."

"Let me guess. Business is improving."

"They don't call you L.A.'s greatest detective for nothing."

After the dancers came the Chinatown Crooners, a peppy male chorus singing the "straight from Shanghai," hit song "Gong Xi Gong Xi." Bea swayed to the infectious tune and joined in singing the simple chorus. According to the parade emcee, the song, translated as "Congratulations, Congratulations," had been written to celebrate China's defeat of Japan, and Bea happily raised her champagne flute to every member of the group. Henry basked in her joy and abandonment, even while knowing they were as ephemeral as the flames of the spectators' sparklers.

Suddenly down the street, two young men started tossing fire-crackers. The air filled with sulfur while the tiny explosives went off like movie theater popcorn. The drumming intensified. Henry looked sideways at Bea. In the dim lantern light, he could see panic pooling in her eyes. "Are you all right? Bea?"

She turned her face away and her breath caught. Fear had paralyzed her. Why hadn't he anticipated this? "Let's go," he said reaching for the glass in her hand. She gave it up without a fight, but clung to the bottle.

Henry headed up Broadway, leading Bea toward his car and away from the festivities. Without warning, a throng of young revelers, some in military uniform, formed a conga line and started to snake across the pavement, pulsing to the driving beat of the drummers. Glancing back, Henry saw Bea enveloped in a firecracker haze, wavering on the other side of the line. He stopped and yelled her name, but got no reaction.

Then out of nowhere, a fist landed on the right side of his face, sending him reeling into the line. He staggered but managed to stay upright and keep his spectacles in place, only to be struck again, this time with a blow to his back. A voice whispered in his ear: "Mind your own business. For Beanie's sake."

Instinctively Henry reached behind to touch the throbbing spot and when his fingers came away wet and sticky he realized he had been stabbed. "Hey! Hey!" he croaked into the crowd. He couldn't make sense of the faces swirling around him but too late he caught sight of two men, one in a brown fedora, hustling away against the tide.

Bea. Where had she ended up? He lurched toward the platform where the drummers were still pounding out their ancestral rhythms. His hand pressed into his back, he staggered up the platform steps, hoping for a better view of the street. Some of the young drummers threw him concerned looks, but Henry ignored the glares and shouted "Bea" into the smoky air. His cry was answered by a woman's scream that didn't belong to Bea. Who she was he never found out.

Henry woke to the smell of a hospital. Years before he had spent many weeks at French Hospital in Chinatown recuperating from his bomb wounds, and its peculiar odors—the antiseptic mixed with garlic and jasmine—were unforgettable.

"I saw your name on the chart and I thought, good God, him again?" Dr. Soong's voice was as brisk and dry as a Musso & Frank martini.

A wave of memories swirled in Henry's head, some pleasant, some painful. Soong, chief of surgery, had operated on him after the bombing, a feat that earned him some notoriety, at least temporarily. Although he knew Henry's body better than Bea, Henry only knew him as Dr. Soong. His round, impish face contrasted with his wiry frame and nicotine-stained fingers. Henry hadn't met anyone who loved cigarettes as much as Dr. Soong, and that was saying something.

"What is it with you and assassins?" the doctor asked.

"What can I say?" Henry whispered, "I'm popular with the hired killer crowd."

"Fortunately the wound wasn't too deep. The knife just nicked your liver. Either they weren't trying very hard, or your scars and fat slowed them down."

Henry struggled to lift his head off the pillow. "Where's Bea? Is she all right?" Then a thought occurred to him. Who would have known Bea's nickname?

"She's with your . . . partner? In the waiting room."

Henry stretched his right arm toward the nightstand. "Where are my glasses?"

Dr. Soong retrieved the spectacles from the nightstand drawer and handed them to Henry.

"Thanks," Henry said as he awkwardly worked the end pieces of his glasses around his ears. Sadly they didn't help with the fog in his brain. "Can I see her?"

"Of course. I'll tell her you're awake." Dr. Soong turned to leave, then stopped. "Do you want to speak to the police?"

"Not yet," Henry mumbled. "Probably never."

"I understand completely." Soong's opinion of the police was about as warm as Henry's.

Bea and Kit sat on opposite sides of his hospital bed, Bea holding his hand with both of hers, and Kit leaning forward as though hard of hearing.

"He told me to mind my own business," croaked Henry. He wasn't about to repeat the warning in full.

"Not very original," said Kit with a snort.

"And not very smart," Bea said. "They obviously don't know Henry Richman if they think a little knife prick is going to slow him down."

"And you didn't see their faces?" Kit said.

Henry shook his head. "They came up from behind and did a disappearing act after they poked me. According to Dr. Soong, the bastards weren't trying to kill me."

"Were they Nazis?" Kit asked.

"I don't know," Henry hedged. "Like I said, I didn't get a good look." He hadn't yet mentioned the blue Ford sedan to Kit and would never have told Bea about it.

"To attack you at a parade though. That's brazen," Kit said.

With no effort to hide her bitterness, Bea said, "Not especially. They must have known the police wouldn't investigate too hard if Henry was the victim. For all we know, the cops were behind it."

Henry couldn't disagree with that, and yet it didn't explain how the attacker knew Bea's nickname. That was the message inside the message—we're on to you, and we know you. He squeezed Bea's hand and whispered. "How are you doing?"

She squeezed his back. "Gong hei fat choy."

He was fighting sleep, losing control in a way that made him anxious. He had to get out of bed, out of the hospital. He rolled onto his left side and tried pushing himself up with his right arm, but a sharp pain across his belly put a quick end to that effort. Defeated, he relaxed into the mattress. A wave of nausea followed by a sudden drowsiness overcame him.

As he was about to succumb to his drug-induced sleep, he tried to make sense of the chaotic moments preceding the stabbing. A memory resurfaced, one from a recent conversation, a half-heard remark uttered by Calvin: "Give Beanie my best."

THIRTY-NINE

KIT

Bag and all, Kit fell into her father's old armchair, whipped from her visit with Henry. Though it had been years since he had last sat in it, the scent of her dad's aftershave and pipe tobacco still clung to the fabric and, tonight notwithstanding, the smell often gave her comfort. She had put up her best brave front at the hospital, but seeing her partner wounded, even superficially, spooked her. He knew more about what was going on than he had let on, she was sure, and she hoped that Bea was the reason behind his caginess. Fort Knox didn't get more protection than Bea Richman, a fact Bea must have hated, Kit thought.

After a moment, nervous energy overcame Kit and she shot back up, carrying her camera bag into the bathroom developing lab. As soon as she crossed the threshold, she sensed something was amiss, but it took her a few seconds to zero in on what.

Lying on the edge of the bathtub she saw a folded piece of paper and instantly recognized it as Army issue. Of course, it hadn't been there the last time she was in the room, and there was no good reason for it to be there now. Even from a distance, she knew it was one of Stanley's letters, letters she had just given her brother for safekeeping.

When she unfolded it, though, she realized she hadn't touched it since it had arrived in the mail months before. It was Stanley's final letter from the front, the one that had come the same day she learned the Army had listed him as M.I.A. She recalled reading it, but not what she did with it afterward. That evening had been a terrible blur.

Kit glanced around the bathroom, but other than the letter, all appeared normal. She hadn't noticed anything unusual when she first returned home, but she had come in through the kitchen door. Instinct drew her to the back door. She rarely used it, but it only took a second for her to see that it had been jimmied with a metal object.

Her fears rising, Kit headed for her bedroom and flipped on the light. Her closet door was opened just enough to call attention to itself and on her bed was her summer handbag. It too was open, and when she touched it, the memory of tucking Stanley's last letter in there washed over her.

Then the reality of the present took over: Someone had broken into her house, found the letter in her closet and left it for her.

Luca found her at the bar at Musso & Frank, sipping a vodka martini with a lemon twist. She had made a point of paying for it before Luca's arrival, not wanting him to feel obligated in any way, or conversely, feel entitled in any way. His smile upon seeing her was sincerely pleasant and comfortable, and she again became aware of his striking features. Once more she wondered about the wisdom of dating her brother's doctor, then refocused her thoughts.

"Thanks for meeting me here," she said as he took a seat on the neighboring stool.

"I just hopped on the trolley. It's nice to get out of there every now and then."

"I bet."

The bartender sauntered over and gave Luca an inquiring nod. "Gin and tonic, thanks."

She removed a folded letter from her purse and placed it on the table. "Like I said on the phone, he was already MIA when I got this. I read it quickly, then stuck it in my purse. I just couldn't face it right then."

"Understandable."

"Anyway, I thought it might be important. Should I read it?"

"Please."

Kit picked up the distinctive Army-issue paper and began to read aloud:

April 3, 1945

Somewhere in Japan

Dear Sis,

First off, thanks for writing to Dewey. You should have seen his eyes light up when I handed him your letter. He put the photo in his bag without showing it to me, but he had a big grin on his face, so I'm guessing it must have been a good one.

We've been moving around so much lately, I haven't had much chance to get my thoughts together. I haven't told Mom and Dad this yet, but the business over here has gotten pretty wild. We barely have time to catch our breath before we're off on another "adventure." Sometimes I wonder if exhaustion, and foot rot, will get us before the Japs do.

And here's the part I can only tell you, Kit: I've started to have premonitions about the platoon. I feel like I can look at a guy and know if he's going to make it or not. I know that sounds crazy. I can't explain it, but my batting average has been almost 1000. Sometimes I wonder whether I could see my own fate, or if there are others who could just look at me and know that my number is up.

Sorry to be so gloomy. It's probably just the weather heating up my brain. Sometimes it feels like this ride is never going to end, even though I know it will and I'm pretty sure we will be the victors. Maybe this will be my last letter because I'll be returning home soon—wouldn't that be killer diller?!

Kit looked up and saw Luca's face go from neutral professional to . . . what, concern, excitement . . . both?

"That *was* the last letter I got," Kit said. Luca stared at the paper, oblivious to Kit's commentary. "What is it?" she asked.

"Curious. That part about the premonitions."

"Why? Do you think it's true?"

"True that he can see into the future? No. That he thinks he can? It might explain some things."

"I have to say," Kit said, "he's usually not this . . . philosophical."

"Do you mind me asking what you said to Dewey, in your letter?"

Kit screwed up her face, trying to recall her words. "Nothing special. Just the usual canteen banter."

"And the usual pinup photo?"

"I had all my clothes on."

"That's good."

"Need another?" Luca said, looking down at her empty martini glass.

'Yes, I think I do. It's been quite a day."

Two martinis later, Kit stood awkwardly with Luca outside the restaurant. "I'm this way," she said pointing in the general direction of her house.

"You're walking?" said Luca. "Let me call a cab."

Kit shook her head and proceeded to head east down Hollywood Boulevard. "My house isn't too far from here. The air will clear my head."

"Of nothing too serious I hope." Luca said, hurrying to catch up.

"This case I'm working on . . . it seems we're tracking Nazis."

"Nazis? In Los Angeles?"

"Crazy, huh? But yes. To hear my partner tell it, the town is crawling with them."

"And you're investigating them? Is that safe?"

"I can take care of myself," she said, pulling her coat tight against the night chill and maintaining a brisk pace.

"I'm sure you can, but is it all right if I worry a bit?" he declared.

She didn't answer. "Do you suppose we'll ever know why? Why people are so cruel and ruthless? Why we keep fighting wars?"

He let out a sigh. "Freud believed violence among men was inescapable and that war was inevitable without conscious group interventions. Humans need enemies, he would say. It's part of our makeup. He was rather gloomy on the topic."

"Do you agree?"

"I don't know about war, but I believe there will always be snakes among us."

"Snakes? Is that the scientific term?

He chuckled and said, "Okay, we call them psychopaths."

"Any tips for catching one?"

"Just remember the old saying: Snakes deserve no pity. They'll have none for you."

Kit slowed as she neared her front door. She knew whoever had broken in was long gone, and she had no desire to involve Luca. She stopped and turned to face him. "We should say goodnight," she said gently. "Stanley needs you."

"Understood," he whispered, his face inches from hers. "Rain check?"

She shivered and said, "Deal."

PISTOL PACKIN' MAMA

Sunday, February 10, 1946

FORTY

LUCA

They had the building to themselves. Some of the patients had headed over to the chapel, others were sleeping in or entertaining visitors in their rooms. Luca had debated giving Stanley the day off, but out of respect for momentum, chose to plow on instead. They were nearing the end.

Stanley wasted no time succumbing to the induction. In contrast to the memories he was about to encounter, he appeared relaxed, serene almost. Luca's final instruction was to "remember everything."

"You're in the cave with Dewey. He's injured, remember?"

"He was losing a lot of blood. I put pressure on the wound. Then I got a tourniquet from my pack and tied it around his leg, like they showed us," Stanley said matter-of-factly, like a witness testifying in court.

"How long were you in the cave with him?"

Stanley's voice became animated. "'Dewey', I'm going to get help. No, no, you'll be fine. I'm going to get help.'" A couple of grunts followed, then silence.

"Which direction are you going in?" Luca finally prompted. "Can you picture it?"

"There's shelling. It's night. They like to attack at night. But I'm a phantom, so I keep going."

"Which direction?"

"West. I'm going northwest. To find the medic." More silence. Then Stanley's face clouded over with disgust.

"Have you found him?" Luca asked.

"No. I, I . . . It's a dead Jap. I fall on top of him, in the mud. But I get up."

"You get up and keep heading northwest?"

"I think so."

"You said there was shelling."

"There's an explosion." Stanley's whole body was shaking now "An explosion. Near you? Did it hit you?"

"I don't know."

"What do you remember after the explosion?"

"There's sun. The light from the sun wakes me up." He squinted and covered his eyes as though shielding them from a bright light.

"You don't recall anything between the nighttime explosion and waking up in the sun?"

Stanley shook his head.

"What do you after you wake up?"

"I run. I run. I run," Stanley panted. "I'm not a phantom anymore. I have to find cover."

"And did you find cover?"

Stanley nodded, his face flooding with relief. "I see a battery area. It's one of ours. I go there."

"So you're safe now."

"Yes, I'm safe." His expression grew dark.

"What is it, Stanley?"

"I don't know if I told them about Dewey. I don't remember."

Luca paused. Should he say nothing, or massage the truth? "You did, Stanley. You told the medic."

"I did? I told them where Dewey was?"

"Yes. They went to the cave. They found him."

"Was he alive?"

"Yes," Luca said softly. "He was alive." Stanley began to weep. "Was?"

He allowed Stanley a few seconds to cry before beginning the trip back to consciousness. Aware of the precariousness of the moment, he spoke in his most even, firm voice. "All right, Stanley. It's time to leave the library. When you awake, you'll remember everything. You'll remember what happened, but you'll understand it's in the past."

FORTY-ONE

STANLEY

He woke shaking from hypnosis and felt the wetness on his cheeks. He groped for his handkerchief, but Doc had already pulled out his own and offered it. His mind was a muddle. Snatches of memory replayed in his head as he wiped his face. He wanted to run, he needed to stay.

"How do you feel?" Doc said at last.

He shrugged. "Tired."

"I'm not surprised. You went through a lot just now." "Yeah, I remember." "Would you like a cigarette?"

Stanley nodded and Doc produced one from his shirt pocket along with a lighter.

"Can you talk about your feelings?" Doc said.

"Feelings?" Stanley said before enjoying a long, relaxing drag.

"How you feel about the things you remember. Retrieving the memory is the first step, understanding it is the second."

"It hurts. Remembering everything about Dewey hurts."

"Anything else?"

"Like what?"

"Other emotions, besides sadness."

"I guess I feel . . . guilty," Stanley mumbled, sensing this is where Doc wanted him to go.

"Guilty. About what? For what?"

He found Doc's ashtray. He needed some time to sort through his thoughts, to back up to the right moment. "I told Dewey that getting letters and care packages from home was the reason I kept going. But he never got letters, so it was a stupid thing to say."

"You thought he didn't have anything to live for and that's why he went off without you?"

"Stupid, stupid. And then I didn't go after him. If I had gone with him . . ."

"If you had gone with him, what?"

"We wouldn't have been caught in the crossfire. Dewey wouldn't have been shot."

"You don't know that."

Stanley shook his head. "It's what I do."

"What is, Stanley? What do you do?" He made his voice as gentle and coaxing as possible, but Stanley just rocked back and forth, unable to explain.

Finally, he blurted, "I make poor decisions. I don't listen. I say stupid things. Think stupid thoughts. I choke."

"Stanley. Did you have a premonition that Dewey was going to die? Is that why you didn't want to follow him?"

Stanley sat in silence for a long, uncomfortable stretch. He heard nothing, not even the usual door shutting and hallway chatter. He tapped the ash off his Chesterfield, then said, "I had a premonition that *I* was going to die. I didn't follow Dewey because I was afraid. I'm a coward. I choked."

"But you didn't, Stanley. You went after Dewey. You tried to save him. You had an understandable moment of self-preservation and you overcame it. You overcame it because you loved Dewey."

At the word "love" he flinched. "I did love him, but I couldn't save him."

"No, Stanley, you did save him. "

Stanley fell back in confused silence.

"Dewey made it out, he recovered." Luca said. "Kit tracked him down. He was discharged last June."

"He's alive? Why didn't you tell me?"

"I couldn't. I needed you to get to this point on your own. Just as you experienced it. Just as you would have experienced it if you hadn't been hit yourself."

"Now what?"

"That's up to you."

FORTY-TWO

HENRY

Calvin was just finishing up his weekly radio broadcast, a mix of gospel music and updates on city business from the reformer's angle, when Henry stormed up the stairs to the top floor of Calson's. Calvin had been producing the show for years, although with less frequency, and fervor, now than in its heyday a decade before. For convenience, he had installed a recording booth next to his office on the upper floor of the restaurant.

Henry paced, waiting for the "On the Air" sign to flick off, and the moment it did, Henry pushed into the booth, shutting the soundproofing door behind him. Calvin regarded him with surprise.

"Henry?" Calvin's voice betrayed no hint of apprehension, and his smile was unforced. "What's going on?"

"Going on? The fuckers stabbed me," said Henry, unconsciously touching his bandaged side.

"Sorry, what? I don't know what—"

"I was warned and attacked."

"Just now?"

"Yesterday afternoon. In Chinatown. At the parade."

"I'm terribly sorry, Henry."

"As you know, I was with Bea."

"I know nothing about it. Honest. Why do you think I would?"

Calvin's ignorance seemed genuine, but Henry wasn't ready to let up. "Just before they stabbed me, they said, 'Mind your own business, for Beanie's sake.'"

"And?" Calvin said.

"You're the only one who calls her 'Beanie.'"

"Are you sure?"

"It wasn't a lucky guess."

"All right, but where would they have heard me say it?" No sooner had Calvin asked the question, when Henry could see the pennies flooding his head. His voice relaxed. "Sounds like I may have another pest control problem." He put his finger to his lips, pointed in the direction of his office, then led Henry out of the booth.

Since his last visit, the boxes had been purged from Calvin's office. Without a word, Calvin picked up the phone receiver on his desk and unscrewed the cover on the speaking end. After a quick once-over, he shook his head at Henry and shrugged.

Henry held up his finger, then pointed at the heavy velvet sofa that sat on the other side of the desk, in front of the bank of windows. Noiselessly he crossed to the sofa, bent over and felt underneath. After a second, his fingers hit pay dirt and he pulled out a miniature microphone with a thin wire snaking out of it. As Calvin watched, he tracked the wire along the floor and up to the nearest window via some discreet corner molding. Henry peeked behind the window's wooden venetian blinds and motioned for Calvin to join him.

Outside, beneath the third-story window, they found the wire cascading down the wall and into the building next door. It stopped outside the first-floor candy store. Apparently the spy operation had been aborted.

"Something tells me the bon-bon ladies just lost an upstairs neighbor," Henry said.

"Businesses come and go out of there." Calvin looked as deflated as Henry had ever seen him. "No one would notice a spy or two."

"They knew enough about us not to bug your phone. Or mine. How did they get in there?" As soon as he posed the question, Henry had the answer. A face flashed in his head. "What do you know about the guy who delivered your food samples the other day?"

"Nothing. I assumed Barzan had hired him." Calvin pushed his glasses back on his face. It was one of his nervous tells. "I was surprised when he brought the boxes up to the office instead of just leaving them at the back with the other deliveries."

"Were you in your office the whole time he was?"

Calvin touched the bridge of his glasses. "Except when I went downstairs to call you."

"Long enough to plant a wire."

"So it would appear."

"Any idea who might have sent him?" Henry said.

"The Army would be my guess. Or the FBI."

"Because of that escaped POW?"

"Maybe they know you and Kit are looking for him and they don't want you to find him."

Henry considered Calvin's suggestion. Superficially it made sense, but it didn't explain the intimate nature of the warning—"for Beanie's sake." Or why they hadn't gone after Kit, who was, after all, an easier target for intimidation. "Or maybe they do want me to find him. "

"What do you mean?"

"What if they need me to lead them to him? They'd have known about Bitenburg, but not about Fisher. Schmidt said the uncle was never seriously investigated."

"Then why the warning?"

"Because they know it will make me more determined, while also letting me know they're right behind me."

Again, Calvin pushed up on his glasses. "They want you to find him but not catch him."

"That's what I'm thinking," Henry said. "But to what end?"

"They're protecting him?"

"Or themselves."

The Bells of St. Mary's—held over for a record-breaking sixth week, according to the Hillstreet marquee—was the sort of sentimental tale he usually avoided, but Bergman had made it palatable, even in the guise of a nun, and even when paired with the doe-eyed Crosby. Henry had come to the theater to catch a matinee before meeting Kit. The discovery of the Calson's bug had unnerved him to the point that he refused to discuss the case in the office or over the telephone.

"Meet me in the Hillstreet's balcony level lobby. I'll pay you back for your ticket," he told Kit.

He parked himself in one of the lobby's plush loveseats and made a stab at reading the day's racing form. The elevator dinged and he looked over to see her exit. She was stunning in her gray wool Hepburn trouser suit, but as she approached, he noticed circles under her eyes, and the crease that snaked along her forehead seemed deeper than the day before. The case was wearing on her. Or maybe it was the shrink she was seeing.

Henry filled her in on Bitenburg and his pals in the dark blue sedan.

"So these government guys have been trailing you and stabbing you and you're just now telling me?"

"I didn't know who they were connected with until a couple hours ago. And even now, I'm not sure what their mission is."

"Other than pushing you out of the way. And maybe me."

"What do you mean?"

"Someone broke into my house yesterday and left one of Stanley's letters for me to find."

"A letter?"

"The other day I gave Stanley the letters he wrote to me while he was overseas, except one that I had left in a purse. Whoever broke in, found it and left it in the bathroom for me."

To hide his concern, Henry folded the racing form and slipped it back into his coat. Kit would resent any paternalistic fussing, but it couldn't be helped. As the pain radiating from his belly kept reminding him, these goons came armed. "I'd say they're wise to

Bitenburg," he said at last, "but maybe not to the uncle. According to Schmidt, the old man hasn't been active in the group."

"Speaking of Fisher, I still haven't heard from Dina. But I know the necklace is hers. A co-worker at the medical office identified it."

With a grunt, Henry rose from the velvety cushion. "C'mon. We need to get back there."

"Not the cops?"

"No!"

FORTY-THREE

Excerpt from "My Escape: A Confession" (submitted to O.P.M.G., February 1946)

My uncle was furious. The woman, Dina, had found them. The foolish woman had come knocking at the door, claiming to be stranded in the storm and in need of a drying off and a telephone. Uncle let her in, being a soft touch for petite women, but when he caught her peeking into the front bedroom with more than a casual curiosity, he became suspicious. He insisted on dialing the number for the tow truck himself. She must have sensed the ruse was up, because out of the blue, she asked about Novak.

The moment she mentioned the doctor, Uncle brought out his World War I pistol from a pocket in his old cardigan and wagged it in her face. She surrendered almost immediately and he led her at gunpoint back to the garage.

"Are you the man who called me?" she said, the moment the garage door was raised and she caught sight of me.

"How did you get this address?" I countered.

Together we bound her hands and dragged her to Uncle's car. In that instant the grimness of her situation overtook her; panic enveloped her and she flailed and struggled against me. I subdued her—she was a slippery little thing—but not before I had pulled a couple of buttons off her blouse and discovered the Star of David hanging grotesquely between her small breasts. I yanked the thing from her neck and shoved her into the back seat. If she thought she was protected here, that the righteous order of the world didn't apply to her, she had just gotten a hard lesson in reality.

The downpour intensified. Uncle had already started the car and was anxious to leave. "Hurry. The road's likely to flood."

"Should we blindfold her?" I said.

"What for?" Uncle said. Then thinking better of it, he tossed a windshield cloth into the back seat.

The drive south had been slow and treacherous. Regardless, we knew we couldn't let her go. As soon as the road was cleared, we had transported her to one of their safe houses, where her fate awaited her. Initial beatings hadn't produced any solid information about possible confidants, but we were operating under the assumption that she wasn't acting alone.

The day after we had taken her, another woman, a reporter (or so she claimed), had come snooping around. Coincidence? Unlikely. The loose end I had convinced myself had been tightened, wasn't just loose, it was unraveling. I knew I would have to leave for Mexico as soon as possible. If I were recaptured, the Americans wouldn't hesitate to send me back to Soviet Germany. I would do anything to escape that fate.

I had stated as much during a camp lunch break with Stefan, a Berliner who had recently joined the Crowder road crew. We had been chatting about their post-camp plans—a favorite pastime among the POWs—and after Stefan declared he was returning to university, I shrugged and said, "Whatever I'm doing, it won't be in Germany. I can't live anywhere controlled by the Russians."

"Why?" Stefan was only nineteen and uneducated.

"Because they're evil," I hissed. "They say the Fuhrer is evil, but the Soviets are much more so."

My mother's paternal ancestors had been Black Sea Germans, I explained, emigrating to Crimea and becoming successful farmers within the German community there. "After the Revolution, the Soviets persecuted the Germans as anti-communist and forced them out of Crimea. They ordered my grandfather to a labor camp in Siberia, and sent the rest of my family to Kazakhstan. My grandfather died in the camp. They said he committed suicide. Perhaps he did, but how would we know? They lied about everything." I sucked hard on my cigarette, my anger rising with each inhale.

"What happened to the rest?" Stefan prodded.

"The rest? Have you ever heard of Stalin's terror famine? The Russians were starving all the Germans to death. Slowly. In my family, only my mother survived. She survived and escaped to England."

"How did she do that?"

I had never spoken about my mother's journey to anyone, but in that moment, I felt a strange need to unburden myself to Stefan. "One by one, everyone in her village started dying of starvation. There were reports of cannibalism."

"Cannibalism?" Stefan said, his eyes wide.

"That's how desperate it got. A Red Army soldier promised my grandmother he would feed her children if she had sex with him whenever he demanded. She held up her end of the bargain, so to speak. The soldier didn't, so my mother stole his gun one night and shot him."

"Afterwards, my grandmother knew it was only a matter of time before she would be arrested. She didn't have the strength to flee and didn't want to leave her children at the mercy of the Russians. So she turned the gun on her two oldest daughters and shot them dead. She was about to shoot my mother when she discovered the bullets had run out. My mother, who was small but strong, ran off and hid in the woods."

I paused. When telling me this story years before, my mother had described her sisters' shootings in so much detail that I had come to suspect she was making at least some of it up. She never spoke about the fate of my grandmother, and in darker moments, after one of my mother's terrifying rages, I imagined it was Mother who had pulled the trigger on her kin, sparing no one but herself.

"My mother hid in a Red Army truck and ended up in Poland. She was sent to a Warsaw orphanage, where an English couple adopted her and took her to England."

"That's quite a story," Stefan said. "Your mother was lucky to have survived."

Survival, that's what it was all about. My mother's hellish past had become my bête noir. The moment I heard the Russians would be controlling my hometown, I knew I would never go back.

FORTY-FOUR

Excerpt from the Journal of Pfc. Stanley Comfort (Birmingham General Hospital, Van Nuys, California, January 2, 1946)

The story of my disappearance now has an ending. I remember it all now. Or at any rate, I remember remembering—if that makes any sense. There are still some things—gaps in the timeline—I don't recall and maybe never will. And then there's the part I couldn't have known until Doc told me, that Dewey is alive.

The real ending of my story, according to Doc, is up to me. Have I escaped the rabbit hole? Have I let myself out? Only I can decide how to use my newfound knowledge. Trust yourself, Doc says, and accept that you've been in control all along. Nice words.

I go through my mental checklist of feelings, just as Doc has instructed. My first reactions after hearing about Dewey were joy and relief. Joy that my friend was still alive, relief that I hadn't killed him. Thinking about him now, however, fills me with . . . what? Uncertainty? Dread? I ask myself, if it were possible, would I want to see him again? Would he want to see me again? Does he blame me for leaving him? You see how it goes.

As for all the rest, the fear is still there. Only now it's front and center in my mind instead of lurking like a phantom in the back. I get stomachaches and headaches whenever I'm reminded of the bad stuff. Doc says there are techniques for coping with these "triggers," and that I'll have to learn them and be patient. Patience is not one of my virtues. Just ask Coach.

Well, I'm nearing the end of my cigarette. That's when I know it's time to stop and get off the porch. I'll stop now and join the others on the path.

FORTY-FIVE

KIT

Henry drove the Studebaker up the hill with one eye on the rearview mirror. As was usually the case, once the rain had moved off, the blinding Los Angeles sun had returned with a vengeance. Kit, riding shotgun, had talked her way into the search of Fisher's property, arguing that, if caught, she would have a better excuse for being there. "I'll tell him I came back for some shots of the cleanup," she said, waving her camera.

To give themselves a nice two-hour window, they had left Kit's house just after seven. Fisher's Furniture opened at ten and was at most a 20-minute drive from Mt. Washington.

"See anybody?"

"Looks clear," he said, then winced as he made a turn onto Fisher's street.

"Are you sure you're alright?"

"They barely nicked me. It was a warning stab, remember?"

"Tell that to the surgeon who stitched you up with a big fat needle," Kit said, scanning the street, then pointing. "That's his house. His car's still there." Henry cruised by and followed the downward curve of the road. Kit pointed to the first turn, a no-through side street. "You can park along there. He won't see us."

Henry parked in front of a salmon pink bungalow, whose lawn was festooned with ceramic flamingoes. With a shudder, he averted his eyes and busied himself with the daily racing form. Kit read her Freud (a gift from the handsome doctor) and kept watch on the traffic. A half-hour later, she spotted Fisher's green Plymouth heading down the hill.

"There he goes," Kit declared, flinging open the car door as fast as she could. "If you see him coming back, honk twice."

"Don't forget the rule," Henry called out, "in in one, out in ten."

Kit gave Fisher's front door a round of firm knocks and waited a few moments for a response. The porch provided some cover, but wary of watchful neighbors, she repeated the knock before confirming the door was locked. With a nonchalant swipe of her hand, she pulled a pin from her hair, then bent it to an L-shape and inserted one end into the knob's keyhole. After she wiggled the pin into what she hoped was the correct spot, she grabbed another pin from her hair and stuck it straight in, moving it gently until she felt the lock give. "Hallelujah," she mumbled. "In in one."

Kit removed the hair pins from the knob and cautiously opened the door. Calling out a friendly "hello" she entered the foyer. Two steps in, she stopped, listening for movements. "Hello? Anybody here?" she said again. Reassured by the silence, she closed the door and reset the lock. She checked her watch. Eight minutes left.

Henry's ten-minute rule was, according to him, "Born of decades of experience, some of them not so pretty. Doesn't matter how long the mark is supposed to be away. You can't count on that. You go in assuming they're going to realize they've forgotten something after they've left and come back. Ten minutes. That's how long it takes for someone to drive off, remember something, and come back. If they don't forget something, you're still good, no harm, no foul." Kit had her doubts about Henry's calculations, but not about his instincts.

She made a beeline for the hallway and popped into the first bedroom she came to. It was a tiny space, with a tidy, narrow bed and an unadorned three-drawer dresser tucked into one corner. A few amateur landscape paintings (Germany?) graced the walls, but otherwise, the décor was minimal and impersonal. A guest room she assumed. If Klaus was in hiding in this house, she felt sure he wasn't sleeping here, right next to the front door.

In the home's connecting bathroom, Kit took a quick look behind the shower curtain but found only one of everything, including linens. Time-wary, she resisted the temptation to inspect the medicine cabinet and headed for the master bedroom.

The bigger bedroom belonged to Fisher, no doubt about that. Everything reeked of strong masculinity, from the deer head trophy that stood guard between a dark mahogany wardrobe and dresser to the burgundy red bedspread. A swastika had been expertly and, dare she say, tastefully carved into the center of the matching mahogany headboard. But Kit found nothing under the bed, not even dust.

On the dresser, in addition to the expected brush and comb, were delicately painted Bavarian-style figurines—a gift from Klaus' mother perhaps or his own? She glanced into the dresser's attached mirror and was startled to see a framed portrait of a dour Adolf Hitler hovering over her shoulder. She spun around and hissed a curse at him, then headed for Fisher's wardrobe. Experience had taught her that the most interesting possessions can be found on the top shelves of wardrobes and closets. On Fisher's top shelf, she discovered an empty box for an old German-made pistol and an unlabeled album of home-processed photos.

The photos appeared to have been taken at a festival of some sort, where the participants were wearing either lederhosen, dirndls or Nazi uniforms. One of the shots featured several young men giving the Hitler salute to the photographer. She didn't notice Fisher in any of the pictures, so most likely he was the photographer. Tucked inside the album she found a membership card for the German Family Association that Henry had mentioned. There was no contact information on it, but she pocketed it anyway and returned the album to the wardrobe shelf.

Between the kitchen and the master bedroom was a door leading to a screened-in patio, a yard dominated by an avocado tree, and the detached garage. Oddly, unlike the well-maintained house, the garage had seen better days. It appeared sturdy enough, but the paint was peeling and two of the bottom slats were broken and hanging down. Torn shades covered the two side windows. Kit bent to look through the slats, but could see nothing of the dark interior. In contrast to the front door, a sturdy padlock held the retractable door in place. Shiny and unmarked, it looked brand new. She gave it a hopeless tug, then checked her watch. She only had two minutes.

The kitchen was her final stop. Having spent time there recently, she didn't expect to find much, but on the oak table where she and Fisher had recently shared a cup of coffee, she noticed a Thomas Guide for Orange County. The spiral-bound book was closed, but she could see that one page had a bent corner. It was a map showing a section of Anaheim.

At that moment, two blasts from the Studebaker's horn blared, stopping her in her tracks. She made a fast and quiet dash out the back door and headed for the side of the house, away from the garage. But after a slamming car door, she heard footsteps on the front porch steps. Fisher had parked on the street. Some time passed before she heard the front door shutting.

Still crouched below window level, she scurried along the side of the house and almost tripped over a Three Star orange crate that had been left under the kitchen window. Just as she reached the front yard, she heard the porch door squeak open. Without thought, she barreled down the yard and jumped in the waiting Studebaker.

FORTY-SIX

HENRY

"The east side of Anaheim. That makes sense, doesn't it, given what we know?" Kit said as Henry pulled into a 76 filling station near the entrance to the Parkway. She had been talking non-stop since making her escape, and it occurred to him that this was the first time he had seen her so hopped up. "Should we head down there?" she plowed on. "We know the general area."

"But not an exact location," he said, cutting the ignition and parking next to a phone booth. "And that's assuming the map connects to the safe house."

"He must have been looking at it recently. I know it wasn't in the kitchen yesterday."

"Fair point." She had impressed him with her focus and observation skills. Unfortunately, they only got them so far. "But without more information, the chances of finding the right spot at the right time . . . You know what they are."

"But if they have Dina . . ." Her desperation was palpable.

"We need more to go on." He pointed to the phone kiosk behind the pay station. "Back in a second."

As soon as he reached the kiosk, he leaned on it for support, but it offered little in the way of pain relief. He lifted the receiver, inserted a nickel and dialed a number from memory. After a few rings, a woman answered with the weary greeting, "Good afternoon. Continental Traveler."

"Senta? It's Tom. Tom Kurzbach."

'Yes, hello Tom." Her voice perked up a notch. "How can I help you?"

"I was wondering how things were going in Anaheim."

"What things?"

"The Association. The dues. I have the money."

There was a long pause before her response. "I'm so sorry, Tom. We've been busy taking care of other matters. Can you wait until next weekend?"

Now it was Henry's turn for silence. Finally, he said, "I can bring the money tonight. Cash. The full amount. I'd like to get this nailed down. Things are getting hot for me."

"I'm afraid that won't be possible." She sounded genuinely dis-appointed. "Tomorrow then."

"No one will be there tomorrow. I'll call you in a few days. Promise." Her tone was warm enough, but firm and final.

Before Henry could say another word, she said goodbye and hung up. He replaced the receiver and rejoined Kit in the coupe.

"Who was that?"

"Senta."

"Alpona? What did she say?"

"I couldn't get a location out of her, but wherever they're going, they're going tomorrow."

"So, we need to get there by today." Kit sighed, drumming her fingers on the console and looking past Henry into the middle distance. She was biting her lower lip, a habit she had when deep in concentration. "Wait. Didn't you say Bitenburg owns a citrus farm down there?"

"He did. But that doesn't exactly narrow it down," Henry said. "There must be dozens in Anaheim alone."

Through the windshield, Kit looked up at the station's giant orange 76 sign, hoping the answer might reveal itself there. When it didn't, she bowed her head and gave Henry a "hold on" signal with the flat of her hand. With closed eyes, she then launched into Luca's self-hypnosis routine, mumbling the alphabet under her breath. When she got to "t", she paused as the image of an empty orange crate, tipped over on its side, filled her brain. She turned, eyes open, and looked at Henry with a smile. "Three Star Citrus. Fisher had an old orange crate from there in his yard. It's in Anaheim. Where's your Orange County Thomas Guide?"

Henry pointed to the back seat. "On the floor."

Kit reached behind her and grabbed the map book. "Let's see what's on page eleven," she muttered to herself.

"Page eleven?"

"With the bent corner. In Fisher's kitchen." Kit flipped the page and ran her finger up and down the map until she found a notation for Three Star Citrus. "Bingo."

The ride down to Anaheim on U.S. 101 had been a quiet one. Afternoon traffic was light. Small talk seemed inappropriate in the moment, and they had no elaborate plan to go over. Every move they were making was a best guess. They could be wildly off, chasing gooses or ghosts. What began as a hunt for a missing veteran had warped into a pursuit of an endangered client.

"Looks like Mutt and Jeff are keeping us company," Henry said with a glance at the rearview mirror.

Kit turned around to check out the blue Ford sedan keeping pace with them on the highway. "Our FBI friends?"

Henry nodded. "Question is, are we ahead of them, or are they ahead of us?"

"We could stop at a filling station and find out."

In response, Henry swerved to take the next exit. The Ford followed, nearly cutting off another driver, who blasted his horn. "I guess we got our answer."

At the end of the ramp, Henry turned left and stayed left. A small truck now separated the Studebaker from the Ford. At the first red traffic light they came to, Henry turned to Kit and said, "Are you ready?"

"Ready for what?"

"Hang on," he said a second before the light turned green. He then floored it—as hard as the old machine could—turning left in front of oncoming traffic. The startled driver of a black Packard braked and sat on his horn, and Kit caught his obscene gesture out of the corner of her eye as they turned and sped away.

"Thanks for the warning," said Kit, as she repositioned herself on the seat.

"Are they still back there?"

Kit eyed the intersection, where the Ford was sitting at the light, waiting to turn. "Yep."

Henry turned right at the next two corners and headed back to the highway. He checked his rearview mirror and, seeing nothing, eased into the onramp and back on the highway, now reduced to one lane.

Once up to speed, Henry switched on the radio, and the car filled with the last bars of "I Can't Begin to Tell You." Even a few bars of Crosby's warbling set his teeth on edge, but KFI was the only station the Studebaker could reliably pull in. Evening was arriving, the winter moon just starting to show itself. Henry assumed they'd be moving Fischer at night, but he didn't want to cut things too close.

Up ahead, traffic had started to slow. An old poultry truck was lumbering along, holding Henry and the three cars ahead of him hostage to its pace. Cars in the opposing lane zipped by, making passing impossible. Nervous, he tapped his finger to the beat of "Opus One." Kit said nothing.

"Christ on a bike," Henry muttered.

Finally there was a break in the traffic, and the front two cars managed to overtake the truck. Henry checked the rearview mirror and grimaced. "Is that them?"

Kit turned and peered out the back window. The blue sedan was behind them. "Christ on a bike," she said. "How did they do that?"

Impatient, the car ahead of them took a chance and steered into the left lane, then floored it, barely clearing the truck before an oncoming car passed, its horn blaring. Kit had her eyes on the sedan. "They're getting closer."

A small truck blew by them, and Henry, seeing a gap, made his move. "C'mon, c'mon," he muttered as his feet smashed into the gas pedal. The Studebaker jerked forward. He flashed his lights at the approaching car, which slowed in time to allow Henry to pass the truck and swerve gracelessly back into the right lane. He wasted no time in speeding back up, but the Ford was soon behind them again. The two cars pulled away from the truck and had the right lane to themselves.

"Where's the highway patrol when you need them?" Henry muttered. "How much farther we got?"

Kit flipped on her flashlight and consulted the map. "About three miles."

"Any alternative routes?"

"Nothing but oil fields."

Oil drills filled the area just north of Anaheim; it was dead man's land. The roads would be rough, winding and open, hardly ideal for losing a tail. Henry assessed the oncoming traffic, a tricky proposition in the dark, gripped the gear shift with his left hand while repositioning his other hand on the steering wheel, slowing a tad. "I've got a better idea."

"Oh dear," Kit said and braced herself against the glove compartment and floorboards. "Did I tell you I don't have a will?"

Two cars passed them in the northbound lane, and a second later, Henry was making a dramatic U-turn. The coupe overshot the blacktop and bounced and skidded into the surrounding scrubby field. A chorus of horn blasts followed. Henry floored it, picking up speed while paralleling the highway.

"What are they doing?" he said with more calm than he felt.

With her arms still locked for impact, Kit looked over her shoulder. "I don't see them." She relaxed a bit and stared at Henry's profile. "Tell me we're not doing that again."

Henry slowed, gently turned the car until it was pointing south again, then braked to a stop. When finally both lanes were empty, he pushed on the gas pedal again and steered them back onto the highway.

"You really need a will, Kit," he said and turned up the volume on "Come to Baby, Do." He tapped his fingers on the steering wheel, "Ellington sure knows how to build a tune."

No sooner was he back on the road and pushing 60 than a Highway Patrol motorcycle slid in behind them.

"What was it you said about the Highway Patrol?" Henry said, glancing at the rear-view mirror.

Kit turned her head to see the motorcycle's flashing lights. "Christ on a cycle."

Henry slowed, pulled off to the side and killed the Studebaker's engine. "I'll do the talking," he said, as they waited for the patrolman to dismount, adjust his gun and belt, straighten his shirt and grab his ticket book. His saunter matched his short, thick legs and potbelly.

"Good day," the patrolman said with a practiced mix of politeness and recrimination. "Taking it a little fast there."

In the dimming light, Henry struggled to read the metal nametag on the officer's starched shirt. "Sorry, Patrolman Walker."

"And I saw that little maneuver you did back there. What was that all about?" Walker said, staring accusingly at Kit.

"Got turned around." Henry said.

Walker, who was already writing the ticket in his pad, grunted. "Looked like you were trying to lose somebody."

"No, just got turned around."

"Driver's license, please."

Henry handed over his license. Patrolman Walker studied it for what seemed an eternity. Finally, he mumbled, "Henry Richman?" He gave Henry a long look. "The Henry Richman?"

"Guilty," Henry said, bracing for the worst.

"The accident fella?"

"The what?"

"The insurance investigator."

Henry paused, thrown. Of the many pursuits he was known for, insurance investigator was not one. "I used to be."

"Your accident reports are legend at the CHP," Walker declared. "We use them in our training manual."

"You do?"

Walker's eyes shifted to Kit. "He's a traffic accident wizard."

"I believe it," Kit said, suppressing a laugh.

"What are you doing now?"

"Private investigator."

"I guess the money's better." Walker looked down at his ticket pad, debating. "How about I let you off with a warning this time?"

"That would be much appreciated," Henry said, as Kit nodded her approval.

"Where you headed?"

"Do you know the Three-Star Citrus grove?"

"Sure do. Got business there?"

"Just visiting." Just then, Henry noticed the blue sedan passing them slowly in the right lane, the two drivers exchanging glares.

Walker clocked the exchange and said, "You want me to pull that guy over?"

"Would you mind? I only need a few minutes."

Walker returned Henry's license with a nod. "If you want a short cut to the grove, take Exit 33 and turn left at the four-way stop. The big house is about a mile down. Can't miss it."

"Thanks, I owe you, Patrolman Walker," Henry said, rolling up his window and restarting the engine.

FORTY-SEVEN

Excerpt from "My Escape: A Confession" (submitted to O.P.M.G., February 1946)

The orange farm was not the safe house I had anticipated, but I couldn't complain. Although there was plenty of activity in the nearby groves, the old family house was situated away from the main road and used only intermittently, according to Bitenburg. Just enough that a car or two coming and going wouldn't attract attention. The growing operation was overseen by a team based elsewhere, which hired mostly non-English speaking laborers. The Bitenburgs owned everything, and occasionally drove down to go riding or take in the sea air, but Bitenburg smartly let someone else handle the day-to-day business.

They were keeping the little Jewess in the stable, away from the house and, hopefully, any prying eyes. The groom, a hopeless fellow named Carl, worked for the Association and could be trusted, according to Bitenburg. He knew how to shoot a rifle and, most important, he knew how to follow orders and keep his mouth shut.

I had doubts about the following orders part, but Bitenburg assured me Carl would not be accompanying us to Mexico. They only needed a few hours to renegotiate the transportation arrangements and then you're home free, Bitenburg said. I deduced the "renegotiations" involved a bigger bribe to move the body across the border.

To say that Bitenburg was unhappy about the Jewess problem would have been a gross understatement. The fake German enjoyed play-acting the part of Hitler ally, and certainly he enjoyed the money that flowed his way from fugitives like me (his love of the Party only going so far), but when it came to the hard stuff, he had proved himself a weakling like most of his countrymen. Yes, he agreed with everything the Party advocated, in theory. At the first hint of danger, though, he equivocated.

After arriving at the grove, Carl and I took turns administering the drugs needed to subdue the girl. During cigarette breaks, I checked her pulse and general physical status. One time, her stillness, her shallow but steady breathing, all but hypnotized me. I sat next to her, my legs crossed, watching her for a full hour. It was oddly relaxing.

I've been asked if I or any member of the escape party abused the Harris girl. I can answer that question with an emphatic "no." For one thing, while most men would describe her as nice-looking, she wasn't my type. Like my father used to say, I prefer the *dunkels* to the *pilseners*—that is, women with some "umph," especially in the breast area.

Secondly, even if she were my type, I would never take advantage. It may seem incredible that after so many years in prison I didn't grab the first woman that came my way. Other men would have—rape being a favorite victor's reward—but other men didn't grow up hearing my mother's tales about bastard Russians committing bastard Russian atrocities. Thoughts of my long-dead grandmother would have destroyed any pleasure I could have conceived of from the encounter.

And then there was the matter of her faith. My father hated Jews and refused to work with them. My mother felt no affection for them, but she tolerated them, believing they shared a common enemy. At that time, I followed my father politically, perhaps because I had grown weary of my mother's diatribes, which masqueraded as her beliefs but were really just her obsessions. She never joined the Party, as my father and I did, but in the end, she didn't object when I told her I had joined the Waffen.

If we had been in Germany, the problem with the girl would have been easily solved. Here, though, it was much more complicated.

The Association's friends in law enforcement (yes, there are some, although I never learned their identities) could only do so much in a situation like this, Bitenburg complained. The profile of the case was too high. The disappearance of a young woman, even an undistinguished one like this Harris girl, would attract attention. And how were we to know whether she had told someone of her plans? She continued to insist she had tracked down my uncle on her own, after their phone call, but her explanations of how she had found him were laughably improbable.

No, she had to be killed. But not until we were ready to go. And at Bitenburg's insistence, the body would not be disposed of anywhere near "his grove."

As I plucked a ripe orange from the tree behind the house and pressed it to my welcoming nostrils, I contemplated Bitenburg's predicament. If they all got caught, Bitenburg would likely be going to prison for the rest of his life, while my life would be over before the doors on the American's prison cell even closed.

FORTY-EIGHT
HENRY AND KIT

By the time they reached the big house, the sun was down. Henry pulled off the road and parked just beyond the long driveway. The two-story Bavarian-style building was dark, save for a few lights on one side of the lower level.

Kit pointed to a horse barn visible in the back. With its colored roof and sashes, it mirrored the main house. "In there?" she said.

"With the ponies?" Henry said.

"They'd be good cover."

"Fair point," he said, opening his door. "Got your flashlight?"

Henry headed across the ranch yard toward the stables and motioned for Kit to follow him. When they reached the front of the building, he whispered, "Stay here and keep watch. I'll go in the back way. If you see someone," he said pointing to her flashlight, "give me two quick flashes through this window."

As with the front, a padlock protected the back double door. He had a hunch that an emergency key was stored nearby, perhaps without the knowledge of the bosses. He ran his hands along the top of the windows and door, but came up empty. Then he noticed a drainpipe coming off the gutter on the left side. He felt around with his fingers and hit pay dirt—the padlock key wrapped in tin foil. A few moments later, he was inside.

He kept his flashlight off and moved cautiously through the moonlit space. He could see four stalls, two on each side. The horses—there were at least two—stirred a little. There was a rising odor of manure and piss, but the place had obviously been recently mucked. What was he expecting to find in here? Other than the horses, he didn't know, but a sense of urgency overcame him and he practically threw himself into the back stall.

At first he thought it empty. He heard nothing and couldn't make out any shapes in the half-darkness. He switched on his flashlight and pointed the beam into the stall's corner. On the floor he could see a large lump covered by a thick horse blanket. His heart flipped and for a moment he was paralyzed. He turned off the flashlight and crouched down next to the bundle. With a shaking hand, he pulled back the blanket. He could make out a woman's form. Strands of dark hair lay across her face, obscuring her features, but he assumed it was Dina. He touched her neck—cool but not cold—and her eyes were closed. Her pulse was barely perceptible. Heavily drugged he assumed. But alive.

He stood up and checked for signs from Kit. All clear. For now. He debated how best to handle the unconscious woman; it had been a while since he had lifted a body, even a petite one. He shook her shoulder gently, then patted her cheek, but she remained dead still. "Dina," he said, still whispering, but with more force. "Dina, wake up."

Her eyes moved under their lids, like she was fighting her way to consciousness, and Henry pinched her cheek a little to help the process along. Suddenly he became aware of the horse in a neighboring stall, now fully alert and relieving itself, the smell of its urine filling Henry's nostrils. Henry scrambled across to the other stall and, before the horse could react with noisy confusion, he grabbed some of its soiled hay and hustled back to Dina. He stuck the hay under Dina's nose. After a few seconds, Dina reacted to the urine's ammonia, jerking awake.

"Dina, it's Henry Richman," he whispered. "We need to move now. Can you get up?"

She nodded like a far-gone drunk and struggled to her feet, gripping Henry's arm for balance. Once upright, she started swaying and lurching, and for a moment, he thought she was going to vomit. "Back this way," he said, pivoting her in the direction of the back door. "We gotta hurry."

Just then, two light flashes illuminated the center aisle, and a pair of male voices echoed outside. Terrified, Dina found her footing and hustled with Henry to the double doors.

Henry hadn't planned an escape route and was grateful to find Kit silently waiting for them in the dark. She signaled for them to crouch and scuttle toward the orange grove that spread out behind the buildings.

"One guy came out, looked over here, and then ran back in," Kit whispered. Then seeing Dina on the verge of falling face-first onto the hard ground, she grabbed the back of her suit jacket and pulled her towards an opening between the orange trees. Dina gasped and Kit put her fingers to her lips.

Henry glanced back to see two men walking briskly towards the stable, flashlights in hand. One was noticeably taller than the other, but otherwise he couldn't make out much in the dark. His bent knees burned and, despite the cool breeze that was blowing across the field, drops of sweat rolled down the sides of his hatless head.

As they reached the inside of the grove proper, he heard a man's barked order coming from the stable: "Check the grove. Over there." Then he saw Kit and Dina running full tilt down a narrow dirt path separating the rows of orange trees. He pushed to catch up.

"There are at least two of them. They'll split up," Henry said panting. "We should too. You go that way," he sputtered, pointing to an out building, where a truck was parked. "I'll razzle-dazzle 'em." He stopped in his tracks, and Kit looked back, hesitating. He waved them forward, then ran headlong in the opposite direction, into the orchard.

A few yards in, Henry stopped and crouched between two of the fuller trees. His still-tender side wound responded with a stab of pain. The trees' branches, heavy with ripe fruit, left little room for maneuvering, and he knew not to get too close—their protective spikes could do damage. He pulled his Smith and Wesson from its holster and held his breath, listening.

Seconds later, a man in gray work clothes—the shorter, slower of the pair—ran past. Henry rose and lunged toward the path. The man stopped, alerted, and Henry fired his revolver in his general direction and ducked back into the trees. A second later, the man got off his own shot, equally off the mark. The report sounded like a rifle.

"Fuck! They're in there," the short man shouted.

On the other side of the stand, Henry could see the beam of an approaching flashlight. He had them going in the right direction, toward him; now he just needed to figure out how not to get shot. "OK, Katzenjammer Kids, come get me."

They had just made it to the truck when a shot rang out. Dina reacted to the sudden noise like she'd been slapped. "What was that?" she croaked with terror.

Before Kit could answer, a second shot, from a different location, stung the air. "Get in and keep your head down." Kit yanked open the driver's side door of the truck and climbed in. Dina followed suit, her head lowered. "The key's not here," Kit said, her on hand on the ignition. She felt along the dashboard, without luck.

"Look under the seat," Dina said in a stressed whisper. "That's where my dad keeps his."

Kit felt under her seat, her fingers brushing against dirt and paper bits but nothing key-like. Was he left-handed? She switched hands and groped underneath, on the door side. Just as she felt the round contours of smooth cool metal, more gunfire erupted. This time, there were three or four shots. "Got it," she said pulling the key out. With a shaking hand, she fit the key in the ignition and turned.

The engine grumbled to life and Kit wrestled with the gearshift to get the truck moving and onto to the muddy, rutted side road.

"Dina, what happened? Did you go to Fisher's?"

"After you told me the uncle lived in Mt. Washington, I looked up his address and took a cab to his house. I told him I needed a tow so I could get inside. I was sure the man who called me was there and if he had any information about Peter, I wanted to know."

Kit resisted the urge to lecture her client about rash acts, especially as she hadn't been a model of restraint herself. "Did you see him?"

"Not there, no. When I mentioned Peter's name, the old man suddenly stuck a gun in my face. They drugged me with something. I don't remember anything after—"

Kit's foot scrambled for the brake pedal. Up ahead, she could just make out Henry's silhouette. He seemed to be waving his arms at them.

Henry zigzagged his way up the stand, stumbling over fallen oranges and suffering thorn stabs as he went. The pursuing duo was closing in, but he knew their visibility was limited, even with flashlights. He squatted, wincing, and caught his breath. Up ahead he could see a dirt road that marked the end of the stand. Behind, judging from the movements of their flashlights, Hans and Franz were heading in opposite directions again. They must have figured out he was alone, he thought. Time to move.

He grabbed two oranges from the ground and willing his dead knees to unbend, he rose to a half-stand and hurled the fruit as far as he could. It was an obvious ploy, but one he hoped would buy him a few seconds. As a flashlight beam roamed the area where the oranges had landed, Henry made his move. Three shots soon erupted, all from a pistol. Hans's aim was better than Franz's, he thought as he kept racing—if you could call his manic stumbling racing—toward the road.

As his foot was about to touch dirt, he heard the sound of an engine revving.

"They're in the truck!" shouted Hans.

Henry noticed the truck, its headlights off, heading his way and ran towards them, waving. Behind him, Franz was thrashing his way out of the stand. The truck accelerated, then slowed to a crawl as it came up alongside him. Inside Kit was gesturing wildly for him to hop on the passenger side running board. As he made his way to the other side, Franz burst from the stand just steps behind them.

With one hand on the door handle and the other gripping the top of the panel, Henry hoisted himself onto the running board. Kit picked up speed just as Franz, running at them, got off a shot. After the bullet ricocheted off the rear fender, Hans, racing up from a distance, fired another round from his rifle. This time, he hit a tree next to the road, splintering the trunk.

Henry saw the whole thing start to fall onto the road and roared, "Kit!"

Kit suddenly swerved to avoid the tree, almost dislodging Henry. Behind them, Franz had pocketed his gun and was running full tilt at the truck. Even in the dark, Henry could tell that Franz was young and athletic. He pounded on the window to alert Kit, but before she could react, Franz heaved himself onto the driver's side running board.

"The door!" said Henry.

Without hesitating, Dina reached over Kit and grabbed the steering wheel from Kit's grip. Kit sped up a little and nodded at Henry. Then in one smooth move, she lifted the lock, pulled on the handle and jammed her shoulder into the door. It flew open, causing Franz to lose his balance and tumble onto the road. As he rolled away, the truck fishtailed a little, testing Henry's strength again.

Up ahead the end of the grove loomed, and to the left of the dirt road was a paved access road. Henry glanced back to see Franz running towards them, his revolver in hand, and flames rising up from the remains of the bullet-damaged tree trunk.

As Kit made a sharp left, Franz fired what Henry calculated was his last shot. Henry heard the bullet splinter some of the bed's wooden side paneling. "Close, Franz," he muttered, "but no cigar."

Henry was looking forward to dismounting when Kit suddenly slammed on the brakes. Standing in the road before them was Hans, one hand beaming his flashlight at the truck, the other on the trigger box of his rifle, which he had tucked under his arm.

Kit threw the gearshift into reverse and started to back up, prompting Hans to fire a one-armed shot that hit the front grill and killed the engine. Frantic, Kit tried to restart the truck, but seeing Hans racing toward them, rifle pointed, she hissed at Dina, "Get down," then raised her hands in surrender. Henry, not convinced that either Hans or Franz intended for them to live, slipped off the running board and, clutching his sidearm, took as much cover as he could at the rear of the truck.

As he sidled toward the vehicle, Hans yelled, "Don't move a fucking inch. Keep your hands way up."

Henry squatted, pressing against the wooden panels, his gun at the ready. He could hear the stress in Hans's voice.

"Where are the others?" Hans barked at Kit. "I'll shoot you if they don't show themselves."

"Harris is in the cab," Franz said, limping out of the darkness, holding his revolver. Was he able to reload it, Henry wondered, or was it just for show? Hans inched toward the passenger side to confirm Dina's presence, pointing his flashlight down into the cab.

As Franz neared the truck's cab, passing him unaware, Henry rose up. He made sure Franz heard the click of the trigger before aiming the barrel at the back of Franz's head. Franz stopped in his tracks.

"Freeze," Henry yelled to Hans, "unless you want a dead Nazi."

"Klaus?" Hans said.

"Yes, he has a gun to my head," said Franz/Klaus. His accent was barely discernable. "What do we do now?" he asked, turning his head slightly to address Henry.

Before Henry could even consider the question, the Nazi spun around and tried to bean him with the butt of his revolver. Henry ducked and stumbled back, untouched, and shifting his stance, fired directly at Hans over the truck's hood.

A yowl of pain filled the air, and in unison, Henry and Hans crumpled to the muddy ground—Hans from Henry's bullet, and Henry from a tackle by Klaus. Pinned down, Henry felt Klaus grab for his revolver, still clutched in his hand, and try to wrest it away. Henry held on until Klaus sunk his teeth into Henry's forearm. With a yelp, Henry let the gun butt slip from his hands.

The truck's doors flew open on both sides. Dina scrambled out and threw herself on top of Klaus with a rage-fueled energy Henry could not have predicted. She pummeled Klaus with closed fists, distracting him long enough from the gun, now slippery with mud and sweat, to allow Henry to grab it back, albeit by the barrel. In one powerful motion, Klaus swept his arm back and dislodged Dina, then rendered her unconscious with a punch. A second later, Kit struck the back of Klaus' head with a thick piece of the damaged paneling, and the Nazi went silent.

Their victory proved short-lived, however, when Hans stood up and lumbered toward them, both hands now gripping his rifle.

Dina was out cold. So was Klaus. Henry was panting louder than she had ever heard him, and she suddenly feared he might be having a heart attack. Before she could assist her partner, though, the German's partner had risen from the dead and was staggering towards them with his rifle aimed at Dina.

Instinctively Henry gripped his gun and repositioned the barrel closer to Klaus's head. "Even in the dark, I can't miss," Henry said, his voice low and firm. He fixed his stare on the rifle, but Kit noticed he had stuck his right leg out slightly, pushing it in her direction. She knew what he was expecting her to do.

At the sound of Henry's voice, Dina started to stir, and Rifleman pivoted to check her movement. In that second of distraction, Kit reached under Henry's pant leg and pulled his derringer from its ankle holster. All previous mocking of the little pistol, which he admitted he never had occasion to use despite years of carrying it, was forgotten as she dove behind the side of the truck.

"Stop, now!" Rifleman yelled in what sounded like Dina's direction.

Kit stopped, but she couldn't keep her hand, the one holding the compact Remington, from shaking. Her firing range skills would soon be put to the test.

"Dina, Dina, it's all right. Don't move," Henry said.

"Shut up!" snarled Rifleman.

"Are we staying here all night?" Henry paused for a response, but got none. "I expect the FBI will be arriving soon. They were tailing us down here." The Rifleman glanced toward the stables and farmhouse. "Bullshit."

"Who's driving down to Mexico? You're in no shape to go," Henry said, indicating Rifleman's wounded side with a tilt of his chin.

"We got a driver for that. Don't worry."

Kit thought she heard some groans—Klaus?—and a moment later, he rolled slightly toward Henry, shimmying like a snake. Then Henry let out a sharp grunt and recoiled, his gun hand suddenly wobbling. Without thinking, Kit spun around and, just as Rifleman was about to squeeze off a round, surprised him with a shot from the derringer. This time, Rifleman, a bullet hole turning red in his chest, crumpled into the mud and stayed there.

She then turned to Klaus as he was struggling to wrest the revolver from Henry's hand, and screamed, "Stop!"

The grove fire must have caught the attention of a passing car, as fire trucks and police cars were roaring towards them. Never had he been so relieved to hear the blaring of sirens. Fischer's knife had struck, literally, at his belt line, and while the belt's leather had reduced the stab's ferocity, he nonetheless was bleeding and in pain.

As Kit held his derringer on Fischer, he saw that her hand was shaking. She had just killed a man. And saved his life. Both facts would soon come to haunt her, he knew.

A pair of Anaheim cops were the first to spot the odd tableau and came lumbering toward them, guns drawn. Immediately Henry threw up his hands, and gestured for Kit to do the same. She looked down at the grunting, fully conscious Klaus and hesitated until a screamed order to "drop the gun!" startled her into compliance.

When the fire and ambulance crews reached them, Dina, Henry and the German were loaded on stretchers. If Klaus had any thoughts of escape, the sheer number of men surrounding him must have given him second thoughts. The uniforms handcuffed Kit and were about to shove her into their squad car, when Mutt and Jeff strode into the grove like Hollywood directors ready to yell "cut." They flashed their credentials and ordered Kit placed in the back of their sedan.

Later, in an Anaheim emergency room, a detective duo from Anaheim PD questioned him about how the fire started, but not about the kidnapping and shootings. Had the FBI already filled them in?

"What can I say, things have a way of exploding when I'm around," Henry told the plainclothesmen. "Even trees."

DREAM (WHEN YOU'RE FEELING BLUE)

(Late February 1946)

FORTY-NINE

Excerpt from "My Escape: A Confession" (submitted to O.P.M.G., February 1946)

We had been bested by a Semite—a female one at that. My blow had only knocked the Harris girl out. The more I thought about that, the angrier I got. Apparently the other two were private investigators. The old man had tricked Senta—the stupid cow—into thinking he was a sympathizer. I supposed the Jewess had paid them well. At least I had the satisfaction of knowing her lover had died by my hand.

After my arrest, the FBI had taken me and, I presumed, my uncle and Bitenburg, to a prison called Terminal Island. It made Crowder look like the Hotel Adlon. The FBI man, Burke, had interrogated me for hours about the doctor and the orange grove. If Dick Tracy were to come to life, I mused, he would look like Burke—broad-shouldered, square-jawed, blue-eyed.

Then Marony, a major from the Provost Marshal's office, took over. Marony topped Burke in height by a couple of inches, but was thin and narrow from top to bottom. Even his hair was thin, I thought, and his chest medals did nothing to distract from his cautious, bookish manner. Periodically, he would look down at his notes, written in a neat, tiny hand in a three-ring binder.

Marony asked a few perfunctory questions about my escape before turning his attention to my camp activities. Curiously, he didn't seem interested in my engineering work, or how the camp maintained security. Instead he focused on my unofficial role as camp translator.

'How often did you act as a translator?" Marony said, clearing his throat.

"Once or twice a week."

'How often were you asked to translate written materials?"

“I did both equally. Written and spoken.”

’How often were you asked to write materials?”

’Write them?" An image popped into my head. “Only once.”

’Once?" Marony said, his pencil poised over his notebook.

’Just the once.”

’What was it for?”

I spoke slowly. ‘A newsletter.”

’What newsletter?" Marony said.

’The newsletter from the Factory,” I threw out at last. At the word ‘factory" Marony flinched.

In the grand scheme, the ‘newsletter story" had been a minor, if curious, event in my camp life. It happened shortly after New Year’s, while I was preoccupied with finalizing the details of my escape. A guard had approached me at breakfast with a summons from the camp commander. Despite my social reserve, the commander trusted my translation skills and frequently requested my services. That particular morning I was escorted to the administrative offices by one of the chattier guards, a hulking freckled boy who felt compelled to comment on the weather (it had snowed heavily during the night) and whatever else popped into his head.

’Missouri’s sure been dry and cold this winter,” the guard offered, pronouncing the state’s name ‘Mizura,” like a local. After a few seconds of what must been uncomfortable silence, he added, ‘Where’d you learn to speak English?”

’My mother was from Dover, in England,” I said. ‘I used to spend summers there when I was a child.”

’You don’t have an English accent.”

’I used to. But after two years in America, I lost it.” It was true the English accent had been replaced with an American one, but the change hadn’t happened naturally. I had forced it after learning my post-incarceration fate. If I were to blend in, I would have to learn to say ‘Mizura" and ‘gotcha" and ‘hot diggity dog" as though born to it.

Inside the administrative building, the guard instructed me to wait at the end of the hallway until called by the commander. Apparently waiting for the commander was a frequent business because two folding wooden chairs had been placed on either side of the door. The guard pointed to one and left.

I was happy to sit and wait even though it meant missing breakfast, but after thirty minutes had passed, my need for a cigarette had overwhelmed me. The back door was only feet away—I would still be visible through the window should the commander choose that minute to summon me—so I saw no reason not to light up in the invigorating winter air.

A few puffs into my Lucky Strike, I noticed an American officer, a captain, approaching. I had yet to meet him, but I recognized him as one of the camp's academic instructors. He was holding a large tan envelope.

"Are you the new writer?" the captain asked without introduction.

I saluted. 'I am the translator," I said in my near-perfect English. "Do you need me to write something in German for you?"

The captain waved the envelope. "The Kearney guys have requested we run an editorial on the Nuremberg trials to complement one that will be appearing in this week's *Der Ruf*," he sputtered, the last in atrocious German. *Der Ruf* was the fancy German-language camp newspaper that billed itself as "made by prisoners, for prisoners." I had tagged it as obvious, lame propaganda. "They want it in our next newsletter, which means I need to get a clean copy to the printer yesterday."

Kearney guys? Was he referring to the POW camp in Rhode Island? And if I was the new writer, who was the old? To buy a moment, I took a long drag on my cigarette. "Does the commander know about this?"

"The commander? He doesn't get involved with Factory matters."

I took a final pull on my cigarette and tossed it into a snow bank. My mind continued to race, wondering how a factory might be connected to a newsletter. Through the window, I saw the commander's door open and his male secretary's head pop out. Confusion clouded the young man's round face as he observed me in conversation with the animated captain.

Impatient, the captain offered me the envelope. "Can I give this to you?"

"I'm sorry," I finally replied, waving him off, "I am just a translator. For the commander." Without a backward glance at the flummoxed captain, I retreated inside. The secretary—a corporal as it turned out and therefore not requiring my salute—ushered me in to the commander's reception area, a strange look of dread hanging in his eyes.

Later, in the mess hall, I found copies of the last two newsletters and checked for names. Most of the content was unattributed, but the editorials—both of which heaped praise on camp administrators—bore the signature of Corporal Dieter Schumann, the same Corporal Schumann who had been driven from camp in the dead of night two weeks before. I assumed the move was protective. Despite efforts to neutralize them, Crowder housed a cadre of "dyed-in-the-wool Nazis," who must have taken exception to Schumann's positions and offered to administer their own painful corrections.

At the time, nothing was said to me about my chance meeting and misunderstanding with the captain. The Nuremberg editorial never ran. But now, as I sat in the bleak interrogation room of Terminal Island, I imagined the three Crowder officers assessing the repercussions and debating how much I had deduced. Not everything, perhaps, but enough. Enough to make me a problem apparently.

In the dank of the Terminal Island interrogation room, I could see Marony weighing his options. We had reached a crossroad of some sort, and I sensed I had the upper hand. "What do you know about the Factory?" Marony said at last.

"I know it's located at Camp Kearney in, I believe, Rhode Island."

"Anything else? For instance, what does the Factory . . ." Marony squinted, searching for his next word, "manufacture?"

I replied quickly, 'Propaganda." It was just a guess, but an educated one. I hadn't put all the pieces together before, but now it seemed obvious. The Factory was a unit dedicated to re-education.

At the word "propaganda," Marony deflated in front of my eyes. The Geneva Convention prohibited the use of propaganda on prisoners, and a program that assigned prisoners to pro-American essay writing would without a doubt cross the line. A silly line, in my view, but a line nonetheless. But why would the victors be so concerned about that violation now? The war was long over. American POWs had been released, eliminating the possibility of reprisal.

And then, it hit me like a ton of bricks—as the Americans would say. Wasn't a form of reprisal happening in Nuremberg right now? Apparently the Allies weren't satisfied with just occupying and dividing up my homeland. They wanted to assert their moral authority as well, a moral authority that for them was defined by their adherence to the Geneva Convention. The Factory's reprogramming project, no matter how tame, would undercut the Americans' credibility at the international court. If word got out that they had developed a far-reaching re-education scheme, their chances at Nuremberg would be zero.

So with little more said, I worked out an agreement with Marony and Burke: I would be sent to Juarez, Mexico, a free man, in exchange for my signed pledge not to leave the state of Chihuahua or to speak to the press for the remainder of my life. The alternative? Death. "Pick your execution," Agent Burke exclaimed. "Lethal gas in California—appropriate, don't you think?—or firing squad in Soviet Germany." I was skeptical about the first threat, but positive about the second.

"The funny thing is," I later told Burke as we waited for the unmarked sedan that would deliver me across the border, "until they were captured, German soldiers hadn't eaten or smoked so well in decades. You Americans only had to keep stuffing our stomachs and giving us cigarettes. You didn't need to fill our minds with propaganda."

Burke looked at me with disgust. "Shut up, Nazi, or I'll fill your mind with my foot."

FIFTY

HENRY

Calvin greeted him at his front door. His usual welcoming smile had been replaced with a slight, tight frown. Henry recognized the pinched expression as worry, not anger. Henry offered his hand in greeting and as Calvin shook it distractedly, he said, "Thanks for arranging this."

"I had to pull some strings to get him here," Calvin said. "I told him you'd make a public stink if he didn't. Your reputation does proceed you there."

"Glad it's good for something."

They entered the sunken living room, where Mutt, a rye in hand, was gently turning the antique globe. He was wearing the same blue suit and brown fedora he had been sporting down in Anaheim. Ever the cordial host, Calvin said, "Henry, this is Special Agent Burke."

The agent looked up and greeted them with a raised highball glass. "Mr. Richman. Good to see you're up and about."

"Are you?" Henry pulled on his suit jacket, which was covering both new and old bandages. "Glad?"

Burke smiled tightly. "I am, your interference notwithstanding." He gave the globe another spin and tossed back the last of his drink. "I gotta confess, I'm surprised you took on a case like this, Detective Richman. Seems like a job for a younger man."

"What can I say? I'm a regular Popeye." Calvin offered Henry a glass of bourbon, but Henry declined. He cut to the chase. "What's the deal with Fischer? Why the escort to Mexico?"

"Rules of engagement say it's a POW's duty to attempt escape," Burke said with a flatness reserved for penal codes, "and the Geneva Convention prohibits extreme punishment after re-capture."

"Last I checked, the war was over." Henry said.

"Doesn't matter, the rules still apply."

"Does the Geneva Convention sanction cold-blooded murder too?"

Burke's lips tightened at the question. "Look, the bottom line is, the OPMG doesn't want Fischer out there. If he goes on trial for murder in California, he'll have a lawyer and a megaphone."

"A megaphone for what?"

"Something Washington doesn't want known just yet."

"Just yet?"

"Not as long as the trials are going on."

"Nuremberg?"

"That's as much as I can say," Burke said. Then with emphasis, he added, "That's as much as I know.

"So, you're saying the Novaks get no justice? Our client gets no justice?" Henry snarled, all pretense at politeness gone.

"It's the Provost Marshal's call."

'How does Mexico feel about having a Nazi psycho running around loose?"

"The local authorities were amply compensated." Burke spun the globe and touched a spot in Mexico. "If it's any consolation, he'll be stuck in Juarez forever."

"Just like he was stuck in his POW camp?"

Burke gave the globe a light slap. "Good point, but have you ever been to Juarez? Even a few months there will feel like an eternity."

Henry debated arguing the matter, but changed tack instead. "Couple more questions."

Burke drained his glass. "Shoot."

Henry fought the urge to smack the glass from the agent's hand. "Was it really necessary to stab me in front of my wife?"

"Your wife's presence was unfortunate, but we needed to deliver our message. You're a stubborn bastard. Severe methods were recommended."

"Recommended? By who? You?"

Burke smirked. "That's above my pay grade."

"You were just following orders?"

"It wasn't me. Knives aren't my style. I prefer fists. But after that stunt in Anaheim, I might have volunteered for the job, knives or fists."

"And the letter? In Kit's house?"

Burke's expression softened and he looked down at his rye to hide his eyes. Finally, he met Henry's gaze and said, "Your partner had obviously forgotten it. I thought it might be helpful to Stanley."

For a second, Henry's disgust melted. Bea often accused him of clinging to moments of grace like a life preserver in a sea of corruption—sometimes to his own detriment—but it was impulse he couldn't shake.

Then Burke said, "This shrink fellow she's seeing . . . how serious is that?"

A few minutes later, as Calvin escorted him to the front door, Henry's mind raced. Burke had been right about one thing—he was a stubborn bastard, and silent capitulation wasn't his style.

"How do you think your pals at the OPMG would feel if I told my pal at the *Times* that our government sanctions the murder and stabbing of its citizens?

"They'd deny it and call you a liar. You know that," Calvin said.

"Sure, but there'd be a great big spotlight shining on them while they did it. And then the digging would start."

"I agree that the situation is unfortunate, but look at the big picture. One criminal here versus hundreds at Nuremberg. One victim versus millions.

"I'm not arguing against that logic. But I was just thinking, maybe there's a way to lessen the pain here. Balance the scales a little?

"What?" Calvin said with sudden concern. "Do you know a guy in Mexico?

"Sure. But that's not what I had in mind."

Calvin sighed. "Then what do you want?"

"I just need you to make another phone call to your pals in Washington."

"That's all?"

"Don't worry, Calvin. You won't feel a thing."

Outside, Henry inspected the Studebaker. It was clean of explosives but not of dirt, mud and scratches. "You and me both," he said as though reading the car's mind.

As he wound his way down the sea of Oak streets, he thought about Bea and the precariousness of happiness. He knew she had been happy as a young woman, when life was full of possibilities. As each possibility became impossible, a little bit of happiness fell away, a little bit of her fell away. But the joy that once defined her still lurked behind her eyes, its shadow still fell across her lips, teasing him with hope. Henry could see it there but he couldn't claim it.

Henry was different. He never had expectations of happiness. Life had been a trial from the start, failures were baked in. Bombs went off, corruption abounded, and more often than not, justice was not served. Life couldn't disappoint him, but neither did it bring him joy.

On Hollywood, he saw the sign for the grand opening of Thompson's Automatic Car Wash—"The World's Finest and Fastest"—and turned in. Emerick came out to greet him, a drying cloth in hand. Though it had only been days since he last saw him, he thought the young vet looked fitter and more robust than before. Seeing his energetic step reminded Henry that he needed to check in with Dr. Soong about his ticker. He had never felt so weak and winded before, not even when his body was full of shrapnel.

"Welcome, sir," said Emerick, not appearing to recognize his customer.

"Emerick. You've restored my faith," Henry said, offering his hand through the open window.

Emerick took his hand and shook it gently. "Mr. Richman?" he said, incredulous that a man from one chapter of his life had suddenly entered the next.

"How's the new job?"

"Fine. I've been doing the books and helping out with the washing." As proof, he waved his drying cloth. "What can I help you with today?"

"A good cleaning. Inside and out."

FIFTY-ONE

KIT

Union Station was as quiet as Kit had ever seen it. The last of the weekend getaway trains had departed, leaving the waiting area awash in discarded newspapers and overflowing ashtrays. Fred Harvey's was nearly deserted. Dina was scheduled to leave on the next Super Chief for Chicago, where Peter's funeral was being held. Having completed the fingerprint match, Judson had released the body and sent it on its way north. Dina was still in recovery mode, and Kit had insisted on seeing her off on the long, lonely trip.

When Kit told her Roland would be working the dining car on that train, Dina asked to speak to him before they departed. Kit was hesitant—it was one thing for her to see things to the bitter end, another to expect Roland to—but she agreed to pass on the request. To her surprise, Roland had said yes without prodding. "I figure the doctor is a sort of war casualty, but she won't be getting a letter from his CO or the President, so I guess I can be the next best thing."

Dressed neatly in black, with a veiled hat that did its best to obscure the bruises left by Klaus Fischer, Dina ignored the pot of tea she had ordered.

"Thank you for seeing me," Dina said. "I know it might seem a little odd, given that you didn't really know Peter."

Roland shifted in his chair, conscious of both the time and the stares of curious travelers. "Nothing odd about it. Your man was a fine person, I could tell. Very respectful and generous."

"Yes, he was."

Roland gave Kit a conspiratorial glance. "I didn't mention this before, but we had a good conversation that last dinner."

"You did?" Dina said.

"We did. He told me all about his work and what he did over there, and how he met you and how much he was looking forward to being with you in Los Angeles."

Dina had given in to her tears, and Kit offered her a dispenser napkin to dry them. In that moment, Kit could see that Roland's words had overwhelmed her with memories. It didn't matter if they were true.

"He told you about our first meeting?" Dina finally asked.

"He was smitten. Didn't want you to know too soon, but he was. You were the one as far as he was concerned. 'I'm going to marry her,' he said."

"Thank you for telling me that."

Roland stood. "I should get going. If there's anything I can do to help on the way to Chicago, just give me a holler."

As Dina, a single suitcase in hand, was about to head for Track 9, where the Super Chief was already boarding, Kit said, "Hold on, I have something for you." From her camera bag, she produced a large button-and-string envelope and handed it to Dina.

"What's this?" Dina asked as she unwound the fastener.

"A present from Henry."

Dina pulled out a document and gave it a glance. She squinted in confusion at Kit. "What is it?"

"It's a French marriage certificate. Specifically Peter's and your marriage certificate."

"Peter?"

"You're now a war widow, courtesy of the War Department."

Dina studied the document. "Where did it come from?"

"Henry," Kit repeated.

"I don't understand. How did Henry get this?"

"He knows people. And he's not above a little . . . forceful persuasion."

Dina suppressed a smile. "I don't know, Kit . . ."

"It's no skin off their noses. They owe it to you."

"Peter never proposed."

"He would have. You know that," Kit said firmly. "Keep it. Use it if and when you need it. Both of you."

Dina said nothing, but as the final call for boarding sounded, she gave Kit a quick hug. "Tell Henry thank you."

She had almost missed Union Station's morning train to Ontario. She had played a hunch about the postwar whereabouts of Dewey Barton. Or rather, she had played a hunch regarding the postwar activities of Dewey Barton, and that hunch had led her to an egg farm in Ontario. Dewey's troop ship had docked in San Diego and from there, he had apparently gone north and east in search of work. Of course, he was going to look for work in the only industry he knew, she thought.

Kit had called several other farms before hitting pay dirt at the Voorhees Family Egg Ranch. The owner's son had been killed in Japan, so as he had explained to Kit over the phone, when Dewey showed up looking for a job, Voorhees didn't hesitate to offer him one. "Kid's a regular Pied Piper, the hens follow him everywhere," Voorhees said, laughing.

As the train pulled into the Ontario station, Kit tried to envision how their meeting would go, but she had no idea how Dewey would react to seeing her. Would he recognize her? Would he want to talk to her? Or to Stanley? As she understood the story, Stanley had left a wounded Dewey in a cave, intending to return with help but never making it back. Medics had, in fact, rescued Dewey and taken him to a field hospital. He had survived, but had lost his leg.

Outside the station, she hailed a cab. To the east, a bank of dark clouds was on the move. Rain was near.

FIFTY-TWO

LUCA

In the veterans' cemetery, Luca and Kit stood close together on a hilltop overlooking a lush field of gravesites. Unlike civilian sites, the graves here were as uniform and neatly ordered as the military units they represented. They watched as, below, Stanley passed slowly through the rows of graves, stopping to take in each headstone before moving on to the next.

"Was this your idea?" asked Kit in a reverential whisper. "To bring him here?"

Luca nodded. "For soldiers, gravesites can be an important point of healing. If the timing's right, it can help them regain control of their thoughts."

"And you think the timing's right?"

"He said he was ready. Come what may."

Kit turned towards him, leaning in close enough for him to catch a whiff of her citrusy perfume. "Has everything come back? His memories?"

Luca met her gaze. "Not yet, and maybe they never will. But he's had a big breakthrough."

"Does that mean he can come home?"

Luca paused, his eyes returning to Stanley, now crouching in front of a flat grave marker. "He could, we talked about it, but he says he doesn't want to."

"Why?" she said, baldly surprised. "Is he afraid?"

He turned the question over in his mind. "No, I believe it's actually the opposite. Going home would be the easy course. It takes courage to know when you're not quite there yet."

"Amen to that," she mumbled. "And speaking of not quite ready, I haven't forgotten our rain check."

"Me neither."

STANLEY

Stanley knew he wouldn't find any of his platoon here. Those that didn't make it had been buried in Okinawa. No one was going to pay to have their humble remains moved from Japan. But there were so many others here, Stanley realized, some who had died in combat, others who had died years later. He read each marker with care.

Arthur Kemp Anderson, Medal of Honor, Sgt. US Army, World War II, Jan 20 1925, Jun 26 1943

John Walter Pecor, Pfc. L, 127th US Infantry, World War II, Dec 29, 1918, Aug 17 1941

Charles W. Gilt, Cook C, 11th US Calvary, World War II, Oct 18, 1910, Mar 8 1942

Arthur Lawngton Walton, Pvt K 7th California Infantry, World War II, May 2, 1920, Aug 4 1941

Stanley never knew any of them, but he felt an odd connection to their resting spots. Each name was etched with precision, standing against time, none to be lost or forgotten. Even in the rain they'll never be phantoms, he thought.

Finally, he found the one he had hoped to see. It was at the end of a row, slightly off by itself. The flat marble marker read:

George Lewis Oshier. New York. Sgt. U.S. Marine Corps, World War II

Above it, a smaller flat marker read:

Blackout, d. 1945.

Dewey's legendary Blackout, the dog who had saved a squad. He grinned with joy and glanced up at Kit and Doc. They had been joined by a thin man with stick-out ears. Stanley waved to him like a man drowning.

Dewey waved back, tentatively. Then he started slowly down the hillside, his right leg hesitating slightly, out of rhythm with his left. Stanley felt a stab in his gut. With each of Dewey's steps, everything about the war, their war, was expressed.

"Dewey. I found him," Stanley screamed to the air. "Blackout. He's right where you said he'd be."

FIFTY-THREE

KIT

Under a still and soft blue sky, Kit led Stanley to a stand of pepper trees on the edge of the military cemetery. Their father had been buried there just months before. A World War I veteran, he had been formally approved for a plot just prior to his death. Since his burial, Kit had visited his grave only once. She wasn't sentimental about such things, even with close kin, and felt sure her father would agree with the notion of "getting on with things."

For Stanley, though, their father's death had been an abstraction. It had happened—the before, during and after—without his input. And she sensed its impact had yet to be felt. Luca had assured her that acknowledging the death would be a good thing for Stanley. It was a "point of healing," as he liked to call it, a bright line underscoring a breakthrough.

Stanley stood silently before the inscription for several minutes. The simple marble headstone noted their father's birth and death dates and his highest military rank, sergeant.

"I never asked him about the war," Stanley said at last. "Did he ever say anything to you about it?"

"No, he never talked about it, and I didn't ask. Mom said something about him having bad nightmares after I was born. Like he was back fighting in the trenches. I think she was trying to make a connection between me and combat."

"That sounds like Mom," Stanley said with a half-chuckle. "Funny that he wanted to be buried here. He never talked about his service to anyone and didn't want me to enlist, but here he is, Sergeant Comfort."

Should she tell him that their father had added the burial request to his will after Stanley's enlistment? He must have seen it as a gesture of solidarity with his son, one that transcended his disapproval. "He was a hard one to figure out sometimes. He was proud of you, though. Proud and scared."

"That's pretty much what Doc said. Only with fancier words."

Kit laughed. "Speaking of Doc, he tells me you had a breakthrough."

"I guess you could call it that."

"He said you're remembering things."

"I have a story now. A beginning, middle and end. That's how Doc describes it. It's different from a natural memory. But it's there."

"You found yourself," Kit suggested.

"I guess. What about you? Did you find the person you were looking for?"

"We found him, yes." She hesitated, not quite ready to share Dina's story.

Stanley fell silent again. "I'm not ready to move back home yet."

"I know. Luca explained it to me."

His eyebrows shot up. "Is it my imagination or has Doc been doing a lot of explaining lately?"

"Strictly professional."

"Yeah, sure," Stanley teased, relaxing for the first time that afternoon. "I won't be returning to an empty house when I get out, will I?"

"Quite the contrary. You'll have a new roommate to get used to."

"You got a roommate?"

"I did. And he's a ginger."

Bomber bumped his fat, scarred head against Kit's calf as she absent-mindedly turned the can opener on his cat food. Then he meowed a meow that could only be translated as "hurry up." She did as commanded and emptied the entire can of Puss 'n Boots into his food dish. Before the bowl even hit the floor, he shoved his head in it and started chomping away at the smelly fishy contents.

"Sorry I haven't been around much, buddy. I've had a hard few days."

In the kitchen sink she found a collection of unwashed coffee cups, the sum total of last week's breakfasts. Had it been that long since she cleaned? She shuddered to think what her hair must look like—she hadn't given it a proper wash and styling in over a week. And her hands. She wasn't fanatical about her nail care, but her homicidal encounter in the orange grove had been brutal to her hands.

She stared at the dirt embedded under the nail of her right index finger. Images of the finger squeezing the derringer's trigger flooded her brain, over and over. She felt her heart start to pound, and her cheeks flush. She knew she hadn't watched her finger pulling the trigger—her concentration, as much as there was, was on the barrel—so where was this picture coming from? And why couldn't she conjure up memories of the real shooting? Why did her recollections start and stop with the derringer's trigger?

She grabbed the bar of Lava from the sink's edge and worked up a lather under some running water. Within seconds her nails had been scrubbed clean, but her mind still reeled with the false memory. She wondered what was worse. Reducing her fatal act to a squeeze of her finger, or recalling the whole deed in detail? How would she react the next time? Would there be a next time?

With another of his pleading meows, Bomber knocked Kit back to the moment. He was bumping her legs again, weaving back and forth, but more gently than before. As he paused to look up at her, she bent over to rub the spot between his ears. He responded with a soft, lazy purr and pressed himself approvingly into her calf.

For the next few minutes, they comforted each other. And then the doorbell rang.

AFTER THE BLUE, BLUE RAIN

Henry was the last person she expected to find on her porch. But there he was, in all his disheveled glory, with what looked like a hatbox tucked under his arm.

"Henry, it's your day off."

"Tell that to my wife."

By way of invitation, she opened the door wide, but he shook his head.

"Thanks, but I'm just here to make a delivery." He handed her the box, which she now saw was embossed with the distinctive Bullocks logo. "Bea saw it in the window and thought it would look good on you. I took her word for it."

"Bea bought me a hat?"

"She did. With gratitude, quote, unquote."

Kit peeked inside the box and almost squealed. Tucked under a layer of red tissue paper was a straw horsehair hat, with feather. *The* hat. And next to the hat lay a shiny silver derringer.

"Tomorrow, nine o'clock, someone's coming in to interview for the Girl Friday job," Henry said.

"What Girl Friday job?"

Henry waved her off and descended the porch steps. "The one we're going to need after today. Nine o'clock, sharp."

"What Girl Friday job?" Kit repeated. When she got no answer, she yelled, "Tell Bea, thank you."

REFERENCES

The following works provided invaluable information and inspiration in the writing of this story:

Hitler in Los Angeles: How Jews Foiled Nazi Plots Against Hollywood and America by Steven J. Ross (Bloomsbury USA, 2017).

In a Lonely Place by Dorothy B. Hughes (NYRB Classics; Reprint edition, 2017; First edition, 1947).

Let There Be Light, directed by John Huston (U.S. War Department, 1948).

Men Under Stress by Roy R. Grinker, Lt. Col., M.C. and John P. Spiegel, Major, M.C. (Pickle Partners Publishing, 2015).

Mollie's War: The Letters of a World War II WAC in Europe by Mollie Weinstein Schaffer and Cyndee Schaffer (McFarland & Company, 2010).

Nazi Prisoners of War in America by Arnold Krammer (UNKNO, 1979).

Available Now
Book 2 in the Comfort & Company Mystery Series:
The Birthday of Eternity

L.A. private investigators Kit and Henry become entangled in the city's robust post-WWII occult trade when they're hired to track down Lillian, the estranged wife of a prominent physician, and her spellbinding "spirit" lover Tashin. Fresh from her training in judo and "dirty fighting," Kit poses as an eager recruit at a Hollywood cult run by the ambitious Reverend, while Henry takes on the city's séance circuit, which has reinvented itself in the wake of war. Assisting them are Kit's psychiatrist lover Luca and her combat veteran brother Stanley, who offer their own brand of expertise in unraveling the tricks of the conmen. Plunged into the strange and deadly world of mediums and gurus, Kit and Henry soon discover that surviving the spirit trade will take all of their cunning and a whole lot of luck.

www.ingramcontent.com/pod-product-compliance
Lightning Source LLC
Chambersburg PA
CBHW070328260626
47160CB00003B/985
* 9 7 9 8 9 8 6 8 9 3 0 8 2 *